1/22   DA

MAR 3 0 2022

PRINTED IN U.S.A.

DISRUPTIVE IMAGINATION

TRANSCENDENT

The Kacy Chronicles Book 4
By A.L. Knorr and Martha Carr

FROM A.L. KNORR

For anyone who ever wished they could fly.

From Martha

To everyone who still believes in magic and all the possibilities
that holds.
To all the readers who make this entire ride so much fun.
And to all the dreamers just like me who create wonder, big and
small, every day.

TRANSCENDENT TEAM

JIT BETA READERS

Daniel Weigert
Micky Cocker
Sarah Weir
James Caplan
Joshua Ahles
John Ashmore
Kim Boyer
Tim Bischoff
Larry Omans
Paul Westman
Nicola Aquino

If we missed anyone, please let us know!

CHAPTER 1

*J*ordan and Sol stood upon the apartment's terrace, watching the tower shadows stretch long fingers over the landscape of Upper Rodania. Sol's arm was looped under Jordan's wings and around her waist. She leaned into his warmth as the late afternoon breeze tugged at her hair. A thin layer of fluffy cloud hung low over the roofs and peaks of the Rodanian towers and palaces. There were patches of blackened ruins where dragonfire had scorched buildings, and timbers and beams jutted from wreckage like broken ribs. It was going to take some time to restore Rodania to its pre-harpy glory.

The peace of the scene before them masked a profound unrest among the citizens. No one knew if or when there might be another harpy attack.

The apartment had been cleaned, and the extra mattresses removed from the bedroom and taken to the ground floor apartment they'd rented as temporary lodging for Eohne and Allan. But there were still missing and broken tiles on the terrace, cracked and broken countertops in the kitchen, and gouges crisscrossing the hardwood floor from sharp harpy talons.

Sol pressed his lips to Jordan's temple and gazed down at her.

"Do you think Eohne and your dad will be happier down there? You haven't just been saying that to make me feel better?"

Jordan nodded. "They'll be happier in their own space and it'll be a lot easier for them to get around, too." A frown tugged at the corners of her mouth. "I wonder what Eohne's plans are, now that my dad is back to normal. I assume she'll be heading back to Charra-Rae one of these days."

Sol made a noncommittal sound in the back of his throat. He didn't like the idea of losing their Elven friend, either. Eohne had become so much a part of their lives, she would leave a gaping hole if she went back to her forest home.

"Look." Sol squeezed Jordan and jutted his chin toward the cloud cover in the east.

A huge shadow darkened the sky, and the clouds disintegrated as the colossal red dragon materialized over Upper Rodania. Her nearly incomprehensible wingspan blocked out the early evening light, casting a long, dark shape over the hills and villages. As she approached, she seemed to grow until she filled half the sky. The red scales of her belly were the color of dried blood. Her wings beat slowly, gracefully, almost lazily, even as her body appeared impossibly light for all its bulk and sinew.

Jordan's heart beat faster as they watched the she-dragon make one of her rare appearances in the skies over Rodania. Views of her had been few since the harpy battle, and Jordan had often wondered if the creature had left Rodania for good. Blue had come to visit every few days, never staying long and always winging away to the west. Jordan figured the dragons had to be living somewhere north of Maticaw, where the wilderness could sustain them.

Jordan briefly tore her eyes away from the dragon to skim the scene below, where the skies had emptied of Strix. Everyone who had been traveling landed to watch with upturned faces. All movement had ceased, save for the dragon's. Her body tilted as she descended.

found them lounging on the grass not far from Sol's apartment tower.

Blue raised his head from the ground as the Nycht landed closer than any Strix had dared since Jordan and Sol had left. Toth approached on foot, hands relaxed at his sides, his dewclaws pointing down in a nonthreatening position.

"Remember me?" Toth asked, as Blue rolled over onto his belly.

Blue lifted his snout and gave three sharp throaty cries into the sky, making Toth blink with surprise, and pause before moving forward again.

"What was that for? Don't like being disturbed on your honeymoon?" Toth reached Blue and lay a hand on his neck.

Blue's jaws clicked together, and the dragon got to his feet in one quick movement. He turned his back on Toth and disappeared into the cave behind the red dragon, who was still laying on her side.

Unafraid but moving with a deferential respect, Toth moved toward the red's snout. She swung it in the grass toward him in an oddly playful manner. Toth crouched to look at her but did not touch her. The red dragon would forever be tied to that fateful battle in Toth's memory; the day Rodania was nearly destroyed under a crush of harpy onslaught, and the day he lost a brother.

A sudden wash of grief cut through him so cruelly it took his breath away. Toth's eyes squeezed shut, and he swallowed. When he opened his eyes, they were misty and red-rimmed.

Caje.

How many nights since the battle had he woken with a start, and the image of Caje plummeting toward that stone tower with his fist down the throat of a devil-bird?

"Don't get me wrong," the Nycht said to the reptile, his voice hoarse and nearly inaudible. "I'm grateful."

The huge red eyes blinked slowly shut and open again.

"But you couldn't have come just ten minutes sooner?" Toth's voice closed up on the last word and he let his head hang for a moment. Some days, it seemed too heavy to lift, his body too heavy to drag from his bed to face the day.

Had the Nycht brothers made the right call accepting Balroc's deal? It had cost Caje his life, and the loss was tearing Toth apart. The vote had yet to be decided, so it was too early to say. Toth's jaw clenched so hard he could hear his teeth grinding. *If Caje's loss was in vain...*

It was too horrific to consider. Winning the vote for the Nychts was Toth's priority. Only when that was done could he fly far away from the eyes of his soldiers and the rest of his family, and mourn properly. Only then could he let himself fall to pieces.

Until then, his soul was tethered together by fraying cords.

The soft sound of claws on grass made Toth look up. Blue made a reappearance, approaching the Nycht with his head down. Something large and pale was clutched in the dragon's jaws, cradled behind his sharp white teeth.

"What have you got there?"

Blue stopped at Toth's side and lowered his snout to the earth, opening his jaw wide, with effort.

A dove-gray egg, mottled with black speckles, rolled onto the grass with a dull cracking sound. It was the size of a human ribcage and had fissures threading across it like forks of light-ning. Toth covered his nose at the smell of death and decay that drifted up from the rotten egg.

"You shouldn't have," Toth said with a half-smile at the drag-on's disgusting offering.

He toed the egg away as he stood, knees popping. He assumed perhaps the red female had lain a dud, though why Blue was presenting it to Toth was a mystery.

Then the egg rolled over, revealing a much larger crack in the shell. Toth dropped his hand in dismay as the egg's contents became visible.

palace staff at the front began to clean up and it became clear that Prince Diruk was finished handing out medals, the realization settled over the dismayed warriors like a heavy, wet blanket.

The ceremony had come to a close, and not a single Nycht had been awarded a set of golden wings.

Jordan, Sol and Toth stood there, mute and enraged. The warriors around them shared looks of hateful indignation. Some of them sent Toth questioning looks, and some of those looks had an accusatory flavor. Jordan felt like she could read their minds. Why hadn't their brave leader stood up and said something against the injustice of it? He was their captain, shouldn't he do something?

Jordan's mouth twisted with the regret of having accepted the medal. If she had known how the proceedings were going to transpire, she wouldn't have flown to the stage in the first place. Juer had said that King Konig was sympathetic to the Nychts' cause, so surely this offense had been manufactured by Prince Diruk.

The prince and the Council members in attendance milled about on stage, murmuring amongst themselves as they watched the crowd disband. Jordan glared at the prince from her place on the green, watching as his cold eyes scanned the crowd. The prince's blue eyes passed over Toth before bouncing back and freezing on the Nycht captain. Jordan felt Sol take her hand as he too noticed the quiet confrontation taking place. It seemed as though someone had sucked all the oxygen out of the air as Diruk and Toth stared one another down.

Prince Diruk spread his wings with a snap, drawing attention to himself. He flew over the heads of the crowd and landed in a fast walk, closing up those golden feathers as he strode to where Toth, Jordan and Sol stood. Jordan had to work to prevent her hands from flying to the hilts of her weapons, so aggressive were the prince's movements.

Prince Diruk's eyes were still locked on Toth and they were

hard with cold fury. His face seemed to be cut from some frozen metal.

Toth did not move a muscle or look away when the prince stopped in front of him.

For a moment, Jordan thought the prince was going to hit Toth. Sol squeezed her hand tighter, and she suspected it was a subconscious and protective movement.

Sol and Toth had had their differences, but the two of them had developed a mutual respect. Jordan could feel the anger baking off Sol on behalf of his captain. She squeezed his hand with empathy.

"I *know*," seethed Diruk, rocking forward onto his toes and shoving his nose into Toth's face. Diruk's voice became a throaty whisper. "I know what you did." His cold eyes swung to Jordan, then to Sol.

Jordan was grateful for the steadying, solid grip of Sol's fingers around hers. It kept her from shoving the prince back and out of their faces——or worse, slapping him across the mouth.

"Soon I'll be able to prove it. Your scheme," his jaw popped, and he again pierced Toth with his gaze, "will not work." With another snap of his wings, the prince lit to the air and made for Upper Rodania without looking back.

Toth only moved when the prince was a small figure in the distance. He uncrossed his arms. Though his expression was impenetrable, his face was pale and shining with moisture. He brought the fingertips of his right hand to his brow, as though a headache was forming there.

"What just happened?" Sol's voice broke like it had been under considerable strain. "What *scheme*?" When Toth didn't answer, Sol put a hand on his arm. "Toth?"

The fingers resting on Toth's forehead flexed open in a gesture which asked Sol not to pry. The Nycht turned away and took to the sky, leaving Jordan and Sol to watch him go in miserable confusion.

such a disaster occur again. We simply will not survive it. The Council is divided about how to proceed, and I fear someone will behave rashly and cause a disagreement between Rodania and the Light Elves." Balroc glowered. "We cannot have that, either."

Linlett was nodding. "Obviously something has gone wrong. But I was briefed before I left our kingdom. The magical engineering of the Rodanian border is invulnerable. There is something else going on here."

"Sabotage," said Balroc bluntly.

Linlett agreed with this possibility with another waggle of his head.

Kehko was nodding, too. She crossed her arms and regarded the Light Elf through half-closed lids, like she'd already decided he had something to do with it.

"Who could have pulled off such a feat?" Eohne posed to the group.

"That's what I'm here to figure out." Linlett's bright gaze fell on Eohne again. "I propose we pool our resources." He rubbed his hands together. "If you're amenable, of course."

"I am," Eohne replied, somewhat dazed. Learning more about Light Elf magic had been one of her lifelong goals. Thus far, there had never been anyone to show her the magic of light; additionally, Sohne had forbidden it.

"Excellent. That's settled, then," Balroc turned to Kehko. "We'll be shutting down your dome temporarily, young miss. Consider yourself on leave, with pay of course." He swept Kehko toward the door.

"But," Kehko threw a glance over her shoulder at Linlett, unhappy to be leaving her dome in the hands of a potential enemy.

Eohne gave her a look of reassurance. "It's alright, Kehko. I'll be here."

The young Nycht allowed herself to be sent on her way.

Balroc excused himself, leaving Linlett and Eohne alone in the dome to begin their work. The door slid shut, muting the sound of the Rodanian Sea and the cries of seabirds.

Eohne watched as Linlett approached the dashboard. "I've been wondering how to..." she began.

Linlett moved his hands in an elegant dance, fingers flicking outward in a symbolic inflection. There was a sound like steam blowing from a kettle.

"...open that," Eohne finished, watching with fascination as the dome lifted away from the floor and hovered there. A bright light emanated from the crack beneath it, beaming outward in all directions. The light flickered and danced with all the colors of the rainbow. Eohne looked down at her own booted feet and discovered that they were completely invisible in the prismatic glare. "Wow," she breathed.

Linlett was rubbing his palms together as if to warm them. "This magic was developed long before I was born by a company of brilliant elders. I have always wanted to see how it worked. The Light Elves have not engineered anything else like it for any other species on Oriceran. It is completely unique." He gave Eohne a warm smile. "So you see, Rodania is special to us. We would never do anything to harm her."

"Then let's figure out who would," the Elf countered.

"Indeed." Linlett lifted his hands and held them poised in the air, preparing to proceed. "Are you ready for this?"

Eohne nodded, not sure what to expect but eager to begin.

"What you'll see will only be visible to us, so don't worry about Strix crashing into one another mid-flight, or ships going off course. I assure you, the optics for Rodania's citizens will remain unchanged."

"What?" Eohne cocked her head, confused by this dialogue.

Linlett's hands danced again, and the dashboard lifted further, the light expanding and brightening. The Light Elf lifted the dashboard aside and let it fall with a clang onto the floor.

Eohne's mouth sagged as she was struck dumb by the beauty of the magic. Suddenly, she understood.

'Optics' indeed.

Her eyes filled with the flare of the border's inner workings as it all became visible. The dome covering disappeared in the glare, and the Rodanian Sea and the horizon beyond vanished from sight.

Slender threads of light in every color of the rainbow shot from the single orb. The orb itself was such a bright light that it could not be looked at directly. The threads numbered in the hundreds of thousands, if not in the millions. The many strands originated from the star and shot outward toward every other dome around Rodania, creating a network of criss-crossing lines. Threads arced high over Upper Rodania, and Eohne could see how every border station was connected to every other one. A network of fine filaments wrapped over Rodania in an exquisite, magical web. Rodania itself nearly vanished from view: the land masses became nothing more than blurry blobs, swallowed up by the radiance shooting from the star hovering near the Elves' shins. The network was beautiful, mesmerizing, and fully intact.

"Hmmmm." Linlett made a thoughtful sound as the two Elves took in the glory of the magical barrier and all its perfection. The pair appeared to be trapped inside a prism; the rainbow of filaments surrounded them and passed harmlessly through their bodies.

"What...?" Eohne's neck creaked as she stared upward, her face filled with astonishment. She couldn't look away from the complex network of magic, and the perfect way it bound Rodania in safety. Never before had she seen work of such precision and elegance.

"There are no incomplete threads––no blights, holes, cankers or misconnections. There isn't a tainted filament anywhere to be seen." Linlett's body was bathed in light, the threads penetrating his figure and shooting out the other side.

Eohne's eyes slowly adjusted, and she was able to better make out the blurry edges of Upper Rodania and Middle Rodania, rendered ghostly by the brightness of the network encasing them. Her eyes fell on Linlett with a new respect for him and his kind.

It was going to take no small amount of effort to set aside the awe she was feeling, and wrestle her inventor's mind into its usual professional place.

Linlett lifted his hands, and Eohne saw that both of them were blue-white apparitions, rather than flesh and bone. His fingertips were illuminated and looked like ten small stars. Linlett plucked at a thread the color of a sunflower at the height of summer. The filament twanged and snapped back into place, and a yellow sparkle appeared in the thread, racing into the sky, following the filament along its length.

Eohne watched the sparkle race from view behind the shadow of Upper Rodania, reappear beneath the island, and disappear again behind Middle Rodania before descending like a falling star behind the smudge on the horizon that was Lower Rodania. Eohne laughed with delight and looked at Linlett. She was about to express her joy at being allowed to witness the bones of this magic, but Linlett's expression stopped her.

"What's wrong? What are you thinking?" Eohne asked, the growing concern on Linlett's face triggering her own inner alarm bells.

"I had barely dared hope," Linlett began, without taking his eyes from the magic barrier and all its complexity, "for some clue to direct us where to look first. Alas, the magic is as I said: intact and perfect. If it is sabotage, it is masterfully done. Possibly by one of our own." He added this last comment in a quiet tone, as though worried Kehko might be listening and he had just confirmed her worst suspicions.

Eohne's eyes widened at this admission. Not only the acknowledgement that it could have been a Light Elf responsible, but that he was saying it out loud to her, a stranger. It showed a level of trust that disarmed her further and galvanized her faith in him. "I'm sorry to hear that. I hope you're wrong." She wasn't sure what else to say.

"Me too." Linlett gazed at his new partner in investigation and let out a breath through pursed lips. "This is going to take longer than I thought."

CHAPTER 4

"Jordan." Toth waved her over to where he sat on one of the rocks that his brother had sat on mere weeks before, eating stew and talking about the harpy threat.

It was late afternoon, and Jordan was winded. It had been a hard day of training for all of them, and the first real day of conditioning since the major battle. The combatants had been busy helping the Strix citizens put their city to rights, but Toth couldn't allow them to let their guard down. No one knew if or when the red dragon would decide to abandon them, leaving them open to another attack.

The physical exertion had been a welcome distraction for all the Strix soldiers, after the insult of the ceremony to honor their fallen. If what Prince Diruk had done was meant to divide the Nychts and the Arpaks, it hadn't worked. The Arpaks were just as livid as the Nychts, for they'd all lost Nycht comrades and friends during the war.

Jordan nodded her thanks to her sparring partner, one of the rebel Nychts who had come back from The Conca with Caje and

Chayla. She put away her dirks and joined Toth, settling onto the stone beside him.

"What's going on?" She leaned forward eagerly, resting her elbows on her knees.

Toth had still said nothing about what had transpired between him and Prince Diruk on the day of the ceremony. Jordan was hopeful he might enlighten her as to what the mysterious 'scheme' was that he'd been referring to.

"There's something I'd like to ask you."

"Anything," Jordan looked her friend in the eye, willing him to feel her respect and support. She was still chafing over having accepted the medal, even though he'd encouraged her to. She felt in some way that she had betrayed her Nycht friends by doing so.

Toth caught Sol's eye as he was saying goodbye to his sparring partner and putting the throwing disks into their trunks for the night. Sol either felt the Nycht captain's eyes on him in that moment, or he happened to glance their way at just the right time to see Toth and Jordan both staring at him. One brow went up with curiosity. Toth invited him over with his hand.

Sol tossed the rest of the disks away and locked the trunk before crossing the green and settling on the stone beside Jordan, his feathers rustling as he stretched his wings. Sweat beaded Sol's brow, and he wiped it away with the heel of his hand. Jordan caught a whiff of sweat and damp leather as he moved.

"Have you seen Blue lately?" Toth plucked at a long piece of grass and caught its stem between his teeth, propping his foot against the rock.

Jordan nodded. "And Red, too."

"Is that what we're calling her?" Toth asked with a smirk.

"Unless you can think of a better name?" Sol challenged, wiping his forearm across his brow.

Toth shrugged. "I like keeping things simple."

"We saw them a couple of days ago, in the park not far from our apartment," Jordan answered more specifically. "Why?"

Toth nodded. "I saw them that day, as well. Blue surprised me with a little present."

"Oh? He didn't give us any presents," Sol replied with a chuckle. "Did he, Jordan?"

"Speak for yourself, he licked my face." Jordan gave Sol a smug smile.

"That's all it takes to make you happy? Good to know." Sol mimed taking out a notepad and licking the tip of a pen before writing something on an invisible page. "Lick Jordan's face after extended time away."

Jordan shoved Sol's shoulder playfully. "You're just jealous."

Toth shook his head. "I'm surrounded by children." His mouth twitched with something that was almost a smile, but the warmth of it didn't reach his eyes.

Jordan and Sol flashed each other a look. Their playing around was a bit forced and they knew it, but they were both eager to cheer their captain up. So far, not much could incite a smile.

"The present gave me an idea," Toth continued, as blithely as though he was ordering a mug of ale at a bar. "I'd like to take the dragons and a squadron of Nychts to Golpa."

Jordan let out a long breath.

Her initial reaction was a fearful one, not just for any Nychts who made the journey to that inhospitable, cold, and dangerous place, but also for Blue. Once she'd acknowledged the fear reaction and pushed it aside to make room for her warrior brain, she immediately understood why Toth would want to undertake such a treacherous mission.

In Rodania, they were always on guard, always being reactive, always guessing, waiting and dreading another attack. If they went to Golpa, they'd be taking their power back. There was nothing worse than feeling like sitting ducks.

Sol was nodding. "Go on the offensive. I like it." His brow furrowed as he unstrapped the waterskin at his waist and unscrewed the cap. The waterskin hovered near his mouth while he said, "Only Nychts? Why no Arpaks?"

Toth had an answer ready. "Golpa is a network of caves. They are vast but they are also deep and very dark. Nychts have sonar; we're built to handle the dark. Arpaks are not."

Sol took a drink and put the cap back on the waterskin. He swished the water around in his mouth and spat it off to the side. "True, but wouldn't it make sense to leave some Arpaks outside the caves to pick off stragglers?"

"Wait a second." Jordan put up a hand. "I think I'm with you, but just for clarity's sake, what precisely is the objective?"

"Exterminate the harpies, of course. Kill them in their sleep." Toth spoke plainly, almost mildly, around the stem of grass between his teeth.

"It's a good idea, Jordan," added Sol. "It's better than waiting around here for them to attack us again." He took another swig, this time swallowing it.

"I agree, but what if Red won't go?"

"I think she will," countered Toth, raking a hand through his sweaty, silver hair and making it stand up in spikes like freshly mown grass. "In fact, I think this is more their idea than mine."

"How's that?" Jordan wasn't necessarily jealous that Toth had had some convivial communication from Blue, but she was very curious as to how it came about. Blue hadn't given her any sign of having formed a plan to go all the way to Golpa with intent to kill. It seemed elaborate, even for an intelligent reptile.

"Blue dropped a harpy egg at my feet," Toth explained. "He couldn't have gotten it anywhere else but Golpa. You saw him earlier that same day——why did he give *me* the egg and not you?"

Jordan made a thoughtful sound in the back of her throat. She had no answer. She had to admit, giving the egg to Toth was a calculated move.

"Blue is not a stray cat," Toth continued. "He's crafty. It strikes me as deliberate, what he did. All the same, I'd still like it if you asked him for me."

"Ask him if he'll go to Golpa with you?"

Toth grunted in the affirmative.

Jordan chewed her lip. The idea of sending Blue, who was still not yet full-grown, straight into the belly of where harpies bred and slept made her mouth go dry. If there were enough of the demon-birds to attack Rodania in the thousands, how many of them lived in Golpa? Or had a large portion of them been exterminated already? No one could answer this. "I'm sure he would go," she said, "but…"

"Red would go too, Jordan." Sol addressed her unspoken fear with a smile in his blue eyes. He squeezed her upper arm. "They're mates. Where one goes, the other follows."

He didn't need to add, *just like us*. The implication was plain enough.

Jordan smiled at him. "Yes, I reckon she would."

Toth was nodding too, but his eyes were alight with something that set a chill in Jordan's bones. Red was who he really was after. Against potentially thousands of harpies, Blue was helpful, but Red… Red was a different story. Red was a force of nature all by herself; she was a flying volcano.

"Without Red," Toth grew serious, as though he could read Jordan's thoughts. "We wouldn't succeed. But with her…" He trailed off, giving a small shrug. There was an abundance of confidence in that shrug, and no small amount of hunger either ——and not for food.

Toth wanted this, wanted it bad.

"You think it will be easy?" Sol crossed his arms over his chest.

The air had grown cool, and the sun had disappeared below Middle Rodania's horizon, sending its rays out from underneath them, as it had not yet passed below the lower island and the blanket of the Rodanian Sea. Their sweat had begun to dry on their skin, leaving the grit of salt on their brows.

"I would never assume any offensive strike like this to be easy, but with two dragons, and Nychts equipped to fight in the dark, we have a good chance of succeeding. And without taking a great number of casualties ourselves," Toth added.

"How would you do it? Have you been there before?" Jordan couldn't visualize how such an attack would go down. With the volume of fire that Red was able to produce, it could very well end in toasted Strix as well as toasted harpies.

"I've spoken at length to someone who has."

"Could Red even fit in the cave? She's massive."

Toth spat out the grass he'd been chewing on and began to talk with his hands. "The caves are enormous. They have high ceilings and there are offshoots and crevices everywhere. Someone once told me they were big enough to sail a whole fleet of Hirola ships into without risk of striking the sides."

"There's water?" Jordan was sincerely alarmed, and pictured a massive half-underwater grotto. Water and Strix didn't mix well. Sonar or no sonar, Jordan had seen what wet wings cost a Nycht, and it wasn't pretty.

"Hirola ships are airborne," Sol explained with a shake of his head. "And big."

Jordan blinked. "Oh." *Airborne ships?* "Wow." There was still so much about Oriceran that Jordan had to learn. "How come I've never seen these airborne ships? Wouldn't they be perfect for delivering goods to Middle and Upper Rodania?"

"Hirola ships are captained by Pirate-wizards from Traft," Toth explained. "Not the kind of people you'd want managing your deliveries." Then he dismissed the matter with an impatient sweep of his hand. "I mentioned them only to illustrate the size of the caves."

"Got it."

"Red and Blue would go in first," Toth forged on eagerly. "The Nychts will stay well behind them. The dragons will ignite the caves with fire, killing eggs and harpies alike, then the Nychts will follow the dragons and finish the job."

"I still don't see why Arpaks wouldn't come in handy," Sol interjected. "We can wait at the entrance to kill off stragglers as they try to escape."

Toth tilted his head side to side in what could be agreement. "If the dragons do their part right, the harpies won't be able to escape."

"But you said the caves are really deep, right?" Jordan was having trouble realistically visualizing the extent of Golpa. "Couldn't the harpies just press back and hide?"

"Maybe," Toth shifted on the stone, "but dragonfire doesn't burn dragons. Red and Blue can push forward into their own flames, and root them out."

Jordan shuddered at the visuals playing in full technicolor on the big screen TV of her mind. It was simple, and simply brilliant.

"Take some Arpaks, Toth," Sol suggested for the third time, his tone quiet. "We lost friends, too. Give us a chance for vengeance, and a chance to end this war."

At this there was a short lull in the conversation as Toth gazed at Sol, and the words hung between them.

Then Toth nodded. "I'll choose some Arpaks, then. You are right. Can I assume the two of you...?"

Jordan and Sol were both nodding furiously.

"When do you want to leave?" Jordan asked.

"We'll need some time to prepare. Four days should do it. I'll handpick the squadron and then everyone will need to be outfitted with cold weather gear——weapons that won't turn brittle or get so cold they can't be handled——and survival packs and food for the journey. I'd send a scout, but Golpa is too far and too dangerous to send anyone there on their own. We'll have to do our best with the intel we have and then finalize our strategy when we get there." Toth levelled Jordan with a look. "So, will you ask him?"

Jordan let out a tense breath. "I don't know if it's really necessary. From the sounds of it, this whole thing is his idea."

"Yes, but," Toth leaned forward, making it clear that it was important to him. "Will you *ask* him? I don't want to make the mistake of misunderstanding his gesture."

Jordan nodded. "I'll ask him."

* * *

TOTH FELT the presence of someone approaching and turned to see the small form of Arth, his half-sister, crossing the lawn behind Mareya's house.

A handful of Toth's large contingent of siblings had come together to honor Caje's memory. While most of them had to leave afterward, a few still lingered in Mareya's backyard. They murmured under the evening sky, and listened to the insects buzz while sharing memories about their brave, larger-than-life brother.

"Care for some company?" Arth plopped down beside Toth, where he sat on the low stone wall that separated the garden from the grass.

Truthfully, Toth had moved to the end of the yard to have a few minutes of alone time, but Arth was a favorite, so he shifted over to make room.

They sat in companionable silence for a time, watching the sky become a blanket of black velvet sprinkled with pinpricks of light.

"Are you——" Arth began, then paused.

When she spoke again, her voice was raspy. "I was going to ask if you're okay, but I just realized it's a stupid question. Of course you're not."

Toth felt his sister's small hand on his back, just under his wing. He could feel the warmth of it even through his shirt. Toth had left all his armor at the door, donning only his leather leggings and a simple, homespun, cotton tunic that laced up the back, underneath and above his wings.

His eyes fluttered shut, and he exhaled. "There is nothing that could make losing Caje okay," he said quietly. "We'll feel the abyss left by him for the rest of our lives. But if we fail to win the vote, or if we fail to prevent another harpy attack..." His voice tightened, and he stopped. He didn't have to say out loud what they both already knew.

If they failed at those two things, or even one of them, then Caje's loss would have been in vain. Neither of them could live with that.

Toth's eyes tracked to where Mareya and her husband Eade sat with their arms around one another. Mareya had her head on her husband's shoulder, and the two spoke with an intimacy that struck Toth with an unexpected longing. It wasn't that Toth wanted to be in love or have a wife; his life didn't afford such a luxury. The desire was simpler than that: to not feel so empty.

One corner of Toth's lips tugged upward in the closest thing resembling a smile he'd mustered since before the harpy battle. "They still seem so in love," he observed.

Arth made a grunt of agreement as she followed Toth's gaze to their sister. "You know what they say. Absence makes the heart grow fonder."

"Absence?" Toth looked down at Arth curiously.

"Mareya spent a lot of years away from home. You know, for her work at the palace."

"She works so hard," Toth frowned. "And for a government who has not done us any favors."

"Not all of us suit the rebel's life, Toth."

"I didn't mean——"

"It's okay. I know what you meant." There was sorrow in Arth's words, but understanding and pride in her voice. "I hope you know that none of us hold it against you. What you did and why you did it. We're all proud of you, proud to call you our brother."

Toth wanted to say thank you, but didn't trust his voice. He hadn't realized how much he'd been wanting to hear those exact words until Arth said them. After all, he'd done what he did for *them*, it had been an attempt to make life better for them. He just hadn't expected it to fail.

If I fail again... Toth looked away and gritted his teeth. He couldn't fail. For the sake of his brother's memory, he would not fail.

"We're proud of Caje, too," Arth added. Then after a moment, "There is something I'd like to ask you." She cleared her throat and forged on. "I'd like to come with you."

"Where?" Toth's heart increased its rhythm a notch. He had a feeling he knew what Arth was going to ask.

"To Golpa. I know you're planning to go."

"No." Toth bit the word out without thinking.

"Toth, he was my brother, too." Arth's expression darkened, even in the moonlight and the dim throw of the lantern hanging by the rear door of Mareya's house. "I have a right to seek revenge, same as you."

"I'm sorry. I understand how you feel," said Toth. "But if something were to happen to you, I'm not sure I could bear it. And I still have a job to do."

Arth didn't reply for a long time.

Toth expected her to continue to protest. His little sister was one of the most tenacious and stubborn people he knew; it was one of the reasons she made such a wonderful engineer.

When she spoke, it was so quiet, he had to strain to hear her. "Alright." Then a moment later, louder, "But will you take Teetch?"

Teetch was one of the brothers in between Arth and Caje, a big, powerful Nycht who had worked on the Lewis guns at the forge before the last battle.

"Does Teetch want to come? He hasn't asked me."

"I think he thinks he's already coming. He hasn't stopped producing bullets since you first announced preparations. He's a good shot, you know."

Toth hadn't considered taking the Lewis guns, not even one of them, all the way to Golpa. They were large and awkward and would tire whoever was carrying them very quickly.

Toth frowned. "Was he going to mention this to me?"

Firing guns in a dark cave full of Nycht warriors was a terrible idea, in Toth's view. They wouldn't be taking them.

"You know Teetch," Arth scoffed, knocking Toth against the upper arm. "He spoke his first word at the age of five, and it was to tell our mother to turn the lights off."

Toth grunted. It was an old family story still enjoyed among Toth's siblings and extended family. '*Off!*' his brother had barked when his mother had roused him for school on the Arpak schedule, which Teetch to this day refused to adapt to. It was the first word he'd ever formed, and their mother had jumped out of her skin. The entire family had assumed Teetch had been born without the ability to speak. He'd been examined by many doctors, and they couldn't find any physiological reason for his silence. He was equipped with a voicebox as well as a sonarbox, just like every other Nycht. But he had never spoken. Until he needed to.

Teetch was not the fighter Caje had been, but he was big and strong and willing.

Toth told Arth he'd talk to their brother about the guns, and then the two lapsed into silence.

Toth had another brother he wanted to talk with before he left. Breo was the smallest brother of the Sazak family, and he worked as a cartographer for a privately held mapping and surveying company. Breo had travelled more than most Rodanian citizens, as he worked first as a surveyor, then as a supervisor. If anyone could give Toth a better understanding of where they were going and what kind of terrain and weather they were to face on their way, it would be Breo.

"I hate them."

The words roused Toth from his mental musings. "Hate who?"

"The harpies. For taking Caje. For killing so many Rodanian citizens and soldiers. I hate them. I never knew hate until now." Arth's words were cold and harsh, but they were calculated and somewhat emotionless in her delivery. Toth knew his sister; she had spent time ruminating on the true meaning of hate.

"Hate is easy," Toth replied. His eyes drifted back to Mareya and Eade, the bond between them giving them comfort, lifting them up, easing the burden of their grief. "It's love that is difficult."

* * *

THE NEXT DAY, Jordan was in the middle of a knife-throwing drill when she spotted Blue gliding high over the landscape of Upper Rodania. There was no sight of Red, but that didn't matter. She took off like a shot after him.

It was midmorning, and Jordan was still fresh; there was little she loved more than a sprint across the sky on strong wings, with the wind tugging at her hair and flowing through her feathers.

Blue spotted her and gave a long, descending whistle.

Jordan was panting by the time she got close. "Hey, buddy," she called, a grin splitting her face. "Just the fellow I was hoping to find!"

Blue seemed to grin before lifting his snout to the sun and sounding off three happy barks. Suddenly, he banked and dove, spiralling downward. Jordan felt a blast of wind as he passed her.

"Hey!" she cried, laughing at his playful movements. "Wait up!" She dove after him.

What ensued was an eye-blearing, hair-tearing, heart-thundering game of chase. Jordan couldn't help the laughter that poured from her throat as she chased her friend across the sky.

Blue had always been quick, but he was bigger and stronger and moved like a starving shark, slicing through oceanic currents. His spine and tail undulated in a sinewy serpentine way as he catapulted through the skies, whistling and barking his own joy.

Jordan did her best to tail him as he carved a path like a theme park ride over Upper Rodania and then out over the Rodanian Sea and toward the training islands. Loops and figure-eights, gigantic upside down arches, followed by plummeting straight down, nearly to the tops of the waves, before swooshing upward again and climbing straight verticals. She wasn't sure she'd ever had a flying workout quite this intense before.

As Blue shot past one of the training islands in a vertical climb, she heard the sounds of the Strix warriors cheering her on, and doubled her efforts. Her heart was pounding, and her wings were burning, but still she pushed herself even harder. She followed Blue in a rainbow-shape over the training islands and back toward his favorite park on Upper Rodania.

"You're going to kill me, bud!" Jordan panted as he zigzagged back and forth ahead of her, his tail whipping across her vision like a flag in her face. "Now you're just showing off!"

Blue gave a barking roar and slowed down, descending toward the green. He still came in too fast, and clawed up clumps of dirt and grass as his talons raked the earth to stop his momentum.

Jordan also came in too fast, and found her bootsoles skidding across the earth. She tripped over one of the gigantic divots Blue had raked out of the soil, and went sliding across the grass on her chest, laughing and gasping for air. She finally came to a halt, her wings spread-eagled in a messy sprawl of feathers, and rolled over, groaning and panting.

"Thanks," she sucked in a big gulp of air, "for that, you brat. You really made me work for this one, didn't you?"

Blue heaved his own gusty breath and flopped over on his side, nosing through the grass like a dog on a scent as he crawled in her direction. He stretched his snout toward her and *whuff*ed in her face, blowing her hair back.

Jordan felt a spray of moisture. "Gross," she laughed, wiping off her face. "Dragon boogers."

The two of them lay there until their breathing went back to normal. Then Jordan rolled to her knees and lay a hand on Blue's neck.

"There's something I have to ask you, Blue," she said, looking into his eyes. "On behalf of Toth."

Blue got up and wandered toward the granite overhang that he and Red had lounged under a few days earlier. He rooted around in the shadows under the cliff and then came back in Jordan's direction, pushing a speckled, gray egg with his nose.

Jordan got a wave of harpy stench and put a hand over her nose. Revulsion clawed at her stomach, and she fought to keep her gorge down. "Eurgh." Jordan's eyes started watering at the smell of rot, but she couldn't stop herself from looking through the crack at the harpy chick inside. "I guess you know what I was going to ask you, then?"

Blue *whuff*ed at her again and sat on his haunches. He lifted one claw and rested it on top of the egg. He shook his head, his wattle swaying back and forth. His shoulder flexed as he stepped down on the egg, crushing it and its contents entirely.

Jordan was blasted with another disgusting wave of stinking harpy scent.

"I'll tell Toth you said yes," she said with her nose plugged.

CHAPTER 5

*A*shley came awake like a siren had gone off next to his ear; his heart was pounding, and his tongue felt coated with a bitter paste. He tugged at the neck of his shirt, pulling it away from his throat as he sucked in air. Rolling over, he reached for the glass of water on his night table. His own feathers tickled the side of his face and poked him in the ear. He let out a bark of frustration, sat up, and slammed back the entire contents of the glass.

He sat on the edge of the bed, glowering and grinding his teeth, listening to the muffled sound of the waves crashing against the stones far below.

He was in a tower that overlooked the lights and harbor of Maticaw. His room was a narrow attic space held together by thick wooden ribs, roughly hewn and as likely to give one splinters as keep the rain off. Part of the ceiling's fat beams were blackened and charred from a fire that had almost destroyed the tower long before Jaclyn had become the building's master. Whoever had patched up the damage hadn't done it artfully, only partially replacing the burnt timbers with fresh ones, and using wooden pegs as thick as a man's arm to cobble the whole thing together. It was not pretty, but it was sturdy.

But it wasn't the half-wasted shell of a tower Ashley called his own that was festering on him like a boil.

It was the dreams. No, not dreams--nightmares.

The dreams were always a replay of that night, the night he chased the frightened, blonde Arpak woman--Jordan--across the black waters of Maticaw in the driving rain.

But he couldn't think of her as just 'Jordan'. He hadn't been able to think of her that way since he'd watched her stagger back across the wet black rocks of the rugged peninsula.

Sister.

His own flesh and blood.

'Don't do this,' she'd said. '*I'll go away and never come back.*' The beauty of her face had been marred with fear. The teal of her eyes darkened to a true sea green in the dim light of the storm, her wet hair plastered to her face and neck. She'd held a knife in her hand, but one knock against her quivering wrist would have sent it flying from her grip.

Ashley put his head into his hands, squeezing his eyes shut and pressing his fingertips into the sides of his skull. A long, frustrated sigh oozed from him like it had clawed its way up from the very pit of his stomach.

In his nightmares, he always finished her.

In his nightmares, there was no armed Nycht nor dragon to protect her; he finished the job he had been given. As the lights went out in her eyes, as her body slumped to the rocks, something cold and hateful would take up residence in his gut. It was a many-legged thing hiding behind a gauzy black drape. The tips of its black legs peeked from under the fabric, each with a long, hooked claw. The thing could reach those hooks into any memory it chose, events long past, mostly to do with Ashley's mother. It could rake them open, spilling the contents of his mind.

The thing was called fear, and its claws were regret.

Ashley stood and began to pace. A dialogue played out in his mind. This too was happening more regularly; enough that Ashley was beginning to fear he might be going crazy.

There is nothing to regret, he thought. *She survived. I didn't kill her.*

But I would have.

Why? The many-legged thing behind the curtain asked.

Because it's what Jaclyn wanted.

Why did Jaclyn want that? it pressed.

Don't ask questions.

I am asking, answered the spider, its hooks tap-tap-tapping against the bones of his skull. Tap-dancing with its relentless, tireless questions.

Ashley let out a scream and drove his fist into the doorjamb, bruising his knuckles and not even noticing.

In the dream that had woken him this night, Jordan died as always. But something was different.

As he had stood over her, at the moment when he always woke up, the dream did not dissolve.

He was staring down at her still form. Her face was pointed toward the ground, her hair covering her cheek, and he sent a booted toe into her shoulder, gently, almost tenderly, rolling her onto her back.

Then he staggered back, choking. Her face was no longer feminine.

The lifeless, lightless eyes were no longer teal, they were brown. Her face had become his own, and the chest which held the steel of his blade was broader––his chest. Rain filled the hollows of his face, making his eyes look larger, magnifying the death in them.

He screamed, and woke up gagging with fear.

Ashley set his forehead against the door and took deep breaths, trying to clear the awful vision.

"Ashley?" Jaclyn's voice was on the other side of the door, so close it made him jump.

His heart bolted around in his chest, and he took another breath before opening the door.

She stood on the landing. Her dewy skin was so pale it almost glowed in the light of the lantern she'd set on the table just outside his door.

Jaclyn never had the flush and color of the sun on her anymore. Ashley wasn't sure if the nut brown mother he remembered from his youth, with the dusting of freckles over her nose, had ever been real. She had never been a woman who laughed, but hadn't she once been a woman who loved the sunshine?

She was dressed in a black tunic, which belted at the waist. Soft camel-colored pants encased her legs, and black suede boots came up over her kneecaps. Her rich, chestnut hair was pulled back into a high ponytail, accentuating the ethereal size of her eyes.

Jaclyn had never dressed like the women in Maticaw. Ashley supposed her taste had something to do with having come from Earth, but he'd never asked her why she preferred the simple, almost androgynous tailoring to the colorful feminine styles of their port-town.

There were a lot of things Ashley had never asked his mother. Questions were not allowed. Not ever. Jaclyn parsed out information like war-time rations.

"I thought I heard you yell." Her eyes probed his face like blind fingers searching his contours for clues. "You're sweating. Would you like me to have Rolea make you that spicy soup?"

"I'm fine, Jaclyn." Ashley's arms drifted across his chest, where only a short time before, he'd dreamed his own sword had run him through. "Thank you."

Jaclyn nodded and held out an envelope with the wax seal of 'Jack', the Port Master at Maticaw. "I need you to deliver this to the courier's office. The next run goes at seven; make sure you don't miss it."

Ashley took the envelope. "I'll leave right after breakfast."

"Good enough." Jaclyn took the lantern, and her steps echoed on the staircase as she returned to her quarters.

Ashley listened until he heard the door at the bottom of the stairs click shut, then he closed himself in his room. He donned his clothing and his armor. *The letter is likely another stall tactic.* He glanced at it and frowned. Yes, it was addressed to Belshar, the Rodanian bureaucrat and their contact for all things trade-related. Ashley had picked up enough conversation around the trade office to know that Belshar was making a nuisance of himself about some mushroom from the other side of The Conca.

Why it had become such a drama, Ashley didn't know, and hadn't ever cared to know.

He flew across the waters dotted with vessels, and landed on the docks in a walk without breaking his stride. He folded his wings away and headed along the boardwalk, turning into a narrow, cobbled alley which led to the steps that would take him into the heart of the commercial district of the city. Ashley had done enough deliveries to find his way to the courier's office in a blindfold.

Barely conscious of his surroundings——the pestering sales-men, the beggars and the mouth-watering smell of street food——Ashley's mind mulled over his nighttime agonies.

The dreams hadn't started right away; they'd crept up on him slowly, at first coming to him as barely-remembered vignettes. He'd wake with an unsettled feeling and a knot in his stomach that would stay with him most of the day.

Then the dreams began to clarify and grow more vivid. He recognized the rugged stones at his feet, Jordan's wet and fearful face, her soaking clothing, the trembling knife held up against his advance.

Her confusion was what pierced him most. Jordan was a lot of things in that moment, but what she had been the most was lost.

How long had you been looking for your mother, Ashley wondered, *only to find Jaclyn and receive a greeting that would make a slap in the face seem like a kiss?*

Ashley's own bewilderment had been fairly well-masked that night. But Jaclyn had not denied Jordan when she had called her *'Mom'*; in fact, she had told Jordan, *'If I thought I could raise you and also do what I was meant to, I would have.'* It was a full admission.

That had been the moment when Ashley was unable to cover his surprise.

He had been certain the young woman was mistaken. She had to be an imposter——someone perhaps employed by their enemies to uncover Jaclyn's alias. But it wasn't adding up; if she had been out to discover Jaclyn's true identity, then why would she pose as her daughter? And how would she even know Jaclyn had had a daughter? Ashley himself hadn't known.

Not that *that* was unusual; Ashley was learning that there was so much he didn't know. And he had always thought himself special, needed, precious and deserving of responsibility in Jaclyn's eyes——it was almost laughable.

It's not too late to turn from this path you're on. An outside voice penetrated his thoughts.

Ashley's lips parted to snarl in annoyance when he saw that the voice had not come from one of the usual peddlers and fortune tellers which clogged the side-streets of Maticaw. A willowy Elf stood in front of a bright blue door along the narrow street. Her pale coloring stood out so starkly against the blue that her image seemed to waver at the edges, as though she wasn't totally there——just an apparition. Her skin was a soft alabaster gray, her hair long and white. Her dress was teal in color and clung to her elegantly, highlighting her tiny waist and long slender neck. Her fine face was expressionless, as though she hadn't just spoken to him. She seemed to look right through him.

Ashley stopped walking, surprised in spite of himself. He squinted at the Elf, uncertain if it really was she who had spoken. But a glance around confirmed it couldn't have been anyone else.

"What?" he said, feeling stupid.

My name is Pohle, the Elf said without moving her lips.

Ashley shook his head once, trying to clear it. Receiving communication telepathically was a new and jarring experience for the young Arpak.

I'm an Elf of Charra-Rae. Her face was as still as midnight, her lips could have been carved from marble. Her eyes seemed to widen and her irises to grow larger as he looked at her.

"Charra-Rae," Ashley felt the crowd bump around him, buffeting him softly, but the feeling seemed far away. "Where the mushrooms are from?"

A soft smile played at her lips. *The fungus. Yes,* she said without speaking.

"What are you doing here?" Ashley's flesh marbled with goosebumps.

I'm here to see you. Pohle's chin tilted slightly. Then her lips finally opened, and she spoke real words with a real voice. "Ashley."

Ashley started, not only at the sound of his name but at how the word felt when she spoke it, like a taut string running from the top of his head to his tailbone had been plucked and sent vibrating. The feeling made his heart leap and clatter, and his groin clench.

"Me?" His voice was a choked shadow of its former strength.

Pohle's pale hand beckoned him, and he found himself staggering toward her, not entirely of his own volition. "I have a message for you from our dear princess."

Ashley felt the blood drain from his cheeks. What would an Elf princess want with him? He stopped in front of her, feeling groggy. "What message?"

"That you are more than this," she gestured to his person as a whole. How she managed to make the movement seem disdainful without changing her facial expression seemed marvelous to him. *The key lies beneath your feet. Free yourself from the web.*

"Web?" Ashley's mind was reeling. "What web?"

The corner of her lip turned up. *Your mother's, of course.*

And the telepathy is back. Ashley wheezed.

Pohle *tsked* and shook her head slowly in what seemed to be an uncharacteristic display of personal opinion about his recent life choices, and Ashley started when he felt her cool fingers slide into his palms. Her face swept forward in a fluid motion, stopping mere inches from his... There was a tightening in his stomach from her nearness.

Is she friend or foe?

"I'm a friend," she said, speaking the words out loud and sending the string inside him twanging.

"You can read minds?"

"It doesn't take a mind reader to see what you are trying to discern. Let me help you along." Her face came closer, her head tilted to the side. For a moment he thought she was going to kiss him, and he knew he wouldn't stop her. If there was a spell or an enchantment in her kiss, he'd already fallen under it.

But she passed by his mouth and put her lips close to his ear. "Listen to me, young son, and listen well."

They stood there in the streets of Maticaw, and he listened. As the Elf whispered, the cracks which had already begun to form in Ashley's trust in his mother spread their forked fingers like lightning clawing through the sky.

* * *

ASHLEY PADDED along the carpeted hallway, silent as death. Huge paintings and mirrors, gathered over the years by his mother, lined the hall and filled it with warmth. Lit torches behind elegant glass sconces filled the hallway with flickering light.

Ashley's reflection passed him by as he made his way to the wide wooden doorway that he knew led into the bowels of the trade building.

'The key lies beneath your feet.'

Glancing to either end of the hall, Ashley grasped the metal handle and opened the door. He let himself down the dark stairwell and closed the door quietly behind him.

Ashley fumbled along the wall for the torch and lit it. Damp air smelling of burlap and seaweed wafted around him like a cloying perfume. His booted feet found the basement, and he held the torch high in the dark space. Firelight threw back the shadows, sending them running for corners and dancing across the floor as he walked past boxes and bags, wooden shelves piled high with goods——either forgotten and left there to mildew, or waiting for some captain's crew to ferry them away.

Vaulted ceilings passed by overhead as the young Arpak explored the space, looking for what the Elf had told him was there. Deeper into the bowels of the building he went. The ceiling sank and pressed down over his head, the temperature dropped, and he shivered. He swung the torch to and fro, reading labels on burlap bags, stamped in several languages.

Crossing over a long, crooked gouge in the floor, Ashley saw a squat door in a far corner and moved toward it like a man in a trance. He reached for the handle, but saw chains barring his way and huffed a frustrated groan. He cast about with the torch for something he could use to break the chain and, when nothing revealed itself, pulled his sword from its sheath. Several sharp hits and the chain gave way. Ashley pulled the chains through the metal rings and let them drop to the floor. He put his sword away, pulled the door open, and peered inside.

More burlap sacks like the ones scattered throughout the basement. He heaved one toward himself and pulled open the ties at the mouth. A smell like black pepper and cloves drifted to his nose as he reached inside and grasped an oddly-shaped, hard lump. The firelight revealed a fungus shaped like a thick half-disk. It was dark brown and lumpy on the underside, and bright fuchsia and smooth on the top-side.

Ashley stared at the mushroom in wonder. *This strange growth is the source of all the friction between my mother and Rodania ——but why?*

His eyes drifted from the specimen in his hand to the mountain of bags which had been shoved into the space that had been relegated seemingly just for this purpose. *How long have the mushrooms been here?*

He held the fungus to his nose and sniffed. It did not have the same mouldering scent that most things in the basement had. It smelled fresh, and even seemed to fill him with a kind of subtle vitality. Tentatively, he stuck his tongue out to taste it. He bit off a small piece and crushed it between his front teeth, letting his taste buds experience it. Mildly spicy. A warm feeling filled his mouth. He spat the bits out, but the warm sensation remained.

The sound of distant voices and the scraping of a boat against stone made Ashley's heart pound. Moving quickly, he put the fungus into his satchel, closed up the bag, and shoved it back into place. He closed the door and replaced the broken chain, hoping that whoever was about to make a delivery wouldn't be delivering more of the fungus and coming this far back into the basement.

Ashley jogged through the basement as the chain on the other side of the outer doors leading to the beach began to rattle. He doused the torch in a barrel of water, replaced it in its iron holder, and was up and out and walking down the hallway of the trade office as though nothing out of the ordinary had occurred, the fungus tucked safely away in his satchel.

CHAPTER 6

"*P*ass the green curlicues, please. The ones with the hair," said Allan to Eohne, forking another bite of orange mash into his mouth.

"You mean the piprian ferns?" Eohne passed him the bowl of steamed vegetables, one elegant, dark brow cocked with humor.

"Whatever they are, they taste like an asparagus mated with a banana." Allan said, cheeks bulging. "They're amazing."

"Normally I wouldn't think that sounded appealing." Jordan speared one of the tightly curled green ferns as the bowl passed under her nose. Each fern was as bright as the inside of a lime and covered in short, silky stalks of yellow hair. "But there is something oddly addictive about this fuzzy veggie. I find it strange how we have some Earth vegetables and fruits here, like potatoes and apples, but none of the Oriceran vegetation made it through the other way."

"That's because over two thousand years ago, Earthlings emigrated here in large numbers, bringing seeds and farming technologies and their languages with them. But that same sort of mass exodus never happened going the other way." Allan shoved a fern into his mouth and chewed rapidly, swallowing so he could get out his next thought. "Explains why there are plenty of humans here but no Elves or Strix on Earth. Except for in books and movies, of course."

Sol was nodding. "Did you also know that an entire legion of Roman soldiers accidentally slipped through a portal and ended up here?"

"Yes!" Allan's entire countenance brightened. "I almost spat out my tea when I ran across that in an old text at the library. On Earth they're known as the Lost 9th Legion; they disappeared from Scotland. They still live in the wilderness on the west side of The Conca, north of the sixty-third parallel. I've heard that it's hostile territory up there. Must have been quite a shock for the Romans, soldiers or not."

Sol nodded. "We studied them a bit at the Academy. They became a warrior tribe whose descendants culled whole herds of feroth from the wastelands, eliminating a peace-loving tribe of healers." He shook his head. "It's a story that seems to repeat itself, no matter which planet you live on."

"Is this what you've been doing with your time, Dad?" Jordan sopped up the last of Eohne's amazing gravy off her plate and popped it into her mouth.

"Never in my whole life could I read all of the books written about Earth history, and it's the same here. The library at the University of Rodania is absolutely stuffed with an entirely new world. I'd forget to eat, if Runcher didn't remind me. It's wonderfully fascinating."

"Who's Runcher?" Jordan leaned back in her chair and rubbed a hand subconsciously over her full belly.

"A professor at the university and the academy," Sol answered for Allan. "Smart man, but if he's still teaching the same way he did when I was there, then he really needs to switch things up or move on and do something else. I love history, and even I fell asleep in his classes."

Allan chuckled. "He does have a monotonous voice, but I

think I can call the fellow a friend by this point. We end up in long discussions whenever I'm there, and I continuously make him late for work."

The apartment they found for Allan and Eohne gave them easy access to throughways for Rodania's wingless citizens. The government of Rodania never prioritized developing modes of transportation for non-Strix, since there were so few of them. Horses and bicycles were used; ponies had been introduced to Rodania before the islands were lifted from the sea, and they continued to be bred in controlled numbers. There were also Strix for hire who would happily carry wingless residents where they needed to go——for a fee, according to the weight of the load.

Overall, it was a tedious affair to get from place to place, if you lived far from your work, so once wingless citizens were settled on one of the islands, they rarely left.

The apartment tower wasn't far from the university library, which drew Allan like a fly to honey. He'd joined a cleanup crew after the harpy battle and was dispatched along with other wingless citizens to put Upper Rodania to rights and help those with damaged homes and businesses recover. After work, he'd walk to the university library to spend hours poring over books and, apparently, talking with Professor Runcher. Gradually, the work that the wingless citizens could do within a reasonable radius was done, and Allan gained more hours of free time.

"You've not been missing Virginia, Dad? No desire to go back?"

Allan scoffed. "I hated my life there."

Jordan smiled. Her father would never have admitted that to her while they were living in Richmond——he wouldn't have wanted her to worry——but she'd known. "I think it was more that you hated your work."

Allan nodded. "Yes, being a politician was possibly the worst choice I could have ever made for myself."

"You can't change jobs?" Eohne asked.

"It would be difficult at my age, and I'm not sure what else I would do."

"You wouldn't teach history?" Jordan knew that had always been Allan's dream.

"I'd have to go back to school to get the proper credentials, and I'm not sure going back to college is really in the cards for me. Why, are you trying to foist me back to Earth?"

Allan was trying to keep his tone light, but there was a vulnerable sound in his voice, like he wasn't entirely sure he was wanted.

"Of course not, Dad. I love that you're here. I just want you to be happy."

"I am happy, Jordy. I mean, if you decided that you wanted to go home, naturally I would go with you." Her dad's hazel eyes held her teal ones; eyes not of his genes, but it couldn't have mattered less. "You're the only family I have; I want to be where you are."

Jordan's heart melted. "Me too, Dad."

"What about you, Eohne? What did you get up to today?" Sol asked as he got up and began to clear the plates.

Eohne's face brightened. "Actually, it's been a fascinating couple of days. I met a Light Elf named Linlett who is here to solve the barrier violations."

"Calling what the harpies did a 'barrier violation' is colossally understating reality," murmured Sol, depositing the dirty dishes into the sink and coming back for a second load.

"It's about time they sent someone," said Jordan. "Just one Elf, though? You'd think they might send a whole team. A nation is in jeopardy here, and it looks as though their faulty magic might be the cause of it."

"I don't think they need to send anyone else," Eohne said, somewhat dreamily. "Linlett is very competent. Light Elf magic is even more spectacular than I thought it would be."

Jordan and Sol looked at one another, and Sol cocked an eyebrow. Did Eohne have a crush, or was the admiration on her face a professional one? They'd never seen Eohne with a love interest before, but there was nothing she was more enthusiastic about than magic, so it was hard to tell.

Allan was smiling at Eohne. "He didn't mind you tampering with his magic, I take it? Didn't you go down to the border specifically to poke around?"

"He didn't mind at all. In fact, he seemed keen to work together on it. Bit of a shock, really." Eohne's voice sounded far away, like she was speaking to her friends but her mind was elsewhere.

"How are you going to tackle it?" Sol sat down again at the now clean table. Curiosity was etched across his features. "Where do you start?"

"Linlett has a way of making the magic barrier visible. I guess that's where we start... Looking for anomalies, gaps, loopholes."

"What about interrogating each of the border guards?" Sol suggested.

"I'm told Balroc is making arrangements to have that done," Eohne replied. She chewed her lip doubtfully. "It does seem a good place to start, but if it was one of the border guards, why would they 'fess up to it?" Her eyes shifted to Sol's. "They wouldn't consider torturing them, would they?"

Jordan's skin prickled with horror, but as she observed the Elf's aversion to such a tactic, she was reminded of the hordes of gnashwitted people back in Charra-Rae. They were in that state as a result of what Eohne had invented: destructive magic she didn't know how to undo. Knowing the Elf better now than when she'd first been exposed to the gnashwits, Jordan believed that Eohne would never have invented such magic unless at Sohne's directive.

Sol frowned. "I don't know." A flicker of an idea crossed his face. "Could you develop some magic that reveals when someone is lying?"

"Like a polygraph!" Jordan immediately thought of Arth. *She's brilliant. Surely she can replicate a polygraph, if we can get our hands on one.*

"What's a polygraph?" Eohne's brows shot up with interest.

"It's a machine that's built to detect lies," explained Jordan.

"Earth has such a machine?" Eohne sounded amazed.

A surprised look passed between Jordan and Allan.

"I would expect your magic could do that better than any human-made device," said Allan. "You've never thought of it?"

Eohne shook her head, still clearly taken with the idea. "Maybe the Light Elves have such a magic, but Charra-Rae Elves don't lie. We're too afraid of Sohne. We can never tell what she does and doesn't know. Plus, it's not in our nature. We're all on the same side, working toward the same goals. Why would we lie to each other?"

"Everyone lies," murmured Allan.

Jordan shot him a somber look. "You sound so cynical, Dad. Of course you would think that, you worked in politics. Lying comes with the territory."

Eohne was one-track. "How does this machine work?"

"I had to take one once," Allan admitted.

"Dad!" Jordan sat upright, shocked. "What for?"

He shrugged. "I didn't mind. I had nothing to hide. It was to clear me of suspicion around Jaclyn's disappearance." He started using his hands to explain the device to Eohne. "They put a strap around my chest——"

"On your skin?"

"Over my clothes. And the machine sat beside me on a table-top, hooked up to the strap by cables. It had a needle that jumped back and forth as they asked me questions, and it would suppos-edly reveal whether I was lying or not. Polygraph machines are, to this day, dismissed by many as 'pseudoscience', but I read up

on it before the test. If the person taking it isn't trained in countermeasures, the test can tell lies from the truth at rates well
above chance." He jutted his chin forward and shrugged. "It's not
perfect, but it's better than nothing."

"What does it measure?" Eohne leaned forward on her elbows,
her big brown eyes locked on Allan's face.

"Blood pressure, pulse, perspiration, things like that. Physiological signs that are known to fluctuate if a person is lying."

"Hmmmm." Eohne mulled this over. "I have never considered
inventing such a magic, but it strikes me that, while lying might
be difficult to detect, deception might be easier."

"Aren't they the same thing?" Jordan asked.

"Not necessarily," Sol interjected. He'd been leaning his chair
back on its rear legs, a toe hooked under the cross-beam beneath
the table. He let the front chair legs drop with a *clack*. "Lying
means a false statement has been made——deceit is when
someone says or does something with the intention to
cause harm."

Eohne nodded. "I might be able to wrap my head around
developing magic that could detect a person's intentions, but
lying?" She made a *tsk* sound and shook her head. "That would be
a big undertaking. Bigger even than trying to synthesize gersher
fungus."

Jordan just stopped herself from adding, '*Or reversing the
gnashwits?*'

Eohne gazed at her worktable longingly. "Thank you, Allan.
You've given me food for thought."

"Speaking of food." Jordan got up. "Anyone for tea and
dessert?"

"You're a ravenous one lately," Allan observed with a smile.

"It's the training," Sol explained. "I'm starving all the
time, too."

Jordan got up to put the kettle on, and as she made her way to
the stove, she passed by the worktable Eohne had set up for

herself. A cluster of tiny white butterflies hovered over it in a tight clump.

"Oh, pretty!" She bent to take a closer look. "They're so delicate and beautiful." Each butterfly had wings of a pale green color on a bright blue body no larger than her thumbnail. A single transparent dot sat in the centre of each upper wing.

"Don't disrupt them!" Eohne's voice was filled with alarm.

"Oh, sorry!" Jordan turned away. "Just looking, I wasn't going to touch them."

Her breath, gentle though it was, passed over the butterflies, and they responded to the light wind immediately by breaking formation. They fluttered outward and then inward, each in their own circle and in perfect unison with one another. They repeated this pattern: swooping out, circling, and coming so close their wings touched.

"Whoa," Jordan breathed, mesmerized.

Eohne let out a soft groan.

"It's time for you to come home, Eohne, my brave friend." Sohne's voice emanated from the cluster of butterflies.

"Sweet fancy Moses!" Jordan cried out and took a step back, startled.

"It's a message," explained Eohne, resigned. "In case you haven't figured that out yet."

"Your human friend has been roused from his magical slumber," Sohne's voice continued. "And you have done more than your fair share to contribute to the war effort in Rodania." Sohne's voice was breathy and musical, soft and sweet sounding. "Come home, Eohne. Come home to Charra-Rae. We are waiting for you. We need you."

"I've never heard her sound so..." Sol trailed off, looking askance at Eohne.

"Nice?"

"I was going to say enticing, almost pleading. But sure, 'nice' also works."

Eohne let out a sigh as she watched the butterflies return to their original formation. Sohne's message appeared to be finished. "She has no power over her Elves when they are not in Charra-Rae. It's why she was so hesitant to let me go in the first place. She cannot compel me to come home, she can only ask. She trusted that I would have returned by now, but I have violated that trust, and the violation becomes more serious with every day that passes. She sounds warm and fuzzy, but inside, I guarantee you she is seething."

"When did you get this message?" Jordan resumed putting on tea and grabbed the biscuits Allan had bought on his way home from the university that day. She returned to the table, opening the carton. "And I'm sorry, by the way, for digging into your personal mail. I didn't realize..."

Eohne waved a hand. "It's alright. You might as well know what I'm up against." She slumped in her chair. "I got it a few days after the harpy battle."

Allan, Sol and Jordan shared startled looks.

"That was almost four weeks ago." Allan put a hand on Eohne's shoulder. "And you've not responded?"

"No."

"*Should* you respond?"

"I don't know," Eohne almost wailed. She put her chin in her hand and propped an elbow on the table in an uncharacteristic posture of hopelessness.

"Do you *want* to go home?" Sol asked gently. "Because you know you don't have to, right?"

"Yeah, you're family," Jordan added with ferocity. The idea of Eohne leaving was a prickly one, and much more so if Eohne had to return to an angry princess. How might Sohne punish her?

"Thank you," Eohne sighed. "I don't know that, either. I mean, sometimes, yes, I miss the wilderness of Charra-Rae. I miss my Elven friends. But if I go home, I'm not sure Sohne will ever let me leave again. And the longer I leave it, the more likely that possibility is. I wish I could just travel in and out of my home as I wished, like all of you can."

Sol glowered. "It's ridiculous that you can't."

"Well, to be fair, most Elves don't have as much trouble leaving as I do."

"Sorry, but how is that fair?" Allan asked incredulously.

"Fair to Sohne, I mean. She doesn't keep everyone on such a tight leash. Just me and a handful of others."

"I really don't like this Elf," Jordan muttered, crossing her arms over her chest. She still chafed about what had happened with Blue the last time she had been to ask the Elf princess for help. The glyphs that wound their way up her arm reminded her on a daily basis that she still owed the Elf whatever she asked for.

"Why is that?" Allan asked Eohne gently.

"Because, well…" Eohne's cheeks tinged with pink.

"It's because she's an absolutely brilliant inventor and magician, and losing her would be like losing a major piece in a game of chess." Sol said it so Eohne didn't have to. It was unlike Eohne to toot her own horn, but everyone at the table knew her value. She was irreplaceable; a major boon to any society lucky enough to have her.

"Basically." Eohne wilted further. "I was thinking maybe I would head home soon, but…" Eohne bit her lip. "But I've met Linlett now, and I'm learning so much from him."

"And he from you, I would imagine," Jordan added.

Eohne nodded. "I don't really want to leave until this problem is solved. Working with a Light Elf can only augment my powers, my understanding of the various languages of magic. It's sort of a dream come true."

"Then *tell* Sohne that," Jordan suggested. "Maybe she would understand?"

The corners of Eohne's mouth turned down. "Sohne doesn't like Light Elves. The fact that we used to be the same people doesn't matter to her. She sees us as the way Elves should be, and the Light Elves as less evolved. She wouldn't approve of me working with one directly, even if I thought it would ultimately benefit the Elves of Charra-Rae."

"That's pretty short-sighted," Allan scoffed.

Eohne joggled her head from side to side in partial agreement. "Sohne is very far-sighted, actually. Remember, she can see some futuristic events. She rarely shares what she sees, but I can at least trust that she has the Charra-Rae Elves' best interests at heart."

"What about *your* best interests?" Allan probed softly.

Eohne didn't reply, but the longing in her eyes was enough to say what she couldn't or didn't want to say out loud.

Eohne wanted to be free.

* * *

"MIGHT I have a word with you privately?" Allan asked Jordan quietly as she and Sol got up to leave later that night.

"Of course, Dad." Jordan's brows drew together at the expression on her father's face. Whatever he wanted to speak to her about, it was clearly of a more serious nature.

Allan and Jordan stepped outside into the cool Rodanian evening. Insects buzzed and sang, and the first of the stars were beginning to dust the sky.

"You know how much I don't like asking you for favors, Jordy," Allan began hesitantly. "You're an adult, and you've been able to make your own decisions for a long time now."

"Dad," Jordan put a hand on his shoulder, concern inflating like a bubble in her gut. "What's this about?"

"I have been wrestling with myself about this ever since I heard of Toth's plan to go to Golpa. At first, I thought I could get over it, but..." Allan tucked his hands in his armpits and hunched his shoulders. He looked like a young boy in that posture, a very uncertain young boy. "I'm not feeling any better about things; in fact, I'm feeling worse. So, I just have to say something."

"Oh?" Jordan had a feeling she knew where this might be going, and her heart fell a little. But within that drop of disappointment was a rush of warmth and love for her father, and no small amount of compassion.

Allan looked into Jordan's eyes, his own hazel ones pleading. "Please, don't go to Golpa." He brought his hands out of his armpits and put up his palms. "I know you're an amazing warrior now, Jordan. You're competent, and strong. But you don't always have to be the one who puts her life on the line. There are others who will go. Toth isn't taking everyone; he doesn't have to take you." His eyes were suddenly glassy-looking, the rims red.

"Dad..." Jordan began, preparing to muster the words needed to give him comfort around the mission. Her lips parted.

"You're all I've got, Jordy," Allan said, taking her hand. "Sitting underground during the harpy battle, wondering what was happening, if you were alright——it nearly killed me. Please, just sit this one out? For me?"

Suddenly Jordan saw the purple smudges under Allan's eyes, the lines of tension and worry bracketing his mouth, the graying hair at his temples. He had been torturing himself over this, she could see now; she'd just been too busy to notice.

He was right, he never asked anything of Jordan.

In that moment, she understood what the request was costing him, how much it meant.

"Alright, Dad," Jordan said. Disappointment was heavy in her, but as soon as she said the words, Allan's face brightened. The lines of stress softened, and Jordan felt that she'd done the right thing.

"Thank you, Jordy," Allan whispered, pulling his daughter in for a hug. "Thank you."

CHAPTER 7

*S*ol hunkered on the floor in the middle of a pile of weapons, satchels, rope, harnesses, armor and clothing. Beyond where Sol squatted, the Rodanian sky was awash with diamonds, and a sweet-smelling breeze circulated through their apartment. In spite of the beauty of the night, Sol was frowning. For the last hour he'd been sifting through the items and making piles, then unmaking them. He could only carry so much to Golpa, and having never faced a journey into the North, it wasn't totally clear what was most important.

Warm layers or weapons? He blew out a long, frustrated raspberry.

Jordan emerged from the water closet squeezing out her damp hair with a towel. She wore a simple, knee-length robe that was custom designed for a Strix woman. It was dark blue and belted at the waist.

Sol's eyes flashed to her, and he smiled appreciatively. "You look so nice in girl clothes," he said.

"Thank you."

Since they'd cleaned up their apartment and Rodania wasn't in such dire straits anymore, Jordan had exchanged one of her gold bars for coins and picked out a few items of clothing from the shops in Keayr--a shopping district on Upper Rodania which vaguely reminded her of Rodeo Drive in L.A.

"How is it going?" Jordan perched on a stool, tucked her feet against the bottom rung and spread her damp wings to help them air dry.

Sol's expression grew serious again as it drifted back to the mess surrounding him. He made a frustrated grunt in the back of his throat. "I'm jumping the gun." His knees popped, and he stood and stretched his back. "Toth will tell us what to bring at the meeting tomorrow, but I was hoping to get a head start. I have never been so far north as Golpa before; there aren't many communities North of Skillen that have anything to do with Rodania, so there was never reason to go. It's going to be harsh and cold. I commissioned cold weather gear from that tailor in Crypsis."

Jordan nodded. "Good. That's good," she said, but her expression was sad.

Sol stepped over the pile of goods and stood over Jordan. She wrapped her arms around his waist and he looped his around her shoulders. He kissed the top of her wet head. "You're doing the right thing, Jordan."

Jordan's eyes drifted shut, and she relaxed into his warmth. "I know. It doesn't make it any easier to watch you prepare for battle."

The sound of flapping made them both turn toward the terrace. As the sound drew nearer, Sol and Jordan stepped out onto the balcony and peered into the dark.

The flapping was shortly accompanied by wheezing, and a dark shape with small wings, clearly struggling to fly, materialized from the nighttime vista. They both squinted, straining their eyes to see who was coming.

"It's Juer!" Sol's voice was filled with alarm. "Uncle?" he called, then spread his wings and went out to meet the old doctor. He wanted to offer his assistance, but the old Arpak made a motion with his hand, signalling he was alright.

He aimed for the balcony and came in for a landing like a bomber suffering from a blown-out engine. He seesawed back and forth wildly for a moment, and Jordan's hand flew to her mouth. She thought he was going to miss the balcony entirely and splat into the granite side of the tower.

From the look on Sol's face, he shared the same concern.

Juer righted himself at the last moment and collapsed on the terrace in front of Jordan. Her hands darted out and she caught him, just preventing his old knees from smashing against the tiles.

"Thank you, my dear," he wheezed, gripping Jordan's arms and leaning heavily on her.

Jordan felt the old Arpak's heart pounding in his thin, bony chest and looked over Juer's fluff of white hair at Sol, who landed on the balcony behind his uncle. They shared a look of concern.

Juer got his weight under himself and stood back from Jordan, breathing hard. "Trouble you for a glass of water?" he asked between gasps. One arthritic hand was pressed to his chest.

"Of course, Uncle." Sol darted inside while Jordan helped Juer into the kitchen.

His wings were even thinner than the last time she'd seen him; she was surprised the old Arpak could still fly well enough to pass between the palace and their tower, even though the two buildings weren't all that far apart. The aging doctor never made the journey to his library in Crypsis anymore. He'd made arrangements to have the books brought up to the palace library, and put the building up for sale.

Sol handed Juer a glass, and he took it and drank greedily, breathing loudly through his nose. Under their artificial lights, Juer looked waxen in color. Dark rings circled his eyes. He looked the way most of the Nychts did in Rodania--exhausted.

Juer handed the glass back, and Jordan pulled out a chair for him to sit on. He nodded, finally getting his breathing under control. His spectacles sat crookedly on the end of his nose from his wild flight. He straightened them with trembling hands.

"What's wrong, Uncle?" Sol set the glass in the sink and came to stand close to the doctor. His uncle's expression put ice into his belly.

"It's gone," said Juer harshly, with a swipe of his hand through the air. "Someone has stolen it!"

"Stolen..."

"The last of the lapita," Juer ground out. His expression was agony and terror. "It's gone. Even now, the king's eyes are dimming. I didn't know who else to go to. I'm afraid I have to ask you to break the law." The rheumy eyes projected palpable regret at his young nephew.

Sol simply said, "Tell me what you need."

"I need Gersher fungus from Charra-Rae. Even now, Cles is waiting for an escort to bring him to the palace so he can process it. We'll have to import it without registering it, it is too important."

Jordan and Sol shared a look. Sol was due at the strategy session with Toth in the morning.

"I'll go," offered Jordan. "Sol leaves for Golpa the day after tomorrow. Besides," she added in an attempt to bring some levity into the moment, "I'm the faster flier."

Sol just winked at her gratefully.

"It may take you longer than usual to get there and back," said Juer with a warning in his voice. "There is a storm moving in from the North, between Rodania and Maticaw. They are always bad this time of year."

Sol was nodding. "I heard this also. If you're going to go, you should leave no later than noon tomorrow to beat it, then hunker down in Maticaw until it passes, and then continue on to Charra-Rae."

Jordan nodded, already calculating what she'd need to take

and if there was anything she needed to do before she left. "Sohne will have to accept gold. After all, this is not a favor for me, it's for the Rodanian King."

"I have gold set aside for it at the palace," said Juer, wiping a hand across his brow. Already, he looked a little better after the short rest, his cheeks regaining some color. "Come by first thing in the morning."

"Who would take your medicine, Uncle?" Sol asked. "Surely you had such a precious substance under lock and key?"

Juer nodded with impatience, his white fluff swaying around his skull like drifting seaweed. "Of course. I kept it in my own private chamber in a locked cabinet. This morning, the cabinet was secure. Less than an hour ago, I went to get the king his evening dose, and the cabinet lock was broken, and the medicine gone." He shook his head. "It is treason." His face grew long and heavy with doubt. His hand clasped Jordan's and squeezed.

"Fly true, little canary," Juer locked eyes with Jordan. The desperation there gave Jordan chills. "The king will not live long if you dally."

Jordan left for Maticaw at first light.

CHAPTER 8

*J*aclyn's desk was neat as a pin. A map of The
Rodanian Sea, including hundreds of miles of coast
from Operyn to Skillen, had been rendered by hand
and painted with vibrant colors. It lay across the dark wood,
pinned down by lead paperweights. Small pawns made out of
different metals had been placed in various positions throughout
the map; they sat on top of each of the three major port cities,
with the most pawns placed in Maticaw. Two pieces sat on the
floating three-tiered cake of Rodania, and Ashley knew who
those pieces represented: Prince Diruk, and Diruk's man, Bryc
—–their only allies in Strix country.

The nature of his mother's relationship with the prince and
the prince's goon was becoming more clear: Jaclyn was a pawn
the prince could use to control the flow of goods in and out of
Rodania. Jaclyn would never have achieved her elevated position
without Prince Diruk's help, and so their alliance was both mutu-
ally beneficial and a secret. No portmaster before Jaclyn had ever
been female; using the alias of 'Jack' while she established her
reputation was a strategic move. The captains of The Rodanian
Sea and beyond were not yet ready for a female portmaster, not

until she had lined their pockets with money and proven how capable and clever she was. Only then would she reveal herself to them.

In a way, it was poetic. Jaclyn envisioned the day she would gather her most powerful captains and let them in on her secret. That day would not come until she had acquired Skillen and Operyn. She even wanted the miserable and remote port of Vischer, the poor relative of all the ports along the coast. It wasn't until Ashley was observing the map spread on Jaclyn's desk that he realized that the ports she aimed to control formed a kind of semi-circle around Rodania, pinning it against the backdrop of the open sea, if one chose to see it.

Each city had always had their own portmaster. Sometimes the masters aligned, other times they butted heads, but having three individuals meant competition, and kept the price of goods down. Having three gave tradesmen, farmers, tailors, and other skilled workers who wanted to sell their goods abroad options.

By bringing each port under her control, Jaclyn would vault herself into a position of power which had previously never existed. She'd have the ability to create a monopoly; control the flow of goods and, therefore, the people and prices. She would be more powerful than a queen, and she would be self-made, having leveraged herself into the position rather than being born into it.

What wasn't clear was Jaclyn's plans for Rodania. Why did Jaclyn care about the flow of a strange pink fungus in and out of the Strix nation? So much so, that she was willing to blackmail a Rodanian bureaucrat to invent a false moratorium on the substance? Belshar had been to visit, Ashley had seen him. The poor thin fellow was as jumpy as a cat in a room full of rocking chairs. No doubt he was experiencing pressure from Rodania to get the fungus cleared, but Ashley knew that Jaclyn was applying her own pressure to Belshar, and the stakes were his life and the lives of his children.

Ashley had been raised not to question Jaclyn's plans, to do as he was told, to be the muscle that helped her achieve their goals of wealth and power. In return, he'd be given whatever he wanted: property, a ship, a fleet of ships, agricultural land in the fertile southern Conca, a bride, or even many women. All this in exchange for his unquestioning loyalty to the woman who raised him and loved him.

Loved?

Until Jaclyn had assigned him the execution of Jordan, it had been enough.

Sister.

Jaclyn had never even told him he had a sister. She had stood there blithely, boldly facing the accusations Jordan had flung into her face. There had been no denying it, no shame.

She'd come all the way from Earth!

Ashley frowned as he stared down at the chess pieces spread on the map before him, staring, but not seeing. What had Jordan been through to find her mother?

When Jaclyn sent Ashley to end her, he'd responded automatically, the way he always had. But while his body moved, his heart told him it was desperately wrong. Jaclyn had never asked him to murder an innocent before——and the young woman was *family*!

Another doubt was steadily chewing through his trust in his mother, like a beetle through rotten wood: if Jaclyn could so easily do away with Jordan, what would stop her from turning against him, too?

Shortly after that awful night, the nightmares had started.

And now the gray Elf from Charra-Rae.

'Ask her,' the Elf had whispered. 'Ask her who you are.'

Ashley squeezed his eyes shut against the bitter feelings and unanswered questions roiling in his gut.

What do you do when the one person you thought you could trust fully, has been caught lying to you? There had only ever been Jaclyn in Ashley's life. It had always been the two of them.

Loneliness swept through Ashley, almost strong enough to bring him to his knees.

"What are you doing in here?"

Ashley looked up, startled, and with guilt stealing across his face.

Jaclyn's long shadow reached toward him from the open door, like a malevolent spirit creeping closer. Her slender hand rested on the broad, iron door handle, her elbow crooked. For a moment she was as still as a porcelain statue, then she moved, slowly.

The door clicked shut behind her.

Her dark eyes locked on her son, soft, but vigilant and discerning. "Ashley?" She crossed the carpet, her footsteps rendered silent by the thick wool rug. The chandelier overhead cast a warped, star-shaped shadow around Jaclyn, which shifted as she walked.

Ashley put a hand down on Jaclyn's desk and leaned forward, looking across the map at his mother. Perspiration had begun to form at his hairline, even though his hands felt clammy and cold as ice.

Lately, his mother's presence had increasingly incited a physiological response from Ashley; and not a pleasant one. A frozen wire wrapped itself around his gut and began to tighten. He was afraid of her, just as she had raised him to be, but he hadn't come this far to cow down. He was gangrenous with questions and doubts, and they festered inside him like a boil.

"Why are you stopping medicine from getting through to people who need it?"

Ashley's question echoed Jordan's exactly, and the mirroring of his twin's words was not lost on Jaclyn. He could see it in her face; the subtle hardening of her eyes and mouth, the flexing of that small muscle just in front of her ears as she clenched her teeth. A blind came down. Her lips pinched together, and she stopped walking. "That is not your concern, Ashley. I know you're not going to make me repeat myself."

"No." Ashley shook his head. "*Repeat* yourself, no. Say something new. Say something real. Tell me the truth, for once."

"What is this about?"

"Who am I?"

Jaclyn resumed her slow journey across the carpet, letting out a low laugh. "You're nobody, Ashley. Until I make you somebody, you're nobody. You are who I tell you to be."

Ashley watched as his mother came around the big wooden desk to face him. She looked up at him, her arms crossed over her chest, her beautiful eyes hard and dark.

"Mom." Ashley grated the word out. He had not called her that in over twenty years.

Her preference, especially in the company of others, had always been 'Jaclyn'.

"You wanted me to kill her. Why?" he demanded.

"Is *she* what this is about?" The hard mask seemed to break, and Jaclyn put her hands on his shoulders, her voice slithering with forced softness. "She was a loose end. You said it yourself: she had seen me. She knows the real identity of 'Jack'. I'll not let all of our hard work be lost because of a girl we can't control."

"Not just a *girl*. Your daughter. My sister. You could so easily sign her death sentence?"

"What do you care? You don't know her. I don't even know her."

"Your own flesh and blood."

"No," barked Jaclyn, dropping her hands from his shoulders. "You are my only flesh and blood. You are all that matters. Everything I do, I've done it for you, for us." Jaclyn turned away from her son. "I did not expect this kind of insubordination from you. Not ever."

"Who am I?" His question was more insistent now. "And don't tell me I'm the son of a merchant."

"Why are you asking me this?" Jaclyn whirled back to him. "Who got to you? Who told you that you were anything or anyone at all?"

"An Elf," Ashley said quietly. "One I had never seen before. She told me about this," he retrieved the lump of fungus from his pocket and held it out, balancing it on his palm for Jaclyn to see.

Jaclyn's eyes dropped to the fungus, and her already pale complexion lost its remaining color. "An Elf." Her brown eyes shuttered, and her neck moved with a swallow. Some inaudible conversation was going on behind those closed lids, or perhaps simply a string of curses. "An Elf from Charra-Rae?" She let out a very long breath and opened her eyes. "Did she have red hair?"

Ashley was momentarily taken off guard. *Who's the Elf with red hair?* "No. She was gray. All gray. Even her skin."

"Oh." Jaclyn brought her fingertips to her temple. "I know this Elf," she said this more to herself than to Ashley.

"She told me to ask you who I am." Ashley took his mother by the shoulders, forcing her to look him in the eyes. "So I'm asking."

"I should have known." Jaclyn's mouth formed a flat, unhappy line. "Damn Diruk and his arrogance." She dropped her face, and her mind went inward, the way it did whenever the gears were turning. Something hadn't gone according to plan, so Jaclyn was strategizing, already forming countermeasures.

Ashley knew the look well.

He shook her. "Mom! Who am I?" Spittle flew into Jaclyn's face and it brought her focus back to her son.

She brushed the moisture from her cheek. "You'd better sit down."

* * *

BRYC HAD NEVER BEEN good for much other than destroying. His own mother dubbed him 'The Destroyer' when he was just a young Nycht. A name that was given in jest ended up aptly describing Bryc's true nature. He wondered how he might have turned out, had his mother not labelled him. *Did the nature result in the name, or the name result in the nature?*

But these were secret things. It was an inscrutable, existentialist question, which, when pondered for too long, made Bryc's head hurt. It was better not to think so hard.

So when Prince Diruk sent his right-hand man to Jaclyn's office to relay the message about King Konig, he bit back a resentful reply about not being a courier.

He understood why palace couriers couldn't be used for any of Diruk's communications with Jaclyn, but thus far, it had been Jaclyn's irksome Arpak roughneck who had done all the boring passing of messages between the allies.

Prince Diruk had no love for Nychts, and Bryc knew it well. But Bryc's modus operandi was to let his kind deal with injustices of life in Rodania as they saw fit, Bryc was loyal only to Bryc. The prince needed an intimidator, a powerful hatchet man, and no one was more powerful than Bryc. Their relationship disclosed the duplicitous nature of the prince: using the superior Nycht assets for his own gain, even as he plotted to keep them oppressed. But Diruk's hypocrisy didn't bother Bryc, as long as he was paid on time and handsomely.

Bryc rounded the corner and strode down the hall toward the foyer in front of Jaclyn's office. The human girl who worked for Jaclyn——Bryc could never remember her name——looked up from her work to watch him come. It was subtle, but Bryc didn't miss the moue of disgust that marred the pretty face. How Bryc would not have minded slashing that perfect skin with one of his dewclaws. But there would be trouble with Jaclyn if he followed his impulses, and trouble with Jaclyn was sometimes trouble with Diruk, so trouble was best avoided.

"It's not a good time," the girl said, visibly cowing as the Nycht filled the hallway with his tyrannizing size. The arches of his wings nearly grazed the ceiling, and his wingtips bumped against the wooden paneling of the hall as he passed.

Bryc ignored the girl and strode toward the double doors behind which the sounds of an argument could be heard. Bryc paused and tilted his head to listen. *How curious, the human pawn is fighting with her lover and mercenary.* A smile creased Bryc's face, and the largest scar on his face, which ran from right temple to left jawline and across his upper lip, puckered, exposing his incisor and gumline.

"Excuse me, I said it's not a good time," the girl at the desk repeated. This time she stood. Though his back was to her, Bryc heard the fabric of her suit jacket brush against the wooden lip of her desk.

He made a small movement—–splaying his fingers out, palm pointed toward her in a gesture of *'shut up'*. His nearly foot-long dewclaws, razor-sharp and gleaming like obsidian, may have curled inward along with the hand gesture. Bryc wasn't always conscious of what his dewclaws were doing. He oiled and filed them, keeping them sharp not only at the tips, but all the way to the base, like scythe-blades. He used them often to climb, stab, cut. That they were also meters of his emotional state to those who knew him was not evident to Bryc. His dewclaws were his only tell.

She fell silent.

Smart girl.

Bryc frowned and strained his ears. The argument was muffled and too far from the door to make out clearly. He crept forward, pressing one scarred ear against the wood. Snippets of coherent language reached him, but fractured and smothered as Jaclyn and Ashley yelled over one another.

Bryc closed his eyes. His hearing sharpened. More came through.

"...everything you've ever asked of me..." This was the Arpak's voice."...lied for you, stolen for you..."

"...arrogance, following blindly..."

Bryc's smile faded. Jaclyn was Prince Diruk's ally, true, but sooner or later their alliance would crumble. It was Bryc's preference that the alliance ruptured when Diruk willed it to, when the timing was right. Perhaps Bryc would even have a hand in it.

"...might object to your scheme! ...not just your goon..."

"Stop this now! I command it!"

"...your son!"

Bryc's eyes snapped open and he straightened, blinking. A low rumble sounded off deep in his chest. *This is news. This is news, indeed. The Arpak mercenary is Jaclyn's boy?* Nothing much winded Bryc, but if he'd had a more evolved emotional intelligence than a junkyard dog, he might have been astonished.

If what he had understood was true, Jaclyn had been lying to the Prince about who Ashley was to her. Bryc didn't care that Ashley and Jaclyn were related, that didn't matter. But *why* had she lied? Lying to Diruk was lying to Bryc.

Remember what Diruk said, if Jaclyn was discovered to be...what was the word the prince had used? 'Deceitful'?

But there were footsteps now. Angry, fast ones. Coming this way.

Bryc darted to the side as the door slammed open and Ashley stalked out, clearly fuming.

Bryc watched the Arpak round the corner without even realizing the huge Nycht was there.

There was the sound of glass breaking from the office.

Bryc peered into Jaclyn's place of business, though it was more like a prison, if you asked Bryc. The woman hadn't seen the light of day in years, as far as he knew.

Jaclyn heaved another breakable item at the wall, and the crystal figurine shattered with an explosive *bang*, leaving a dent in the wood. Her chest was heaving, her pretty face pink with rage and her teeth bared. She caught sight of Bryc in her periphery.

"What are you looking at?" she snarled. She snatched another item from her desk, this one an iron paperweight the size of a Maticaw dockrat. She hefted it, preparing to throw and eyeballing Bryc's head, when a shimmer of real fear passed over her face. It was fleeting. She hastily composed herself.

But Bryc had been trained to spot fear——to smell it and to use it. She didn't know how much or what Bryc had heard, that much was clear. *Probably best to let her think I heard nothing of relevance.*

"Having a bad day?" Bryc's voice was a throaty murmur. He sauntered into the office and closed the door behind him, casual as a Sunday morning.

"Even the most loyal of partners can sometimes step out of line," Jaclyn said, tugging her vest down and smoothing the velvet. She swept a hand over her hair. Some of the high color had not yet left her cheeks.

Bryc thought she looked like a girl of seventeen when she was angry. Jaclyn's was another face he wouldn't mind leaving a mark on. It was too perfect, too unspoiled.

"He did seem rather upset," Bryc observed, his voice almost gentle. "Where do you suppose he's headed in such a… piqued state?" Bryc was so pleased to have found an opportunity to use the word 'piqued' that his dewclaws gave a jovial twitch.

"Nowhere important," Jaclyn said, the words coming out in a rush. She seemed to realize she sounded perturbed and slowed herself down. "He likes to drink at The Oyster & Clam after work. He'll be back before midnight. All will be well."

"Maybe," Bryc grunted. "But I wonder if you remember what the prince said about the four of us?" Bryc stroked his grizzled chin. "Working together, I mean. How we're only as strong as our weakest link."

Jaclyn's cheeks drained of color. "Ashley is still trustworthy."

"That didn't sound like a conversation you have with someone you trust," Bryc intoned, wandering toward the desk. "Forgive me for overhearing, but you were on the emphatic side. Hmmm, not quite the right word. You were on the… vociferous side, let's say." He picked up a weighted quill and fingered the feather tip, feigning disinterest. "It sounded like a…" he paused, theatrically searching for words. "Parting of doctrines, if you will." Bryc had always liked the word 'doctrine'. He wasn't entirely sure if it was appropriate in this instance, but it had a nice ring to it. One of the perks of working for Prince Diruk was the constant exposure to lovely words. "What was it about, I wonder?"

"Ashley is simply tired of not being let in on the plan," Jaclyn replied, crossing her arms over her chest. She watched as Bryc poked around her desk, picking up chess pieces, putting them back in the wrong place. Jaclyn's upper lip twitched.

"So did you?"

"Did I what?"

"Let him in on the plan?"

"No, of course not," Jaclyn snapped. "We agreed it was better he wasn't aware of the overall scheme." Her voice calmed and she added, thoughtfully. "*He's* too good for that." She eyed Bryc, watching for a sign that he'd recognize a barb when it was sent his way.

Bryc chuckled. "Be that as it may, it seems the lad may need a *scaring back into place*. What do you think? For his own *good*?"

Jaclyn's mouth flattened, and she didn't respond right away. She was squirming mentally, like a worm caught on a hook. Bryc could smell her writhing, smoking thoughts.

"He'll not be trouble again. I can guarantee it."

Bryc cocked a cynical eyebrow but remained silent. Her words hung in the air. They were betraying her, exposing her more and more with every moment that wandered past. If Jaclyn didn't want Ashley harmed, it would look as though he meant more to her than she had previously let on. Jaclyn had consistently presented Ashley as a pawn and a bedwarmer, nothing more.

"Fine," Jaclyn amended with a shrug, but then swallowed with an audible click. She cleared her throat. "Perhaps it is just what he needs."

"Very well." Bryc put down the letter opener he'd been twirling between his fingers and strode purposefully for the door. He paused and looked over his shoulder. "Oh, by the way, the prince says *'it's time'.*"

There was a sharp intake of breath at this, but Jaclyn did not otherwise react.

"Bryc," she said just as he reached for the door handle.

Bryc paused but did not look back.

"Just a scaring. That's all. None of your getting carried away."

A smile crossed the Nycht's face, one that did not reach his eyes. "Of course." He swept through the door and let it slam behind him, leaving Jaclyn in her cell to rot.

As the Nycht took to the air over the trade office, headed for Maticaw, he had every intention of getting *'carried away'*. He'd already secured permission to get carried away from the only one who mattered.

The prince's words echoed in his mind, what he said after the meeting with Jaclyn where they had first met her henchman and lover——*but apparently not, apparently he is her son; won't Diruk be pleased to learn she's been caught, and that I've already eliminated the problem?*

After that meeting, the prince had said, *'I don't like him. I can smell a conscience a mile away. If you catch so much as a whiff of artifice on that kid, you end him. He's only good for us so long as he doesn't ask questions, and I know his type. Sooner or later, he'll ask questions.'*

Bryc remembered the moment well, he remembered it because he'd liked the word *'artifice'*. It was a nice word. He wasn't entirely sure what it meant, but he was pretty sure it applied in this case. And if it didn't... well, he wasn't one to carry a dictionary around with him, and better safe than sorry.

CHAPTER 9

*S*omething huge moved in front of Ashley. Like the stormfront rolling in outside, the thing was dark and oppressive, and swept in from out of nowhere. It took a moment for him to piece together what he was looking at through the haze of alcohol, but the jigsaw finally meshed into the puckered and seamed face of Bryc.

The giant Nycht slid onto the stool at the adjoining corner of the bar, the wooden seat giving a creak of protest under the warrior's weight.

Despite everything, Ashley found the will to be surprised by the goon's sudden arrival. Glancing at the other patrons in the bar, a flock of them now seeking shelter from the storm, he could see that they were all watching Bryc and wondering if the storm had just come inside. Ashley wondered drunkenly if they weren't right.

"You lost?" Ashley slurred as he swung his head around to meet the dark eyes glinting from beneath Bryc's craggy brows.

Bryc's face split into a smile that would shame some of the sharks prowling the harbor. Another squeak issued from the stool as Bryc leaned in close enough for Ashley to feel his hot breath pass by his face. The stench of partially digested onion and garlic had Ashley fighting back the urge to retch.

"Ohhh," he purred, his voice sounding like a gravel tumbler, "I've found what I'm looking for."

"What's this then?" Ashley growled at a volume only a drunk would think was reasonable. "Jaclyn sent you here to bring me home? Talk some sense into me? Maybe... maybe teach me a lesson on the way back?" Ashley sneered.

Bryc's ugly face seemed ready to split, he was smiling so big. "Yeah," he said in a voice so soft it was barely audible over the mutter of patrons and the rain pelting the warped glass windows. "Something like that."

It would be just like Jaclyn to send Bryc, someone I have no love for, to slap me around a little after my display of insurrection. Not that there are a lot of other messengers she could send who are actually capable of 'slapping' me around. In retrospect, the prehistoric-looking Nycht was the perfect choice to send after her wayward son.

Ashley almost laughed at his own inner dialogue. He dipped his head down and sighed.

It was an exaggerated posture of surrender. A ploy to put Bryc off his guard.

It almost worked.

Ashley stood up as fast as his inebriated brain and body would allow, knocking over his stool. He'd intended to bolt for the door, but ended up clutching the bar for support instead, as the world suddenly spun and tilted.

Too much to drink. It never fully hits until I get to my feet. Ashley moaned and squeezed his eyes shut.

Bryc chuckled and didn't move, still smiling.

That quiet, calm mockery stung Ashley like a sloppy smack across the mouth. His eyes flew open, and he opened his mouth to insult Bryc, jabbing a finger toward his nose. But language failed him in that moment.

"You're weak." Bryc ignored the finger in his face. "Soft in the mind as well as the body."

Even though he was still a young man, Ashley was thick in the chest and back and corded with muscle. His hands were calloused and capable, his skeleton straight and strong, his wings enormous and limber. He peered at Bryc through bleary eyes. Something about the grizzled henchman reminded him of feroth jerky——so tough you could hardly bite through it, and when you did, it took ages to chew. By the time you swallowed it, your jaw was sore.

Next to Bryc, Ashley actually did feel about as gooey as a soft-boiled egg. He struggled for a witty retort and came up blank.

"I despise frailty." Bryc hooked the handle of Ashley's mug of beer and took an enormous swallow.

Ashley belched out a strained laugh that was more beer than mirth. "I'm not afraid of you." Even as he said the words, a small, cold voice whispered that it was a bald-faced lie.

Bryc put the mug down with a *clack*. Beer sloshed over the bar. "You should be, boy."

"Don't you dare!" Ashley roared, sending patrons jumping away from the pair as he jabbed his finger into Bryc's unyielding chest. "Don't you dare call m——"

In one fluid motion, Bryc lay hold of Ashley's hair and drove his face into the bar.

It happened so fast, there was no time to breathe or even think. Stars of light and pain exploded and then meshed into a single blinding sheet. Ashley's legs gave way, and he slid from the bar down on to the floor, landing in a boneless heap. He tasted blood. When he tried to suck in air, his nose hurt so much he gagged on the pain. It felt like a spike was being driven into his sinus.

"Sorry to interrupt," Bryc's tone was flat, remorseless. "It's just that the last man to lay a finger on me like that had to eat that finger. Then the others. Then his hand."

Ashley groaned and groped at his belt, somehow finding the floor with his knees. The world spun, and his stomach clenched, fighting to keep his last meal and his beer on the inside. Ashley sucked in a deep breath through his nose and closed his eyes, going inward, finding the warrior's instincts that had been chased away by the alcohol. They were there... somewhere.

"You see, boy, appearances matter in my line of work." Bryc loomed over Ashley, reaching down with one scarred paw to grip him by the hair again. "After all, what would it look like if I let some snot-nosed runt lay hands on me without teaching him a lesson? What would others think?"

"Please! Please!" The hoarse cry came from the barkeep, an older man whose shoulders drooped from years of lifting barrels. "Good fellows, not here! No fighting. Go outside. Take it outside!" The barkeep's hands were outstretched in a plaintive gesture, but he did not touch either of the fighting Strix.

"Shoo, little fly, before you––"

Ashley surged into action, yanking his shortsword free from his belt in a reverse grip. He punched upward and gouged a furrow across Bryc's forearm where his bracers did not cover. The grip on his hair loosened, and the younger Strix rose from his knees with a hooked slash that drove Bryc back a step.

The entire bar, at first frozen by the sudden violence of Bryc's initial assault, exploded into frenzied movement at the sight of drawn steel. People were getting out and quick, giving the quarrelling Strix a wide berth. In the din of movement and voices, the protests of the barkeep could still be heard. They were ignored.

"Do not touch me again," Ashley growled, swaying on his feet but finding he still had access to his reflexes. He felt a trickle of hot blood run down over his upper lip and chin. He glared at the Nycht, ignoring the rush of patrons passing them by.

The bartender wailed inaudible words over the roiling crowd.

Bryc took a second to examine the bloody wound on his forearm before barking with laughter. "Good!" Bryc bellowed, his smile still fixed, wide and unnerving. "I am glad this gets to be business and pleasure." He made for something on his own belt.

Ashley couldn't afford to give the monstrous Nycht a chance. Darting forward, he feinted a head-high swipe with the blade jutting from his fist. Bryc was taller, heavier, stronger, and infinitely meaner, but Ashley was certain that he was faster, even with beer in his belly. He couldn't let Bryc get the upper hand again. The Nycht may have come here to beat him back into line, but he wasn't going to make it easy for him.

Bryc didn't duck or backpedal as Ashley was sure he would, but instead stepped into the shallow swipe. The sword pommel and Ashley's fist thudded into Bryc's meaty chest. The angle was all wrong, and the blade turned, pinched by the flat between Bryc's body and Ashley's arm. The two were so close that Ashley could see every knot of scar tissue on his enemy's face before Bryc's head snapped downward.

Unable to deny the cry of pain from having his crushed nose so mistreated, Ashley fell back and tried to keep the blade point up between himself and Bryc. His eyes were full of light and tears, so he never saw the hand that swept in beneath his guard and wrenched the sword from his grip with a savage twist.

"Enough, sirs, please!" the barkeep begged.

Ashley's eyes cleared enough to see Bryc look at the barkeep for the first time.

"Would you mind holding this for me, friend?" the brute asked, before he rammed Ashley's sword through the man's outstretched arm and down into the rough wooden bartop. The barkeep looked like he might have screamed if he could get over the shock of seeing himself pinned to his own bar.

Ashley's skin crawled at the ease with which the Nycht had been able to injure the innocent barkeep. Fury flushed his face, but he no longer had a weapon to avenge the poor man with. He took a few steps backward as Bryc drew his own sword. The bare steel glittered in a way that matched Bryc's glistening smile.

Bryc picked up Ashley's mug from where it sat next to the pinioned barkeep and threw back the remaining beer in one gulp.

"Now," Bryc intoned with a casual flourish of his blade. "Where were we?"

Ashley kicked a stool at him in reply.

Bryc batted it aside and advanced.

Eyes darting every which way, Ashley searched for something, anything he could use as a projectile. Spotting a pitcher on a table next to the bar, he scooped it up and hurled it at Bryc's face. Bryc tilted his head to one side, and the glassware bounced off one thick shoulder and tumbled behind him to crash upon the floor.

Bryc kept coming.

"Come now, boy, don't give up yet."

Ashley's eyes shot to the exit, but he was on the wrong side of the building. To go out the front, he would have to get around Bryc, and that was not looking likely. Instead he retreated further into the bar, among tables arranged around a big brick fireplace. He snatched up an overturned tankard and another from a pool of ale on the floor.

"What's in your head, boy?" Bryc chuckled as he slid between the tables after his prey. "You going to batter me with pewter since you've got no steel, or you just looking for one last drink?"

Last drink?

Ashley's stomach twisted around its liquid contents as he realized he may have underestimated Bryc's plans for the evening. That realization, alongside some merciful seconds since the last time Bryc bludgeoned his head, brought a clarity and energy to Ashley he desperately needed. He shuffled backward, keeping his eyes on Bryc, until he felt the rough texture of the fireplace against his heels.

With terrifying ease, Bryc tossed a table out of his way as he closed the distance between them. "Looks like you are going to have to do something now, Ashley," Bryc remarked sagely. "Nowhere to run."

"You talk too much," Ashley snarled before he hopped up to plant both feet on the brick, and drove himself forward.

The ceiling was too low and the room too cluttered for Ashley to open his wings fully inside the bar, but all he needed was a quick, shallow pump to send him sailing over Bryc's skewering sword. As he passed overhead, Ashley brought one tankard down across the back of Bryc's outstretched swordhand, knocking the weapon from his grip. Then he brought the other tankard hard across the side of the brute's head as he completed his leap. Ashley might have been proud of the acrobatic move—–well executed, even in an inebriated state—–if he hadn't been so frightened. Adrenalin pumped through his system and seemed to have more control over Ashley's faculties than Ashley did himself.

Bryc staggered to the side and collided with a table and pair of chairs, which drove him to one knee. Pouncing, Ashley was on top of the big Nycht, punching down onto his head, neck, and shoulders with the tankard that hadn't already been crushed against Bryc's skull.

As he rained down blows and felt the satisfying crunch of each impact, Ashley dared to think that he might come out ahead in all of this.

Until Bryc's hand shot out and wrapped around Ashley's fist.

Ashley groaned and tried to twist away, beating his free fist against Bryc's arm. Iron-fisted, Bryc tightened his grip on Ashley's hand as he rose to his full height. Ashley ground his teeth against a scream as he was forced again to his knees.

The good humor was gone from Bryc's dark eyes. "How disappointing," he hissed between his bared teeth, giving Ashley's fist a fresh twist.

Bryc's other hand snaked out and took hold of Ashley's throat. Incredible pressure closed off Ashley's airways, his head filled with blood, his eyes bulged. He was lifted into the air and slammed down on a tabletop. Pain sparked along the primary bones of his wings as they spread wide and took the brunt of the blow. His armor and wings had kept Ashley's spine from snapping, but the table gave way with a crash. Wood splintered beneath him, and something stabbed Ashley in the side, slipping between the ties of his leather armor. He gritted his teeth against another scream.

Bryc released his grip on Ashley's hand and throat, but it did the Arpak no good, as he could barely move. He lay on top of the broken wood, desperately sucking in air. The pain which had struck between his ribs seemed to go numb. *At least there's that.*

Bryc appeared over him, his sword recovered, and sank down to place a knee on Ashley's laboring chest. Ashley wheezed as the considerable weight of the Nycht pressed him against the rubble of the table beneath him.

"I have a message for you," Bryc sneered as he held the blade in front of Ashley's face. "From your mother."

Ashley's eyes widened at the reference to Jaclyn as his mother. It had been a secret they'd kept for years, and Ashley had only just himself learned why it was important no one know. Apparently, Bryc knew.

Ashley's mind whirled with shock.

With aching slowness, Bryc brought the blade tip down, pressing its needle-sharp point to Ashley's lips. Ashley tasted blood and steel as the very tip of the blade cut the corner of his mouth with cruel promise.

"It might not matter to you," Bryc mused as he held the sword blade in Ashley's mouth, letting the edge cut a little deeper. "But when I report back to your mother, I would like to tell her you said goodbye. For closure, you understand. Go on now," Bryc pressed coolly. "Say it. Say goodbye to mommy."

"The lad was right, you talk too much," came a ragged voice from behind Bryc, just before a stool exploded across the back of the Nycht's head.

Bryc and his sword rolled free of Ashley, and the latter took a little more blood on its way out. Ashley got to his feet in time to catch the hilt of his sword, which the barkeep tossed to him.

One arm hanging useless and bloody, the poor man looked ready to collapse. Instead, he fixed Ashley with a steady stare. "Run, lad. I'll have no death in my bar tonight."

Without thinking about it, Ashley rose and staggered toward the door. He was halfway across the bar when he heard a bestial roar. He looked over his shoulder in time to see Bryc plunge his sword into the chest of the barkeep. The old man took it, back straight, head up, before dropping to the floor of his bar. A crimson stain spread across the hardwood floor.

Ashley gasped in horror, astonished that Bryc would actually murder the man for helping him. Shame burned in him, turning his eyes into two hot coals.

Pain laced through Ashley's body. His vision bleary, his crushed fist useless, and his wings badly bruised, Ashley seized the chance the man had died to give him. He bolted for the door, as a peal of thunder ripped across the skies of Maticaw and shook the bottles of liquor behind the bar.

He felt the sword in his hand and spied a bundled fishing net, hanging as a decoration over the doorway. Legs pumping, Ashley raced. Behind him, he could hear the sound of Bryc crashing through the furnishings like an enraged bull. Ashley doubted such collisions would slow the hulking Nycht in the slightest, but he found enough room in his diminished consciousness to hope Bryc tripped over a stool and fell on his own blade.

Bryc did not fall, but all the same, Ashley knew that he was going to beat the Nycht to the door, if only by a hair. Ashley flew through the door, raking his sword across the net's fastenings as he did so.

With a sound that, to Ashley, was as beautiful as music, there was a slither of rope and cord unwinding. The Arpak burst out onto the storm-wracked streets of Maticaw. Rain stung his skin with cold fury, but Ashley felt only relief as he heard a crash and bellow as Bryc became caught in the net. It wouldn't take him long to disentangle.

With an internal promise that a reckoning would come, Ashley moved like a silent shadow through Maticaw's soggy alleys, disappearing into the endless maze of narrow streets.

CHAPTER 10

*H*unkering against the rain, Jordan arched her wings over her head in a makeshift umbrella and made her way to the Silver Pony. Her boots splashed in the rapidly rising puddles, and steam rose from the soaking stones as the heat of the day was diffused by cold droplets. The storm had moved in faster than anyone had expected, and though it was only mid-afternoon, the sky was so pregnant with thunderclouds that it seemed like night.

The Silver Pony was nestled a few streets back from the harbor, and Jordan made her way toward it without thinking. It had been a haven for her once; it would do for tonight, as well. She was cold, wet and hungry after a fast flight from Rodania, weighed down with gold coins for Sohne.

Turning left down a narrow alley, Jordan was jostled by a couple of humans moving quickly and muttering to each other in hushed and fearful voices. She put her back to the wall to let them by. The sound of muffled crashing noises several streets over made her cock her head and listen. A peal of thunder raked across the skies of Maticaw, then all returned to quiet, and the patter of rain and sloshing of distant waves was the only soundtrack.

She continued on.

The alley opened into a small square sheltered by a large tree in the center. The yellow glow of four streetlights, one in each corner, threw criss-crossing shadows across the cobblestones. Jordan made for the alley straight across the square.

A large, winged shape came barrelling from the alley. With a thud, and the smell of beer on the wind, Jordan and the Arpak hit chest-to-chest, hard enough to send her staggering and the other sprawling onto the ground.

"Oh, I'm so sorry," Jordan said with a gasp. She bent over the fallen Arpak man and held out her gloved hand to help him up.

Her answer was a groan. The tangle of wet feathers moved aside, revealing a bloody face.

Jordan staggered back in shock.

The familiar brown eyes of Ashley blinked up at her. Blood ran down his chin, one lip was puffed up, and an impressive goose-egg had sprouted from his left temple. His eyes were bloodshot and one of them was half-closed with swelling. Blood caked the side of his face and trickled from his mouth.

"Jordan?" he gasped, his voice ragged. He held a palm out. "I won't..." he panted, but didn't finish the sentence explaining what he wouldn't do. He seemed in a daze.

"Ashley!" Jordan drew one of her blades and stepped back into a fighting stance. Her wings opened out, framing her as she snarled at him like an avenging angel. Every nerve in her body was suddenly afire, and the desire to leap forward and send her dirk into his chest was nearly overwhelming. Jordan bared her teeth. "Come at me," she hissed. "Give me one reason."

Ashley was on his feet in a flash, his eyes full of her steel. He cradled one hand across his chest and held the other out at her defensively, the fingers splayed.

His expression made her hesitate, took her off-guard. He was Ashley, of that there was no doubt——but the expression on his face was so different from the last time she'd seen him, not to mention the wounds, that she was a bit disarmed.

Ashley had not drawn a weapon. He only looked at her, eyes wide and seeking to predict what she would do next. One of his shoulders drooped as though injured. His chest heaved as he worked to catch his breath. He stole a glance into the alley he'd come from and then stared back at Jordan.

"Sister——" he began.

The word set Jordan off like a bomb. *How **dare** he call me 'sister'!* She lunged forward and slashed at Ashley.

He moved just fast enough to block her strike. His training lay hard in his muscles, and he danced by her, sending the power of her stroke harmlessly to the side. Jordan spun, sending her fist toward his head. Ashley ducked and ran his shoulder into her ribs, sending her reeling back and off her feet.

"Not here!" he cried. "I understand you want to kill me," his words came out on a long, pained groan that was thick with the scent of hops.

Jordan brought her elbow down on the side of his spine, and he grunted.

Rain dripped from the leaves of the tree down onto the Arpaks, running into Jordan's eyes. The sound of heavy boots on the pavement came to Jordan's ears as Ashley carried her backward into the alley at the far corner of the square.

"Shhhh," he whispered into her ear as he crammed them into the dark space of a doorway. His hand came up to cover her mouth. "I don't want to hurt you."

Jordan's nostrils flared as she struggled for breath. Ashley's bulk pressed her into the hard wood of the doorway, crushing her. Light from the streetlamps were blocked out as Ashley's wings spread wide to hide them from view. The feel of his hand over her mouth sent her into a panic, and she was only vaguely aware of the sound of leather bootsoles scraping against stone as the footsteps passed by them and continued down the same alley she'd come from only minutes before.

Jordan brought her knee up into Ashley's groin. Hard.

The hand fell away as Ashley crumpled soundlessly. His frame curled inward like an armadillo, and a long, low wheeze of pain came from the back of his throat as his hands clutched his genitals.

Jordan set her blade against Ashley's neck, and the two of them froze there. Her teal eyes bore into his brown ones as her twin stared up at her with Jaclyn's eyes. Even with one of them nearly swollen shut, they were the same eyes that had haunted her for years.

"Go on, then." Ashley ground the words out. He lifted his chin, giving her better access to his jugular. "I deserve it."

Jordan gritted her teeth and stared down at him. Rainwater ran down her neck, plastered her hair to her face and dripped from her chin and nose. A chill settled into her bones and she shivered. With a snarl of frustration, she took her blade from Ashley's neck. His right eye was now completely closed and swollen, and his left was bloody in the inner corner from a burst blood vessel.

"What happened to you?" she gritted out.

The corner of Ashley's mouth turned up, just a little, twisting his lips with irony. "Our mother tried to have me killed."

He made to get up, and Jordan raised her swordtip to his throat again. He froze, his eyes on the blade. Slowly, he raised both hands, palms out. "I'm not going to hurt you. I swear."

"Your word means nothing to me," Jordan spat.

Ashley's good eye left the steel and trailed upward to her face. The irony which had twisted his expression melted away. He frowned, his eyes heavy with sorrow. "I know."

Jordan stepped back and allowed Ashley to get to his feet. Indecision about what to do next settled over her like a cloak.

Should I just turn my back and leave? Is what he said about Jaclyn trying to have him killed true? Is this some kind of trap?

She sheathed her blade and shook the water from her wings, watching him through narrowed eyes.

"There's something——" Ashley began, but paused to take a heavy breath. His hand clutched at his side and then pulled away, opening palm up and shaking. Even in the dim light of the alley, Jordan could see it was covered in blood. "Something..." he wheezed, looking down at the hand. "You should know," he finished, before his eyes rolled up in his head and he collapsed face-first onto the pavement.

* * *

"Can you help him?" Jordan asked the Dwarf who hovered over Ashley's still and ashen form.

"Depends," the Dwarf mumbled, probing Ashley's side.

Ashley had been hoisted onto a narrow wooden table by Jordan and the Dwarf——not an easy job even between the two of them. It had taken a burly sailor recruited from the docks, as well as two gold coins from the purse Juer had given Jordan for Sohne, to get Ashley's unconscious form carried to the Dwarf healer's clinic. The storm had not let up, and Maticaw was swathed in the dark and violence of a proper seaswept storm.

The stranger Jordan had hired to carry Ashley knew about the Dwarf healer, and told Jordan in lilting and a very old form of English that the Dwarf was better than any doctor. Jordan didn't know if she had been foolish to believe the sailor or not.

The Dwarf's hut was built high up in the side of a steep hill. It had been a long and exhausting day. Jordan was bushed.

The Dwarf levelled her with a crafty look. "Gold, have you?"

Jordan nodded wearily. "How much?"

He let out a long, low growl that could have been a sound of rumination, before slurring into the words, "Four gold coin." He snatched up a seriously hefty pair of shears and snipped at the ties holding Ashley's vest on. The boiled leather parted like a crack in the earth. Blood spilled onto the wooden table from a ragged stab wound in Ashley's ribs.

"No, five," he amended.

The Dwarf barked in a foreign tongue to no one in particular, but almost immediately, a small door in the corner cracked open and a younger dwarfish face peered out. She responded in kind, her garbled tongue sounding to Jordan more like a chicken clucking than anything else. The door opened further, and she came out carrying a stack of folded white linen cloths. The healer took one and pressed it to Ashley's side.

"Hold this," he directed Jordan. She moved to the table and pressed the linen into Ashley's wound.

The healer went to a trunk against the wall and knelt in front of it. "Needs magic," the Dwarf growled over his shoulder at Jordan.

"I'll pay," said Jordan. "But I can't stay longer than tonight. I have to continue on first thing in the morning. I'm not his friend, I'm just his..." *Sister.* The word bounced around in Jordan's skull, forming ice wherever it landed. "I'm an acquaintance. I didn't want to leave him to die in the streets."

"Did this?" the Dwarf asked as he rummaged through the trunk of goods, tossing aside fabrics, leather bags, small weapons, and other strange implements.

"Me? No." Jordan sagged against the table, keeping the cloth against the cut. "I don't know who did this."

"What weapon? Poisoned?"

"I don't know. Looks like a very messy knife wound, or maybe a jagged stick. I have no idea if it was poisoned."

The Dwarf snatched up a vial and grunted. He spread Ashley's armor wider and took over the job of holding the now blood-soaked linen to the wound. He pulled it away very slowly, and Jordan winced at the slash in Ashley's skin. It looked as though whatever had stabbed him had ripped the skin, rather than cutting it cleanly.

"Hold head."

Jordan moved to the table and held Ashley's head still. His hair was wet and matted. She kept her fingers away from the crusty blood on the side of his temple.

"Hold mouth open."

"He won't be able to swallow."

"He will."

Using her other hand, Jordan pulled Ashley's jaw down until his lips parted.

The Dwarf dribbled liquid from the vial between Ashley's slack jaws. Jordan expected it to spill over, but it disappeared inside.

"Step back. Hands off."

Jordan moved her hands away, holding her palms up to show she was no longer touching him. There was a popping sound, and a cloud of blue smoke jetted from Ashley's mouth and nostrils.

"No poison," the Dwarf grunted, satisfied. "Leave the coin there." He pointed to a shelf above the fireplace. "Five. Five coin." Then he barked again, and the lady Dwarf reappeared.

She grasped Jordan by the hand and tugged on it, leading her toward the door.

"We have bed for you," she said in her clicky, clucking way. "He need time."

"I was going to stay at the Silver Pony," Jordan protested. The Dwarf continued to cluck like a chicken, and Jordan had the feeling she was trying to be comforting. Jordan allowed the Dwarf to take her into a small room with a cot. The woman tugged on the laces at Jordan's back, and Jordan let her help her out of her armor and wet clothing. She was handed a shirt with an apologetic look. It was a tunic, which Jordan would have to put on backwards, as it wasn't made to accommodate wings. It had five ties that would normally be fastened up the front, and a boatneck collar.

"Thank you. At least it's dry." Jordan smiled at the Dwarf gratefully.

The shirt barely fit across her shoulders. Jordan was laced up the back and handed a towel for her wet hair. Then she was made to sit and, with a gentle push on her shoulders, to lay down.

"Only until the storm stops," Jordan mumbled. "And, thank you."

The Dwarf nodded and clucked. She gave Jordan a sloppy pat on the forehead then took Jordan's wet clothes and hung them on a rack in front of the fireplace to dry. She slipped from the room, and Jordan was left alone with only the sound of rain lashing the small round window above her head.

Jordan tried to sleep but couldn't. She tossed and turned, leaving the sheets and blankets in ruins, and her backside exposed to the chilly air.

What if Ashley dies? How will that make me feel? What would Jaclyn do?

Even though he had tried to kill her, Jordan had to admit that she didn't wish death on Ashley. He was her flesh and blood. And besides, if he was in the mood to talk, which it certainly seemed he was until he collapsed on the cobblestones, he could have some very enlightening things to say about their mother.

If he dies, whatever puzzle pieces he can provide will be lost with him.

Several hours later, the storm still had yet to lose its power, and the door to Jordan's room opened. The Dwarf healer poked his head in.

"Lady," he said. "Better now. Come, come, come."

Jordan rolled over and put the soles of her feet on the chilly stone floor. Her jaw cracked wide with a yawn. She looked down at her bare legs and feet, thinking.

"There." The healer pointed to a pair of stockings hanging on the rack next to her clothing.

Jordan pulled them on, thinking they weren't quite what she was after. "Have you got any pants?" Her own leather ones were still soaking, and would be nearly impossible to put back on until they were dry.

But the healer was gone, leaving her door open.

"Okay, then." Jordan pulled the long stockings up as high as they would go and frowned down at her ridiculous appearance. She checked to make sure her rear end was covered by the tunic. Just before she headed through the door to check on Ashley, she snatched up the holster with the throwing blades.

"Just in case," she muttered.

* * *

JORDAN WALKED into the room where she'd last seen Ashley laying still and ghastly pale on the narrow table. Her brows shot up to her hairline when she saw him slouched at the low table near the fire, a fuzzy blanket wrapped around his shoulders, and sipping something hot and steamy from a thick, misshapen mug.

"You look remarkably better," she said as she padded across the floor in her stockings and sat across from him. The table was kid-sized, and the two Arpaks looked ridiculous, squatting on the low seats with their wings splayed out over the floor like overgrown feather-dusters.

Ashley was still pale and his eyes were fever-bright, but the dried blood had been cleaned from his head, and his eye was no longer puffy. The hand holding the mug seemed stable and strong again.

He smiled at Jordan, and his brown irises were soft as he looked at her. "Thanks to you," he croaked. His eyes fell to her bare forearm, where the Elven glyphs looped around the limb. One brow picked up with interest. "I didn't suspect you to be the tattooed type."

"How do you feel?" Jordan asked, ignoring his personal comment.

"A little bit like I have the flu, but doc says it'll pass by morning, and I should be as good as new. Maybe a little tired, but much better."

Jordan's eyes dropped to his side where he was swaddled with the blanket.

Ashley moved the blanket aside and lifted the white linen shirt to show Jordan where he'd been stabbed.

"Wow!"

The wound was nothing more than a thin pink line of scar tissue that looked to be already several weeks healed.

"You're a wizard!" Jordan said to the healer, who was packing his tools and instruments into the trunk.

He looked back and winked at her. "Not wizard. Simple magic from botanics south of Skillen. I import." He closed the trunk and got to his feet. "Am the only one in Maticaw who can do this work," he nodded his oversized head toward his patient, "without Elf magic." He shrugged modestly. "It not perfect, but it is good. And much cheaper."

He snatched up the small bag into which he'd deposited Jordan's gold coins and shook it at her. "Thank you for business." He shoved his small spectacles up his nose and put a pinky finger into his ear, twisting it and winking like a dog getting a good scratch. "You stay until your clothes are dry and storm goes. There is broth on fire, there." He pointed to the cauldron hanging over the small but cheerily crackling fire. "Help self to."

"Thank you." Jordan watched the Dwarf healer waddle to the exit.

"He need rest," he said from the door. "Take him home. Let

him sleep few days. Good as new." And with that, their host slammed the door and left the twins alone.

"I don't know how to repay you," said Ashley, taking another slow sip of the hot drink. "I mean, I will. The gold is not a problem, but..." He took a breath in through his nose. "You had no reason to help me. In fact, you had good reason to leave me alone in that alley and let me bleed to death." He looked her full in the face, his mouth a line of misery. "But you didn't."

"I'm not like you, and... and Jaclyn," Jordan stuttered over her mother's name. "I would have done it for a stranger, let alone my own flesh and blood."

Ashley's eyes shuttered closed for a long moment. When he opened them, they were nearly as pained as they'd been in the alley before he'd collapsed. "I don't want to be like Jaclyn, either," he mumbled.

These words surprised Jordan into momentary speechlessness, which was followed rapidly by a healthy dose of skepticism. "This had better not be some sort of trap."

Ashley rubbed a hand over his weary face. "If it is, it's a damn poor one. Why would I get myself beat up and stabbed just to trap you? I didn't even know you were in Maticaw."

He was right. If it was some kind of trap, it was a ridiculous one that had yet to reveal the punchline.

"You said you had something to tell me?"

"Did I?" Ashley looked thoughtful.

"Right before you passed out in the alley." Jordan got up and took a mug from the set of hooks hanging over the fire, and ladled herself some broth. She sat down again, looking at Ashley expectantly. "You also said Jaclyn tried to have you killed. Is that true?"

Ashley nodded and his gaze dropped to the floor, but not before Jordan caught the line of moisture gathering along his lower lids. He brushed at his eyes angrily, pinching the bridge of his nose. "She sent a goon after me." He let out a long exhale. "Jaclyn doesn't like being questioned."

"What did you question her about?"

"Everything. All her motives over the last several years. I've been following her blindly, just the way she raised me to. The only reason I dared question her at all is because an Elf enchanted me to." He looked doubtful about this even as he said it. "Or something."

"An Elf?" Jordan let out a disbelieving laugh. "Are you serious?"

Ashley nodded. "One of the ones from Charra-Rae. You know it?"

"Yes, I know it." Jordan's eyes narrowed. "Did she have red hair?"

Ashley's face paled, and his eyes widened. "No. Who is this redheaded Elf? Jaclyn asked me the exact same thing!"

Jordan grunted and took a sip of her broth. "One of the more devious Elves on Oriceran, I suspect. If she wasn't redheaded, then I'll wager she was gray. And beautiful."

Ashley nodded. "That sounds like the one."

"Pohle." Jordan breathed out the name with wonder. So there was an Elf that Sohne allowed out of Charra-Rae. Jordan didn't know what the gray Elf's talents were, but she didn't doubt that Pohle was important to Sohne, one of her right-hand Elves. She chewed her lip thoughtfully. "Why would Sohne send Pohle to enchant you?"

"Who is Sohne?"

"The redheaded Elf, but nevermind about her right now. What did Pohle say?"

Ashley scratched his head. "Do you know, I can't really remember? But after the encounter, I knew that there was something in the basement of the trade office that I needed to see. And more importantly, that Jaclyn has not been truthful with me about my identity."

"Your identity?" Jordan bristled. "What do you mean?"

Ashley let out a long sigh and stared at his sister. "Our mother is a wonder."

"That's an interesting word for her. I might use 'disappointment', 'sociopath', or 'power monger'. Take your pick."

"All this time," Ashley continued, without reacting to Jordan's stream of consciousness, "I thought that Prince Diruk and Jaclyn were scratching one another's backs because they were on the same side."

"They're not?"

Ashley shook his head. "Jaclyn is planning to betray him when the time is right. All this time, I thought she was bending to his will because once on the throne, he would be able to give her the position she wants."

"Which is?"

"Master of four ports." He numbered them on his fingers. "Skillen, Operyn, Maticaw, and Vischer. No one person, let alone a woman, has ever achieved this; the ports have always had one master each. Jaclyn has already shown that she doesn't care about the flow of goods, even medicines needed by the people."

"A monopoly on trade?" The implications of this were evident. Monopolies on Earth were never good for the people, and it would be no different on Oriceran. If Jaclyn could control the flow of goods, she'd be more powerful than any monarch. That kind of power in the hands of someone with so little regard for life would be frightening. Jordan's forearms swept with goosebumps.

"Yes. But Jaclyn's ambitions are far greater than that," Ashley went on, his expression still incredulous about what he had learned.

"She wants to see Diruk take the Rodanian throne?" Jordan guessed, thinking back to when she'd seen the prince stalk from her mother's office. Since the two of them were allied, it would only make sense that Jaclyn would want her partner in crime to be as powerful as possible.

Ashley gave a laugh with no humor in it. "She cares about putting *someone* on the Rodanian throne. But it's not Diruk."

Jordan gave her twin a confused look. "Who else could it possibly be?"

Ashley looked at her, his mouth a sober line, his expression grim. "Me."

CHAPTER 11

*J*ordan and Ashley raced over the Rodanian Sea, riding high on gusty thermals, their eyes squinting against the bright light reflecting off the water below. The Dwarf healer had told them Ashley needed rest, but the situation wouldn't allow it. Since he had no intention of ever going back to Jaclyn, his choices were to be left behind to convalesce in some Maticaw bed and breakfast, or to accompany Jordan on a breakneck journey back to Rodania in an effort to save the king.

Ashley didn't hesitate, and they left as soon as the wind and rain had died down enough to make it possible.

Jordan had stolen many secret glances at her brother––his freshly shaven face still jolted her, the similarities she found there to her own bone structure. They shared Jaclyn's chin and cheekbones, her high brow and generous bottom lip. She had felt his eyes on her also, and wondered what was going through his mind.

Jordan also kept an eye on the strength of his flying and the color of his cheeks as they travelled. He looked a little peaky, but she could hardly tell he'd been close to death the night before.

My twin is strong, she admitted grudgingly.

The air was crisp and cool after the prior night's storm, and flotsam and jetsam crowded the docks and beaches of the coast. Once over deep water, however, one could hardly tell there had even been a storm. The sky was blue and the sun was doing a decent job of baking away the remaining clouds.

Jordan's thoughts were a jumble of amazement. When Ashley had told her Jaclyn's intention to put him on Rodania's throne, she had laughed fit to burst. It was a wild delusion, a fool's paradise, which made her think her mother had to be clinically insane--until he told her the truth about their biological father.

Jaclyn had had a relationship with King Konig himself--*they were his children.*

This had left Jordan breathless; she'd placed her head between her knees as her vision fuzzed to black. Listening to Ashley's story was like being hit repeatedly with a big sack full of flour; each revelation accompanied by a dull thud to the chest.

Rodanian royalty?

Half-sibling to the wretched Prince Diruk?

Jaclyn and King Konig?

It was simply too much, especially after everything that had happened already. Jordan's mind raced back through time across the events that had brought her to this moment of stupefying revelation.

Jordan asked Ashley if the king himself knew of their existence--after all, they'd been born on Earth. He'd answered that, according to Jaclyn, yes, he did.

When Ashley had produced the fungus from his satchel to show Jordan what he'd taken from the basement of the trade office, Jordan was galvanized. She had snatched it from his palm and stood up so fast that Ashley had to catch her as she nearly blacked out for a second time.

Priorities reshuffled like playing cards in the hands of a card shark. She explained to Ashley that she had to get the fungus to Juer as quickly as possible. It wasn't a large piece, but she weighed the options and decided that it was better to get even a small amount to Rodania posthaste. She could then go back to Charra-Rae for more.

The twins didn't speak during the trip until Jordan saw the three-tiered, off-kilter cake shape of Rodania on the horizon. Her lips parted to ask him if he had been to Rodania before, but the way his dark eyes focused on the masses of land ahead of them gave her the answer. He had, otherwise he'd not be able to see it.

She focused front and closed her mouth, demanding a little more speed from her wings. Jordan's hand drifted to her satchel where she felt the lump of fungus under her palm. She'd already checked a dozen times to make sure she hadn't lost it.

The Arpaks headed straight for Upper Rodania and the palace. Landing on the white marble terrace, their boots skidded across the smooth surface as they closed up their wings, sending gusty drafts and dust whirling into the air. They passed through the pillars to the palace interior, Jordan's eyes darting about for someone who could help.

She spied a Nycht dressed in servant's garb carrying a small tray, and she called out, her voice sharper than she meant it to be. "Juer, the king's doctor. Which way?"

The Nycht dropped the tray and slammed his back up against a pillar, clutching his chest. The clank of metal against marble echoed through the space as an empty cup rolled in a wild circle on the floor, and he bent to retrieve it and the tray. "Oh, you gave me such a fright!" he exclaimed, panting.

"I'm sorry. We're in an awful hurry."

"No problem." The Nycht pointed down a long hallway lit with tall, crystal torches, each topped with a flickering white light. "That way. Third door on the right. But I warn you, Juer isn't taking visitors."

"He'll take us," Jordan threw over her shoulder, as the twins made their way down the hall, their boots tapping out a brisk pace.

They passed by two large doors before approaching the third, which was flanked on either side by two of the royal guards. Their grim faces broke with relief when their eyes fell on Jordan's blonde hair and bright yellow plumage. Though they'd never seen her before, they'd obviously been told to watch for her.

"Jordan?" one of them said in a leaden voice.

Jordan nodded, her chest still rising and falling with the strain of the flight. Her hand clutched at the precious lump in her satchel.

"Juer is expecting you."

The guards stepped aside and opened the double doors for them. The one with red hair and freckles led them into a circular windowless antechamber. The room was dark, lit only by an ethereal chandelier that cast a soft red glow over the room. It made everyone's eyes appear black.

"Wait here," he instructed before crossing the carpet to a narrow door, and rapping on it with a knuckle. When it opened, he muttered, "Jordan," and stepped aside.

Juer rushed into the room and made a beeline for her. He looked frazzled and old, even under the softening effects of the red glow. Jordan reached into the satchel and produced the fungus. She held it out to the doctor, and he snatched it up greedily.

"Oh, you've done it, and so quickly, you clever girl." He sniffed the fungus and nodded. "Fresh. But, is this all?"

"It's a bit of a story. It was either this much today, or more in two days."

Juer nodded. He put a hand on the redheaded guard's shoulder and tucked the fungus into his hand. "Take this to Cles as fast as you can. He's in my laboratory in the east tower. If there is anything he needs, anything at all, you have my permission to get it for him."

"Done," the guard said, and left the room, swift as a shadow.

Juer turned to look at Jordan, and took her face in his dry, thin-skinned hands. "Thank you. It is up to Cles now." Physical details were soft in the red glow, but Jordan could easily see the worry etched in his eyes.

"How is the king?" She added *'my father'* in her mind, and the room seemed to sway before settling still again.

"Not well. Anything but red light is too harsh for him. His eyes are so dim." Juer shook his head. He finally noticed Ashley, standing behind Jordan. "Who is this?"

Before Jordan could introduce him, Ashley stepped forward and tilted his chin down in a sign of respect. "Ashley Kacy, sir." Ashley's face was pale as a moon, and grim.

"Kacy?" Juer's eyes drifted back to Jordan. "A relation of yours?"

"My twin, in fact."

"Twin!" Juer's bushy white brows shot up. "You never told me you had a twin." His gaze flicked between them. "I can see it now, you are very similar. Does Sol know? He never mentioned it either."

"He knows, but they've never met."

"Good doctor," Ashley said, and his tone was pregnant with austerity. "It is of great importance that we see the king before he gets any worse."

Juer was shaking his head before Ashley had finished asking the question. "This is impossible, he is far too ill. I am allowing no visitors——not even ones who may have possibly extended his life. I'm sorry." The doctor cocked his head. "Why? Is there some-thing amiss? Something I can help you with?"

Jordan and Ashley looked at one another, and she knew her twin was wondering the same thing she was. They hadn't had time to discuss how to reveal who they were, or with whom it would be safe to do so. Jordan shot Ashley a warning look and shook her head subtly. Making such a wild claim would shake Juer's trust in her. They had no proof.

Juer's question was still hanging in the air.

"Would you be willing to pass him a message for us?" Ashley asked.

Juer let out a long breath. "That depends on what it is. I'll not be giving him any information which will raise his stress levels. He has already lost the power of speech and he can't sit up without assistance."

"Just tell him that his medicine was brought by the twins."

"Only this?" Juer looked baffled.

"Only this."

Juer shrugged. "This is simple enough, and is the truth. I will tell him." He put a hand on Jordan's arm. "If you'll excuse me, I'll be getting back."

Jordan gave the doctor an encouraging smile, and the twins watched as he disappeared through the narrow door and closed it with a soft click behind him.

They left the antechamber and walked back down the hall at a much slower pace than when they'd arrived. A beetle of anxiety trundled through Jordan's stomach, and she put a hand over her belly.

"We have to tell someone." Ashley whispered the words once they were out of range of the remaining guard.

"And how are you going to explain your part in it?" Jordan whispered back. She wanted to add, 'Our mother was plotting treason, and you were her right-hand', but wouldn't risk even whispering it while still in the palace.

Ashley's cheeks were pale, but he spoke stoutly. "I'll tell the truth. I had no idea what Jaclyn was doing. She kept me in the dark."

"Wait!"

The twins stopped whispering and turned to see the other guard staring at them from down the hall.

"Come back, please!" He was beckoning them with rapid hand movements.

Jordan and Ashley shared a look of trepidation. Jordan's stomach felt as though it had frozen solid.

They were escorted back to the antechamber where Juer met them with wringing hands. A slash of anger and worry pinched the skin between his brows.

"What did you mean by that message, boy?" the doctor snapped and grasped Ashley by the forearm. "King Konig is asking for you. Insisting." Juer leaned in toward Ashley's face. "Demanding," he bit the word out. "You knew this was going to happen. Who are you?"

"The king knows who we are," Ashley replied. "I am sorry for the upset it has caused, but I told you it was important. May we see him?"

Juer gave Ashley's arm a shove. "Go," he snapped, his face twisted with disgust. "And if you upset him, you'll have me to answer to. You have five minutes only." Juer's eyes levelled Ashley with a glare. "Five minutes."

* * *

THE ROOM WAS cool and dry. It was lit with the same red glow as the antechamber, emanating from a dozen sconces around the room. The sound of ticking could be heard from a tall grandfather clock against the wall opposite the door. Heavy drapes blocked the light from the towering windows on either side of a simple bed. Jordan had expected a room gilded with rich furniture, a massive four-poster bed with gauzy curtains, behind which the king's shape could be seen. But the room, though large, was sparsely furnished and simply decorated. A table not far from the bed was covered in a collection of bottles and instruments. *Juer's*, she guessed.

Two glowing slits opened in the dark shadow of the king's head. Jordan's flesh crawled at the sight of those dimly glowing eyes turning in their direction. The shape in the bed lifted a hand and beckoned them closer.

The twins went to the bed, and the king's features became clearer. He looked almost the same as when Jordan had seen him from the balcony in Crypsis after the first harpy attack. He wore no hat and his shoulders were bonier, but the same high cheekbones and broad forehead spoke of a man who had once been strong and handsome. His wings were cradled in a specially made headboard that supported his spine, but even so, it was easy to tell that his wingspan was broad.

He'd been a good flier at one time, their father.

One of the king's hands reached out and grabbed Ashley by the fingers. Ashley jumped. King Konig's other hand gestured to the window.

"You want me to open the drapes?" Ashley guessed.

The king nodded. He let go of Ashley's hand and held his palms apart, showing him how wide he could bear them to be.

Ashley fumbled in the dim light for the cord and pulled the drapes back several inches, sending a shaft of sunlight into the room and illuminating their faces.

King Konig was holding a hand over his eyes as the light in the room changed. Ashley and Jordan waited while the king parted his fingers, allowing his eyes to adjust slowly. Then the hand came fully away, and their father looked up at them.

Jordan's mouth went dry as she took in his face close up and in detail. In the natural light, it was clear that the glow of his eyes was much more faded than it had been when she'd seen him last. His pupils and irises had not been visible at all before, but now they were a suggestion, a shape in the white spaces between his lids. His expression was no longer vacant, but full of understanding and intelligence. The king's lower lids filled with moisture. He knew he was looking into the faces of his children. The king took a shuddering, raspy breath. He lifted shaking hands and held one out to each of them. His brows drew together, furrowing his forehead.

"You know who we are," Jordan said softly as she took his hand.

The king's face tilted toward her as his eyes passed from Ashley to her. He nodded, his head moving slowly as though it asked a lot of him to do it.

Jordan clasped one hand and Ashley took the other. King Konig's grip was weak, and Jordan could feel the tremors passing through him. The light in his eyes dimmed further, even as they stood there with him, holding his hands.

The king brought Ashley and Jordan's hands together and forced them to clasp, he put a hand over theirs and squeezed. The message was clear. He wanted them to be united.

The door opened behind them, and Juer came in. "Your time is--" the doctor's words faltered as he saw the king holding hands with Ashley and Jordan. His eyes flew to the drapes with horror. "Light," he hissed. He composed himself and approached the bed. "Your Majesty, I must insist you rest."

The king's face went stiff, and he gestured at the side table.

Juer retrieved a small, shiny black ring from a bowl sitting at the king's bedside. King Konig lifted his hand and extended his index finger. Juer slipped the black ring over the fingertip, and it lodged just above the first knuckle.

King Konig moved his finger through the air, slowly, laboriously. In response to his movement, a line of illuminated text appeared just beyond the foot of the bed.

The words made Juer gasp and his already pallid complexion turn to wax.

"These are my children."

Juer's eyes grew so wide they seemed to bulge from his head.

He stared at Jordan, his mouth opening and closing like a fish out of water.

But the king was still writing, slowly, the letters crooked and appearing as though written by an inebriated hand.

"I need to recognize them. Get Darber. Now."

King Konig hadn't added a second name, but Jordan suspected he meant the same Councilman who had spoken alongside Prince Diruk at the ceremony where the Nycht warriors had been so thoroughly insulted. Her heart fell, and she began to get a bad feeling in the pit of her stomach, like she'd swallowed something rancid.

"Right away, Your Majesty," said Juer. The doctor left the room at a speed that would have made a younger man envious.

Jordan's heart was pounding so hard that she pressed her palm to her chest and closed her eyes. This was all happening so fast. She felt like she was on a theme park ride that had gone out of control––a ride that hadn't been fun to begin with, and had gone from tolerable to nauseating to terrifying.

The sound of a labored breath and a cough drew her eyes open. King Konig's body stiffened as he struggled to breathe. The rattle in his chest was awful. Jordan went around the bed to his other side so she didn't have to lean over Ashley, who had gone to his knees beside their father.

"What can I do, Your Majesty?" Jordan asked, panic rising in her chest.

King Konig shook his head but found a wan smile for her. He raised his index finger again, slowly, and it visibly trembled as he spelled more words out in the air.

"I loved your mother."

Jordan and Ashley read the words and then looked at one another, mirroring shock.

King Konig lay his hand on the coverlet, his chest rising and falling with the effort that the spelling of the words was taking him.

"What happened?" Ashley's voice was thick and rough. "Why does she…" He swallowed hard and his adam's apple bobbed several times. He opened his mouth to continue, but no words came out.

King Konig's head rolled across the pillow as he looked at his son, the lapita-induced light in his eyes was nearly gone. He lifted his finger and spelled what Ashley could not say.

"Hate me?"

The words appeared slowly and then faded, but Jordan thought they might be burned into her retinas forever. Emotion choked her throat closed.

Ashley nodded, his eyes like that of a beaten dog.

King Konig lifted his hand again, but it trembled in the air. He lowered it and closed his eyes. His breathing grew heavier.

Jordan wanted to scream for Juer to hurry up.

The King rolled his face toward Jordan and gazed at her. As she watched, the last of the artificial glow from the medicine faded from her father's eyes. No longer were his irises obscured by the light; in the natural glow from the window, she could see the color of his irises without trouble. Teal. Just like hers.

Jordan's vision blurred with moisture, and tears spilled over her cheeks.

A sound emerged from King Konig's throat——not words, but a sound of protest at the sight of her tears. He lifted his hand and passed the side of it clumsily over her cheek, wiping the moisture away. His hand continued on, into the air, to spell. The words were so messy, they were barely discernible.

"You're home."

The King took a few breaths before lifting his hand again.

"Ask for"

The letter after the "r" became lost in a long line, dropping down like a squiggly tail as their father's hand fell to the coverlet again. The light of the words faded.

" 'Ask for'?" Ashley put a hand on the king's forearm. "Ask for what? Who?"

"Where is Juer?" Jordan choked, tears now running freely down her cheeks.

The door banged open, and the doctor rushed in with Darber on his heels. Both men were perspiring and breathing heavily. Juer clutched a small bottle of black liquid in his hand. He ran across the room.

"Out of the way!" he cried, and Ashley leapt aside to make room for him.

Juer unstoppered the bottle of medicine with a squeak and brought the bottle to the king's lips.

The lips did not respond.

"Your Majesty, you must drink!" Juer shook the bottle, and a few drops of the medicine splashed onto the King's lower lip.

King Konig's face had gone slack and still. His teal eyes were half-closed and his lips open, the black medicine glistening on them. There was no breath left in him.

Juer let out a long, low moan and dropped his forehead into his free hand.

Darber stood a few feet from the bed, taking in the scene with a somber expression. He crossed to the grandfather clock, opened the glass door and reached in. He stopped the pendulum and the room fell silent.

* * *

"I WITNESSED it with my own eyes!" Juer cried, his eyes flashing and his face rigid with anger. "You must recognize them. It was King Konig's will——"

"I believe you," replied Darber, but his expression was thick with the very opposite. "But I cannot take the word of the king's doctor and a couple of kids who appeared out of thin air with a claim to the throne."

"We haven't made any claims," argued Jordan.

In fact, she and Ashley had hardly spoken since they'd been ushered from King Konig's chamber. They'd been made to wait in a stuffy room full of dim paintings and musty furniture, while Darber consulted with the royal lawyers. Jordan wanted nothing more than to go home to Sol, Eohne and Allan, and forget everything that had just happened.

Instead, since Darber had returned, she and Ashley had been watching the two old Arpak men argue, the twins' heads vaulting back and forth like they were at a tennis match. Jordan almost wished she had popcorn, but she didn't have her appetite anymore.

"I'm telling you," Juer lifted his finger, and on it was the black ring the king had used to communicate his dying wishes. "He spelled the words 'they are my children'. We all saw them."

Darber let out an impatient sigh. "And maybe they are, but we are bound by Rodanian law, doctor. Your speciality is medicine, mine is upholding the legal tenets that keep Rodania from sinking into the abyss of corruption and chaos. I have consulted with no less than four lawyers in the last hour, Arpaks who know our edicts inside and out. As long as a child is formally recognized by the king, regardless of whether they are of the queen or not," Darber's voice tightened, and his lip curled ever so slightly. "They have legitimacy and a claim to the throne."

"Yes!" Juer was nodding his head vigorously, his jowls quivering. "And he did recognize them. His intention was to do so legally, which is why he summoned you," he poked a twisted finger into Darber's chest with not inconsiderable force.

"But the recognition didn't happen," Darber hissed, knocking Juer's finger aside. "Not formally. I was not there when this so-called message was scrawled into the air." His voice was now taking on a heavy tone of sarcasm. He raised his own finger into the doctor's face. "And if you think that I'll take the word of Solomon Donda's uncle…"

Juer's eyes widened, and he blustered, "Wh-what does Sol have to do with anything?"

"He's the dragon woman's lover!" Darber barked, shooting Jordan a look of loathing. "For all I know, this is a scheme the three of you cooked up to unseat Prince Diruk. Mighty clever of you, but it won't work. You have no proof!"

"This is outrageous," Juer whispered, his eyes bulging. "I have been the king's loyal servant and personal physician for five years." His voice seethed with barely controlled anger. "How dare you insinuate this treason. It is not to be borne!"

"What else am I to think?" Darber clipped the words off like he was cutting hair.

Juer spun away from him in a huff, rolling his eyes and throwing up his hands in frustration. "This is a disgrace!"

"I'll say it is," boomed Darber.

Ashley leaned over and whispered to Jordan, "It's going well, don't you think?"

"Might I be of some assistance here?" A calm voice made every head swivel to the door. A broad, short Arpak with blue wings and an open expression entered the room. He nodded to Juer and Darber.

"That's Balroc," whispered Jordan to Ashley as she nodded at the Councilman. "He's one of the Council of Ten."

"Doctor, Councilman." Balroc crossed the room and extended a hand to Jordan, which she took. He didn't shake it, just held it in both of his. His hands were warm and dry. "Nice to see you again, Jordan."

Jordan nodded. "You too."

The Councilman's eyes turned to Ashley, overflowing with curiosity. "You must be the brother?"

"Ashley." The young Arpak stood and took the proffered hand.

Balroc nodded. "The mysterious twin." He chuckled as he shook and then released Ashley's hand. He opened his palms out. "Quite a situation we find ourselves in. Not to worry. Even now the couriers are delivering their messages to the Council, calling the ones who are abroad right now back to Rodania. The death of the king sets in motion many things; this hearing will be just one of many meetings that now must take place."

"We cannot begin until Prince Diruk arrives," Darber said, his voice sharp.

"Actually, the prince is not permitted at these proceedings," Balroc contradicted Darber. "And it will be at least a few days before we can hold a proper hearing."

Darber began to protest, his chest puffing up and his jaw working with indignation.

Balroc continued before his councilmate could form words. "Being a man of the law, surely you'll recall that, when there are multiple claims to the throne, neither the heir apparent nor the claimant——in this case, claimants——once their arguments have been heard, are permitted at the hearing. I understand the royal doctor was there when King Konig used his ring to communicate that these," he gestured to Ashley and Jordan, "Arpaks are his children?"

"Surely you don't believe this rubbish," Darber scoffed, his gray feathers rustling like those of an upset hen.

"Doesn't matter what I believe," said Balroc, rocking on his heels and clasping his hands behind his back with confidence. "What matters is what is true. We have a duty to unearth the truth, no matter our personal feelings or political position."

Balroc turned to Jordan and Ashley and held a polite hand out toward the door. "You may as well go home. The hearing cannot commence until all of the Council members are in attendance, and several of them own businesses abroad and aren't home right now. There is no use in waiting around here. A courier will come to retrieve you, if your claim is supported."

"We didn't make any claim," Jordan repeated, but it seemed to fall on deaf ears.

"And if they are not?" Ashley asked the Councilman as he escorted them to the door.

"If they are not..." Balroc hesitated. "I don't know. This is very unorthodox, as you can imagine. But I think there would be an investigation."

Jordan's mouth went dry. "Of us? An investigation of us? I haven't done anything. I got pulled into this mess when I went to fetch medicine for the king and ran into him." She jerked a thumb toward Ashley. Her heart was sprinting around in her chest like a frightened rabbit. The last thing she wanted was the eyes of Rodanian government on her, even though she'd done nothing she needed to hide.

"Try not to overreact," Balroc advised gently. "We don't know anything at this point."

"What do you need, to ensure a claim is upheld?" Ashley asked.

"Normally, a king will give a public and formal recognition for the heir, irrefutable proof for all to witness. If he truly wants to pass the throne to a beloved offspring, he will do it far earlier than this. This is actually not uncommon. Kings often have many illegitimate children whom they are fond of." Balroc said all this impassively, without any display of personal feeling or emotion.

"But King Konig didn't know where we were, our mother has been keeping me hidden," Ashley's voice grew more insistent. Evidence of an idea crossed his face. "What about the word of our mother? Would that be enough?"

"I'm afraid not," Balroc said patiently, although two pink spots had appeared on his cheekbones. "You can imagine what a mess we would have, if every royal lover who'd had a child was able to make a legitimate claim for her offspring." Balroc chuckled. "No, that would be absurd."

"The proof has to have come from King Konig himself to be ironclad. Do you have anything other than the word of Doctor Juer? A document with a signature and seal, perhaps?"

Ashley shook his head. "Surely a paternity test would do?" he suggested.

Balroc was shaking his head now. "Proof of paternity is not what is in question here, only your recognition as legitimate heirs. Now go home. Nothing can be done until after the hearing." He ushered them from the room, their hearts and minds reeling.

CHAPTER 12

*J*ordan's knuckles rapped on the wooden door of Allan and Eohne's apartment.

"No lights," Ashley murmured.

Jordan opened the door and went inside. "Eohne? Dad?"

"They don't lock the place?" Ashley asked as they wandered into the ground floor apartment. It was neat and tidy except for Eohne's worktable, scattered as it was with all manner of strange things. The little white butterflies still fluttered tirelessly in a cluster over the table, reminding Jordan of Sohne's message to Eohne.

"The border magic has the ability to track people. If anyone misbehaves, they can easily be found and kicked out permanently," Jordan explained. "Rodania is very safe."

"Except for the harpies," Ashley muttered, wandering through the galley kitchen and poking his head into one of the bedrooms. "You sure they won't mind me crashing with them?"

"Better than staying with Sol and me," said Jordan. "He won't be impressed that I've been fraternizing with the enemy." She smiled at Ashley so he knew she didn't actually see him as the enemy any longer. But it was only fair to warn him that her

129

friends wouldn't be so quick to forgive him, after he had tried to kill her. "I'd steer clear of him and Toth, if I were you."

Ashley's look was sincere. "For what it's worth, I am sorry about that. If I could go back, I would do things differently."

Jordan grunted in response. Somehow, a verbal apology just wasn't quite enough for the terror that Jordan had endured as Ashley had pursued her with murder in his eyes. "Well, I'm alive, at any rate." Jordan slumped into one of the chairs, and watched as Ashley wandered by Eohne's worktable.

He stopped at the butterflies and lifted a finger.

"Don't touch that," said Jordan, her chin in her hand.

She hoped someone would be coming home soon. She was completely exhausted and wanted nothing more than to sleep off the shock of the day's events, and then help Sol and Toth make preparations for Golpa.

She wished more than ever that she was going with them. Somehow, facing off with harpies was easier than dealing with politicians who thought she was scheming for the throne.

Footsteps could be heard approaching, and the door swung open. Allan entered the apartment, his hair windblown and his cheeks flushed.

"Jordy! You're back. What happened? Did you get the fungus? You were so fa..." Allan stopped midsentence when he saw Ashley standing in front of Eohne's table, staring back at him. Allan's face became ghostly, and his freckles stood out. His lips softened and his face grew long as recognition transformed his features. Allan let out a long sigh of understanding. His eyes devoured the young man standing across the room from him. "I've not seen you since you were a toddler, but I would know you anywhere."

Ashley shifted uncomfortably from foot to foot, his eyes going to the floor, to Jordan, to the ceiling, and back to Allan. "I... uh..."

"It's okay." Allan set the book he was holding down on the table and took a few steps toward Ashley. He held out his hand.

"I'm Allan. It's amazing to see you again, Ashley." Allan's voice grew tight with emotion. "You've gone and grown up."

Ashley took Allan's hand and the two men shook, eye to eye.

Jordan wondered what was going through Ashley's mind. He was shaking the hand of the man who had started out as his father, before Jaclyn had taken him away. As far as Jordan knew, Ashley never had a father figure after Allan.

Allan turned toward Jordan, and her heart ached for him. His eyes were full of a heavy, breathless pain, in spite of the smile of welcome on his lips. He pulled out a stool and sat down. He gestured to a seat, inviting Ashley to join him.

"How did——" His voice went hoarse, and Allan coughed to clear it. "How did this happen?" He pointed between the twins and then folded his hands together, but not before both Jordan and Ashley noticed that his fingers were trembling.

"I landed in Maticaw for the night and was on my way to the Silver Pony to wait out the storm when I ran into him."

"Quite literally," Ashley added.

Jordan nodded, giving Ashley a crooked smile. It was surreal, having her twin and her father in the same room. She watched Ashley, scanning his expression for anything hostile. Protective-ness of Allan loomed in her heart suddenly, like a lumbering movie-monster. But her brother's expression was open and soft and, if she wasn't mistaken, a bit embarrassed.

"How is your mother?" Allan asked, his voice gentle.

Ashley let out a laugh that didn't reach his eyes. "Jaclyn and I... we didn't part on the best terms."

"She tried to have him killed," Jordan supplied. "He was a hot mess when I found him."

Allan's face went wooden. "Truly? Jaclyn is far from perfect, but I can hardly believe she would be capable of killing——" His hazel eyes flashed to Jordan, and she knew what he was thinking; Jaclyn had already tried to have Jordan eliminated. "Her son," Allan amended miserably.

"Believe it." Ashley's words were bitter. "If it weren't for Jordan, I'd probably be dead."

For a moment, Jordan could only see a scared and lost little boy sitting across the room from her. The only person he'd ever trusted, the one he thought would have loved and protected him above all else, had betrayed him in the deepest way possible.

She felt a small amount of acerbic satisfaction that Jaclyn had treated Ashley the same way she'd treated Jordan.

"What happened?" Allan prompted.

Ashley rubbed a hand over his face, and there was red in the corners of his eyes. "I confronted her about my identity and about some of the things she was doing to position herself for power. I didn't understand why she had set me against Jordan that night," Ashley nodded at his twin, his face lined with regret. "Old habits die hard, and when she commanded me to kill you," Ashley was speaking candidly to Jordan now, "I didn't think, I just acted. The way I'd been acting my whole life. Jaclyn brought me up to do her bidding, treating me more like a soldier than a son. I thought all sons were raised this way, until I got old enough to go out into the world and observe different. Anyway," he shrugged his shoulders, "it is not an excuse. I only hope it can shed some light on the circumstances and my mentality... that night."

It was on the tip of Jordan's tongue to ask Ashley why they should trust him, but the image of him bleeding out in the rain that night in Maticaw silenced her. Her instincts told her he was being truthful.

"Jaclyn has been conspiring with Prince Diruk to weaken the king," Ashley said to Allan. "And kill him when the time is right, once they've got their chess pieces in place."

"Treason," whispered Allan, and his face went pale, his freckles standing out in contrast. "You're sure?"

"I'm sure. The plot has been so tightly managed that even I, Jaclyn's right-hand, was never entirely sure of what was going on.

Now I'm certain. Jaclyn exposed herself in a bid to get my trust back." His eyes turned calculating and cold. "It backfired."

Allan and Jordan shared a look. Jordan fought the urge to jump in and tell Allan what Ashley had already told her, back in Maticaw, but she kept her lips sealed. It would be better coming from Ashley.

"Why would Jaclyn conspire to kill the king, though? She wants Diruk on the throne because he can give her security and power?" Allan put forward the same exact reasoning Jordan had back in Maticaw.

"Jaclyn doesn't want Diruk on the throne. She's plotting against him, too. Her goal was always to put me on the throne."

"You?" Allan straightened. "How is that even possible?"

"We are King Konig's children," Ashley's eyes drifted to Jordan, but she only had eyes for Allan.

Allan's hand covered his mouth, and his eyes lost focus as he went somewhere in his mind, letting this news soak in like liquid soaks into cotton. "Jaclyn and the Rodanian king," he said with awe. Multiple emotions played across the surface of Allan's face, and then he reacted in a way that startled both of the twins.

He laughed.

"Oh, marvelous," he said through belly-shaking, genuine laughter. "That woman! It is beginning to make some sense now. I don't know how she did it, but only Jaclyn——" He interrupted his own diatribe to slap his knee and laugh heartily again.

"Dad?" Jordan's gut tightened as she wondered whether he had finally snapped under the shock of everything his wife had done.

"I'm fine, Jordy. Your old dad is much heartier than he looks. Jaclyn cannot hurt me now. I know you worry about this. But it has been a long time since Jaclyn had any hold over my heart, sweetheart. Don't worry." His eyes crinkled at his daughter, and she was happy to see that they were calculating and precise, not frail or uncertain. They shifted to Ashley. "How did she do this? Did she tell you? I mean," Allan gestured with his hand, "not the baby-making part, but... a king? She is beautiful, sure, but beauty is not enough for this. This is like magic."

Ashley watched Allan, his mouth slightly open, his expression uncertain. Allan's reaction had startled him. He finally collected himself. "She did tell me some of the story, amending some details. But I'll tell you what I know."

"Did she fall through the portal accidentally, the first time?" Allan shifted forward, his elbows on the table, leaning eagerly into the story.

"Yes. She couldn't get back to Earth, and had come through with nothing——only the clothes on her back and a locket she'd been wearing."

Allan nodded and glanced at Jordan. "Locket."

"I think this part of her history is something she is very proud of," Ashley continued. "How high she was able to rise, when she'd started with absolutely nothing. She was captured by a band of gypsies and sold to a merchant at a slave auction."

"Oh, she wouldn't have liked that," Allan chuckled. "Not at all. Go on."

"The merchant was a man she referred to as Torpizar, a wealthy man with many agents and connections up and down the coastline, including Rodania and beyond. Her job at first was simply to serve, but she soon endeared herself to him. She demonstrated how well she could help him buy and sell——"

"She's no dummy..." Allan muttered.

"And Torpizar gave her more and more responsibility. Jaclyn never said so, but I suspect the merchant fell in love with her."

"They always do." These words were laced with bitterness, and it was clear that Allan counted himself among this ensnared number.

"But he was shrewd, too. He never married her, which is what she tried for. He never released her from her bonds; he never really trusted her."

"Then he's a smarter man than I."

"Don't say that, Dad." Jordan put a hand on his forearm. Allan patted the back of her hand.

"When their seasonal circuits would bring them to Rodania, Torpizar always had an audience with the king, as his goods came from places on Oriceran that were exotic and unique. This was before the system relied on portmasters to regulate everything. Since then, the laws have changed, and merchants like Torpizar don't exist in the same way anymore. Anyway, the variety and quality of his goods surpassed all other merchants of the time, so he was welcome on Upper Rodania. And of course, Jaclyn came with him."

"And when King Konig got a look at those big, brown eyes..."

Ashley nodded slowly. "This is the part of the story I feel holds Jaclyn's greatest wound. You say that men always fall in love with her... Well, I think King Konig finally got the better of her, and *she* fell in love with *him*."

Allan made a noise of disbelief in the back of his throat.

Ashley sensed his incredulity. "I have no doubt about this. King Konig bought her freedom and welcomed her to live at the palace. He showered her with expensive gifts, an apartment, whatever she wanted."

"What about the queen?"

"She turned a blind eye. According to Jaclyn, she always did when it came to King Konig's mistresses."

"And then what happened?"

Ashley's mouth flattened. "Jaclyn didn't tell me why she left Rodania. There is a black hole in her story wherever she wants there to be a black hole. She'd told me my whole life that Torpizar was my father, that she traded herself for freedom. She didn't want me to know of my true heritage until it suited her."

"Why not?" Jordan asked.

"Because, what would have stopped Ashley from leaving Jaclyn to make his claim in Rodania years ago?" Allan theorized.

"Ashley was her most valuable asset. Naturally, she would want to keep him where she could control him."

Ashley nodded. "But everything has changed now. King Konig is dead, and I'm no longer under Jaclyn's control."

"Dead?" Allan let out a long breath through pursed lips. "How do you know? Surely I would have heard the announcement at the university?"

"We know because we were there," explained Jordan. "Ashley had some of the fungus I went to Charra-Rae for. He took it from the stores Jaclyn has been keeping in the basement under the trade office in Maticaw. We delivered it to Juer together, but it was too late. It only happened a few hours ago."

"Did you actually *see* the king?"

The twins nodded.

"He knew who we were," added Jordan, her voice quiet and sad. "He even told us he loved Jaclyn."

She explained to her father what had happened when they were in the king's chambers, what he wrote in the air, and how Juer, Darber, and Balroc had each reacted. She explained there was to be a hearing to determine whether or not the twins' right to the throne would be upheld or not. Allan's face grew serious as the position the twins were in became clear. His shock at their true identity transformed into worry for their safety as Jordan told the story.

"So now what?" Allan asked through stiff lips.

Jordan spoke first. "We will either be coronated, or…"

"Or, what?"

"We don't know. Banished? Left alone to live our lives? Accused of treason?" Ashley and Jordan's eyes connected, their fates linked. "We have to wait and see."

CHAPTER 13

*E*ohne stood at her worktable, eyeing the butterflies
miserably. She let out a long sigh and lifted her fingertips to her temples where the beginnings of a headache were
stirring.

For days, she and Linlett had been working together on the
barrier magic without success. They had taken apart whole
sections of the magic and reassembled them, looking for traces of
tampering. Linlett had to do the actual physical work with the
filaments, since only he had the ability to touch them, but Eohne
was there, making notes and using her powerful memory to help.

It was frustrating, because Eohne knew what she was capable
of; she just hadn't yet been able to bridge the Light Elves' magic
with her own. It was like trying to communicate with someone
who didn't speak the same language; basic concepts came across
roughly, but full understanding was nuanced and as elusive as
the tide.

Linlett had tried to show Eohne how to transform her fingertips into the stars that would allow her to feel the filaments, to
move and read them, but thus far she seemed incapable of this
kind of magic. It was disheartening. After all, the Elves of

Charra-Rae were descended from the Light Elves. Surely the residue of their magic would still reside within Eohne's body, there to access if she learned how. Perhaps she'd just been in tune with frequencies for so long that any other magical language she might have been capable of had gone dormant.

They had visited more than half of the domes. Linlett would remove the dashboards, and the same beautiful web of threaded color and light would shoot into the sky, intact and perfect. Linlett worked tirelessly, without complaint or any display of discouragement. He was convinced that as long as they didn't give up, they would find the source of the problem. It had to be there——some trace, some clue... they just hadn't found it yet.

Time was passing, and Eohne still hadn't responded to Sohne. She was unsure of what to say and unsure of how long she could remain absent from Charra-Rae without the Elf princess getting impatient enough to punish her.

No more messages had come; it wasn't Sohne's style to repeat herself. Eohne had begun to wonder if the Elf princess would send someone to retrieve her, or worse, come herself.

Sohne rarely leaves the safety of our forest kingdom, but might she? For an Elf subject as valuable as me? Eohne didn't know. She just kept telling herself that she'd go home in another week, just one more week.

Somehow, that week would roll by, and still Eohne stayed.

And now, Linlett. Another reason to stay.

The work was fascinating. It was frustrating, but the feeling that they were on the edge of a breakthrough increased every day.

Eohne's eye fell on her leather belt containing the small vials of vibratory essence, the same one she'd been wearing when she first left Charra-Rae.

The same belt I tracked Toth and Caje with, she thought with a pang.

She smiled as she next remembered all the work she had done

cutting down harpy venom in a bid to save Allan, which had thankfully worked.

Eohne picked up a vial and glowered at the clear liquid inside. She enclosed the tiny vial in her fist, then shut her eyes and tuned in to its contents.

She could feel the subtle, barely detectable vibration which told her its origin--harpy. No other creature shared a vibration like it. Every creature, every plant, every living organism had its own unique signature.

Eohne opened her eyes and gazed at the vial, still feeling the tingle in her skin.

Then she got an idea.

CHAPTER 14

*L*eaving Ashley at Allan's for the night, Jordan said goodbye and took to the air, headed for home. Her mind swirled, and her gut roiled on the edge of nausea as a rat of worry had its way with her insides.

The sun was kissing the horizon, and the colors of Rodania had turned into a palette of pastels. As Jordan landed on the terrace of her apartment with Sol, she closed her eyes and sucked in a long, steadying breath.

"Jordan? Is that you?" Sol's voice called from the bedroom, his tone incredulous.

"It's me," she answered. Just the sound of his voice was enough to steady her.

"That has to be some kind of record," he said with a laugh as he emerged, his hands full of boiled leather armor. The moment he saw Jordan's face, his own melted into a mask of concern. "What's wrong?"

Jordan gazed at him, her vision growing blurry. Sol knew nothing of what had transpired over the last day. She was loath to complicate his life further—he needed to focus on Golpa, on doing the job and getting back safely.

Jordan began to speak but her throat closed up. Sol's loving face was enough to bring all of her emotion rushing to the forefront, and she finally felt allowed to fall apart a little.

"What is it?" He put the leather and the knives on the nearest stool and came over to where Jordan stood on the terrace. He put his hands on her shoulders. "Jordan, what's happened? Is it something to do with Sohne?" His voice hardened. "What has that wretched Elf done now?"

At his touch, a sob broke from Jordan's throat, and she sagged against him, willing herself not to bawl like a baby. Tears came anyway. Sol wrapped his arms around her and squeezed, his warmth soaking into her, and she closed her eyes and drank it through every pore. Sol didn't pressure her to talk, he just held her as the remaining day's light leaked from the sky.

When she was ready, Jordan wiped her face. The kitchen was full of supplies, so she pulled Sol into the bedroom where they could sit on the bed. Sol listened quietly while the story spilled out of her; she told him everything that had happened and everything she had learned. When she revealed to him who her biological father was, he didn't seem as surprised as she expected him to be.

"You're not shocked?" she asked, watching his face.

"I am," he said, shaking his head. "It's just that I actually had the thought once before, that you might be related to the king. I didn't suspect you were his daughter, but... something in his family tree."

"You did?" Jordan was startled by this admission. It was the first Sol had ever mentioned it. "When? Why?"

"Way back, when we spent that first night on Oriceran together. Remember?"

Jordan smiled. "When we had giant crab for dinner and took turns staying awake? How could I forget?"

Sol nodded. "When you started to talk about how your mom

had to be on Oriceran and I had to help you find her. That it was the reason we met."

"Oh, yeah." Jordan looked a little sheepish. "I was pretty insistent."

Sol chuckled at the memory. "I first noticed the color of your eyes in the parlor of your house. Such an unusual shade," he murmured, tucking her hair behind her ears. "Yet it was so familiar, and I couldn't figure out why."

"King Konig's eyes."

Sol nodded again. "Yes. As courier I'd had occasion to be in the same room as him a few times, picking up messages and whatnot. But I couldn't put you and him together in a way that made sense, so when I met you, it wasn't obvious why your eyes were so familiar to me. King Konig was far from my mind at that moment in time. But when you talked about your mother being on Oriceran somewhere, that's when I remembered where I had seen eyes like yours before. Only it was too farfetched to believe, so I just dismissed it."

"Wow."

"So, what do they intend to do with you?"

She explained that the Council was meeting to discuss her and Ashley's legitimacy for the throne, and that Juer had been the only witness. She left out the disdain that Darber had shown toward Sol; there was no point in bringing up the Councilman's personal feelings.

Sol's bright blue eyes darkened. "What happens if they decide against you?"

"I don't know. I don't know anything, Sol. But I hope they do decide against us."

Sol's brow wrinkled. "What? Why?"

"I don't want to be a ruler! I don't want any more power or responsibility than I already have. I have never wanted that. Having power made my dad miserable and corrupted my mother, if she wasn't already corrupt before. If she was, power just made her worse."

"Jordan."

She kept talking. "I don't want to be anything like her. I just want to be happy. I want to be with you. I want to make Rodania safe, make sure my father is healthy and happy. That's it. I'm not complicated, even though I seem to bring complication with me wherever I go."

"Jordan." This time Sol's voice was sharp enough to make her pause. "If you do not do everything in your power to claim your inheritance, then I don't want anything more to do with you." His eyes had gone sharp.

Jordan gasped. "What?" Her voice quavered, she could hardly believe what she was hearing.

Sol got up and began to pace, his wings flexing in and out with agitation. "How many times have you pinned me down, asking me why I never did anything to help better the Nychts' situation? How many nights since we first talked about it have I spent awake, trying to think of one way I could help make life in Rodania better for them?"

"You've spent nights awake?"

"Of course, I have! Jordan, I spent most of my life thinking that working in service to my government and my king was the best thing I could do, the way I could have a positive impact on the world. I know better now. Governments and monarchies are only as good as the people who make them up. And right now, Rodania's government is sick, it's bloated with its own arrogance." Sol's voice was rising. "Where do you think this country is headed? You were at the ceremony. You saw with your own eyes the nature of our next ruler, and those of the Arpaks who support him. Do you want all the Strix who died during that battle to have died in vain? Because that's how it's going to be if Diruk takes the throne."

Jordan blinked at this impassioned version of Sol. She was stung, but deep down, she was also ashamed. Sol wasn't wrong.

"I don't care if you don't *feel* like taking on the responsibility that your birthright thrusts upon you. To cast it aside or treat it with disdain is foolhardy to the point of immoral. It's the equivalent of being given an unbeatable weapon in the middle of a harpy battle, and purposefully dropping it into the sea."

Jordan's mouth parted with shock, but words failed her. She'd never seen Sol like this before. Her heart pounded at the righteous fury in his eyes. She understood that it wasn't directed at her, but at a decision she might make, an outcome that only *may* come to pass.

"Jordan," Sol came back to the bed and took her face in his hands. "There aren't very many people I know who could wield power responsibly, but you are one of them. If you are given this gift, or burden——because yes, it is both——then grab it with both hands and use it to help those who need it. Don't run away because you're afraid of it. Don't be weak." He brushed the moisture from her cheeks, his voice softening and the anger passing out of his eyes like the clouds of a passing storm. "Be a queen."

Shame burned Jordan's cheeks. Sol was right, and she loved him for it. "Well," Jordan croaked, taking his hands. "We know where you stand, don't we?"

Sol smiled. "Sorry. I can get a bit carried away when the future of my country is at stake."

"I understand that. But Sol, I have no cards to play. Yes, King Konig admitted that Ashley and I are his children, and your Uncle saw it, but I don't think the Council is going to acknowledge it."

"They might," Sol said, hope lighting his eyes. "You don't know what is going to happen."

Jordan nodded, squeezing his hands with hers. "You're right, we don't know. So until then," she got up from the bed, shaking off her anxiety, "we've got some work to do. Let's get you ready for Golpa."

* * *

To an outside observer, Eohne and Linlett might have looked as though they were doing some strange dance. Eohne stood facing Linlett's back, her eyes closed and bound with a kerchief to shut out the pervading light, her palms on the bare skin of his ribcage.

She still flushed when she thought about her suggestion that he remove his shirt and allow her to feel the subdued vibrations of each filament as they passed through his body.

To her pleasant surprise, Linlett had not cocked a lusty eyebrow or smirked arrogantly at her suggestion. He'd simply nodded, elegant brows drawn together. "That makes sense," and doffed his tunic.

Eohne had suspected that Linlett's skin changed color, but she had never guessed how drastically. She tried not to stare but it was nearly impossible.

Linlett's skin was very pale in hue on his face and hands, but the terrain of his body changed color the closer it got to his heart. The skin over the left side of his chest was the color of cinnamon, but it grew lighter in color as it radiated outward from his heart. The dashes that ran across his cheeks and hands also ran across sections of his chest and stomach.

Linlett's pale green eyes observed Eohne scanning the canvas of his bare torso. As he turned to toss aside his tunic, she saw that the same coloring and patterns were mirrored on his back.

"It's a sign of my calling," he said by way of explanation.

"Your calling?"

"I'm an Etheriast. It's why the Light Elves sent me." He looked down at himself. "I can access the invisible medium that permeates the universe and allows light to travel. Every time I do it, I get more markings and this," he put a hand over the cinnamon skin on his heart, "gets darker."

"Like a tan."

Linlett nodded.

"I've never met anyone like you," blurted Eohne.

"The feeling is mutual, I can assure you." Linlett smiled at her. "Shall we continue?"

Eohne nodded. Linlett turned his back to her and she put her blindfold on and set her hands on his ribs. Linlett's fingers illuminated as he touched and held one filament at a time.

When they'd first begun this exercise, it had taken Eohne a long time to feel the vibration of the filament as it passed through Linlett's body and into her fingertips. Linlett needed to hold a filament between the brightly-lit ends of his fingers for nearly a minute before she would tell him to go on and select another. But the longer they did it, the faster Eohne got until Linlett was touching the filaments at a rate of one per second. Eohne's mind found the frequency and categorized it; Arpak, Arpak, Nycht, Arpak, Elf, human, Arpak. And so on.

"Wait," she said, detecting something entirely different.

"What is it?" Linlett waited with bated breath, hoping it was what they had been searching for.

A slow smile spread across Eohne's face as she registered whose vibration it was she was feeling. "It's Blue."

"Who is Blue?"

"He's Jordan's dragon."

"A dragon?" Linlett was so startled he took his hands down and looked over his shoulder at Eohne. "Dragons aren't allowed in Rodania!"

She lifted the blindfold and looked up at him. "This one was, because they thought he was a Predoian Miniature."

"They *thought* he was?" Linlett's brow arched. "What was he actually?"

"Not a miniature," laughed Eohne. "We thought for a while he was going to get kicked out, but then the harpies attacked, and Blue and his mate saved the country."

Linlett turned around fully to face her, amazed. "*Another* dragon got in?"

"Yes, thank goodness."

"Where is she now? I haven't seen any dragons flying around."

"Toth has taken her and Blue to Golpa, to kill the harpies where they nest."

Linlett frowned thoughtfully.

"You didn't know how we survived the harpy attack?" Eohne asked. "No one told you that it was two dragons who saved us?"

He shook his head. "Seems a glaring oversight on someone's part." He rubbed his palm over his mouth. "We've been at this for days now; we've touched tens of thousands of filaments, wouldn't you agree?"

Eohne nodded, and she knew where he was going with this line of thinking. She'd been thinking it herself.

"You've found one of only two dragon filaments in the barrier. But how many harpies did you say attacked in the last big onslaught?"

"In the high hundreds," said Eohne. "Possibly as many as a thousand."

"So why haven't we located any harpy filaments yet? It's against the odds."

"We haven't located Red's filament either," Eohne pointed out.

"Red?" It took Linlett a second. "The other dragon? You call her Red?"

Eohne nodded.

" 'Red' and 'Blue'. Really?"

She nodded again, a smile tugging at the corner of her mouth. "Sol named them. The man never claimed to have much imagination."

"I'll say. Poor names aside, we might not run into Red's filament. She was never inducted legally, right?"

"No. But she passed through the barrier, so shouldn't that mean she has a filament? Otherwise, why are we spending all this time looking for harpy filaments?"

"Because of the sabotage," Linlett explained. "Passing through the barrier illegally, if that were even possible, wouldn't magically result in a filament. Only going through the proper channels——submitting blood and so on——would create a filament that would then become a permanent part of the barrier, allowing its root being through as many times as he or she likes."

"Someone would have to have legally inducted every single harpy, if what you're saying is true. That seems near impossible."

Linlett nodded. "Seems like it, yes. Nevertheless, it's what I suspect happened. So I'm just wondering why we haven't run across any yet." He turned his back to Eohne and raised his hands again, his fingers lighting up. "We're bound to very shortly. It's mathematically certain."

Eohne pulled down her blindfold and rested her hands once again on his torso as they resumed their task.

CHAPTER 15

The Strix squadron of eighty-three Nychts and a baker's dozen of Arpaks flew over the forest of dreesha, a monstrous narrow-leafed species of tree that towered above a secondary canopy of smaller trees. The long, thin dreesha leaves allowed narrow slices of sunshine in geometric shapes to penetrate and feed the forest below.

The force passed not far from where Sol had been pursued by two harpies before crashing through a portal and meeting Jordan.

He couldn't help the smile that touched his lips at the memory of that fateful day.

How much had changed since then, not just in his life but in his country and with his people? No longer was he a courier for the aristocracy——now he was a soldier, following a Nycht leader, no less. He never would have believed it possible.

His eyes found the back of the bat-winged man they had all sworn to follow on this mission, possibly to their deaths.

The heavy sound of huge swaths of air being pushed aside by enormous wings drew his gaze from Toth's back to the shadow passing overhead. The yellow belly-scales of Blue passed through the cloud cover, just visible through the wisps of condensation.

Red and Blue made their presence known once a day. They rarely passed so close; most often, they were serpentine shapes on the horizon. An echoing roar would bounce off the landscape, reassuring the party of soldiers, and then the creatures would disappear until the next day.

A dragon couldn't be bent to someone else's will; they were either in, or they weren't. The Strix just trusted that the dragons would be there when they were needed. Without them, the mission was doomed.

Harpies they met on the way were swiftly cut down, if not by the dragons then by the Strix warriors. The demon-birds were met in singles and doubles, occasionally in threes, and the frequency with which they were seen increased as Golpa neared and the temperatures dropped.

The Strix kept a steady pace, set by Teetch, Toth's quiet brother. As the light changed and the shadows became long, he would break out ahead with three companions, scouting out a suitable camp for the night. When it was time to rest and refuel, he'd arrow downward, heading for a sheltered break in the landscape that could accommodate them. They'd descend, set up a collection of tents, and stoke a dozen fires or more——enough to provide a hot meal and warm their bones before sleep took them.

When they camped, six Strix always remained awake, keeping watch over the rest... though predators were few. Even if there had been gypsies or slave-traders around, they wouldn't dare tangle with a group of winged soldiers armed to the teeth.

Arpaks took the first shift, watching until the moon rose high in the sky. They'd switch with the Nychts just past midnight, and they'd watch the camp until the morning sun became a suggestion in the sky. The group would then break camp and be off before the sun had hoisted itself fully past the horizon.

After three days of flying this way, the landscape changed drastically. Rolling, barren foothills crusted with broken rocks and scrawny, twisted trees passed by below, and majestic mountains loomed where the sky met land. Towns became villages, which became nomadic camps populated by tents made of animal skins. Herds of the lumbering, multi-tusked feroth became more frequent. Lifting their heads and giving their deep, bellowing cries as the shadows of the Strix passed over them.

The winds grew strong and bitter. The Strix pulled out their cold-weather gear: rough-spun scarves and hats, fingerless gloves with little caps that folded over their fingertips, thick boiled leather or oiled canvas jackets lined with fur and woolen insoles for their boots.

Their breath hung in clouds as they sat talking around their fires at night. Chayla wrapped her neck and head in a thick black cowl, leaving only her glittering green eyes visible, staring out with flinty resolve. She was never happier than when she was on a mission to kill an enemy; her anticipation oozed with a seething militant patience.

They passed over the rocky foothills and into the rugged mountain territory. The deep gorge of The Conca lay fifty miles west of them, drawing closer slowly, bit by bit, as they kept a trajectory for its northern end, where the gorge became huge yawning caves.

Teetch and the scouts led them into a narrow valley to set up camp for the night. Word passed quickly from mouth to mouth: tomorrow they would reach Golpa. Tension in the camp mounted as they worked to erect their shelters, heat their rations and get them into their bellies. Hats were pulled low over their ears in the sharp chill of evening. Icy shadows soon swallowed them as the last light of the sun vanished, and the glow of the fires threw a cowl of heat over their faces and bodies. Weapons were sharpened, and conversations were low and guttural. Unlabelled bottles were passed around, the belly-burning liquids inside offering a different kind of warmth.

Sol put away his razor-sharp dirks and blew warm air over his frozen fingertips, watching how his breath formed a jetstream. He'd never experienced such a cold and hostile environment as this before. Rodania was hospitable and temperate, never requiring more than a vest and leather leggings to keep warm. He scratched at his forehead where the skin itched under his cap. He didn't like wearing a hat. After a few hours, what once felt like a soft hug around the temples became a vise which he yearned to remove. But removing it left him vulnerable to stabbing headaches from the freezing winds. It was better to suffer with the hat on.

How he ached to be at home curled up with Jordan in their bed, their feathers making a cocoon around them. The sooner they got this job done, the sooner he could go home. If he could help it, he'd never travel this far north ever again.

He spied the tall, straight shape of Toth as he passed by the fire, heading for where Teetch sat with a map laid open on his lap. Sol watched as the Nycht mercenary stepped over a large log and sat down beside his brother, accepting a plate of food from Chayla as he did so. Toth was always the last one to eat, never taking in a morsel until he knew all the rest of them had had their portions.

Sol got up and went to join them, stepping over the same log and sitting on Toth's other side.

Toth glanced up, his cheek bulging with bread and cheese. He gave Sol a nod and shifted closer to Teetch to give more room.

"Didn't see Red today," Sol said, crossing his arms tightly over his chest and hunkering against a breeze that kicked smoke into their eyes.

"She's around," Toth spoke around his food, swallowed, and tore off another huge bite from the chunk of hard cheese Chayla had given him. "She and Blue made a big kill yesterday."

"That feroth herd we passed, after the lake with the wrecked ship on the shoreline?"

Toth nodded. "They're always slow after." Toth's chewing became labored, and he glanced down at the rind of cheese in his hand, frowning. He swallowed, with some difficulty it seemed. "Like eating a shoe," he muttered. "Hand me that water, would you Teetch?"

Teetch passed him a bottle, and Toth took several long swallows before coughing explosively. He looked at the bottle with shock, as though a label might reveal itself.

"That's not water," he wheezed.

A gale of laughter rose up around the fire, and even Toth's eyes crinkled at the corners as he thumped his chest and coughed.

"Who's responsible for this vile liquid?"

"My uncle has a still in his backyard," explained one of the Nychts, a tall, slender man Sol knew as 'Breaker' because he'd snapped more javelins in practice than anyone else. He didn't know the Nycht's real name.

Toth handed the bottle to Sol, who took it by reflex. Breaker's eyes followed the bottle and tracked up to Sol's face expectantly.

"It'll set fire to your insides," Breaker offered as a benefit and desirable outcome. The other Strix, squinting with good humor, watched Sol and waited.

Sol lifted the bottle to his lips and took a swallow. His tongue and throat were immediately aflame with a ghastly burning sensation that was more chemical than anything else. It scorched his esophagus all the way down and pooled in his belly like lava. He coughed hard, grinning at the pain, and the Strix around the fire bellowed laughter, including Toth.

He handed the bottle to the next Strix, who went through the same painful routine. In this way, they were united by the heat and pain. No one enjoyed it more than Breaker, who laughed uproariously every time a wheezing cough echoed through the valley, and streaming eyes were wiped. The bonding over the noxious liquid did more to lift their spirits than hearing Red's roar in the distance.

Sol stayed up to take first watch as the Nychts broke for the night. As he and five other Arpaks moved to their stations at the perimeter of the camp, Sol's vision swam. The warmth of the liquid began to creep outward, warming his torso, then his limbs. A good-humored calm stole over him as he settled against a thick stump of a tree. A slow grin crept over his face, as his mind lifted and played memories on the screen of his mind. A much tinier Blue crawling under a bench at his Uncle Juer's library to sleep among the dustbunnies. Jordan's face after he'd fashioned those ridiculous leaf shoes for her, before they'd reached Nishpat.

At thoughts of Jordan, the strong and regular beats of his heart seemed to turn juicy and soft, flooding his body with a love-drunk feeling. Sol passed the hours of his watch playing over the blossoming of their romance: their first kiss, the trip back to Richmond to retrieve the gun and her family's gold, the beautiful night they'd spent in front of the fire before they returned to Oriceran. It had just been the two of them—no danger of harpies, no Rodanian politics, and, as much as Sol loved Eohne and Allan, no one to interrupt them. Sol had never felt happier.

The changing of the watch happened before Sol had even realized how much time had passed. He recognized Toth's shape as the Nycht made his way over to switch with him. There was a slightly lumbering, liquid quality to Toth's movements that Sol had never seen before. As the Arpak watched the Nycht approach and sit opposite him, he was filled with a never-before-felt desire to connect.

When Sol didn't get up and head for his sleeping quarters, Toth cocked an eyebrow at him. In the hard blue glitter of moonlight, Sol could see that the Nycht's eyes had a softness they didn't normally have. It struck him only then that they were drunk from the small amount of awful moonshine that Breaker had shared.

"Not tired?" Toth shoved his hands into his armpits and settled back against the tree.

"Do you love her?" Sol blurted the words, not even realizing what he was going to ask before the words were out of his mouth.

Toth went still as stone.

Sol did not have to clarify who he was talking about.

When the Nycht didn't respond, Sol fought hard not to apologize and retract the question. His cheeks flushed in spite of the cold night; *I won't take it back... I need to know.*

He'd been wanting to know the nature of Toth's feelings toward Jordan since the Nycht first came into their lives. He pressed his lips shut and waited as the silence grew thick.

Toth's expression remained still and unsurprised at the question, his eyes unguarded. He let out a long breath, and it hung in a cloud in front of his face. He focused on this cloud and watched as it dissipated. Then he boldly met Sol's gaze.

"I do," Toth finally replied, "but not in the way you think."

Sol waited.

"I have eleven siblings," the Nycht continued.

Sol nodded. He knew this.

"Had. I have lost two." Toth held two fingers up.

"Caje, and..."

"Caje and Nieve." Toth let out another sigh. "She was not so strong as Jordan, but they have the same spirit, the same idealistic world view, the same compassion."

Sol's heart thudded with a heavy, painful ache for the Nycht. He would have felt pain for Toth even had he not been affected by the strong drink, but the alcohol brought all of his emotions to the forefront.

"I wish you and Jordan well," said Toth. "But when I met you, I didn't think you were good enough for her. While we're being honest."

"I wasn't," Sol agreed, surprising even himself with this admission. "I had a girl once. I failed her."

Toth cocked an eyebrow. "Really?"

Sol nodded. "A nice girl. Raya was her name. She was a lawyer's daughter, and a sweet girl."

"What happened?"

"I was always gone. Obsessed with my work. Committed to king and country. I had *important* work to do." His tone dripped sarcasm. He pulled his cap down over his forehead, then tucked his fingers up under it and scratched. "I was foolish. Too young to understand what love really was, or what putting someone else first looked like. I broke her heart when I ended it." Sol frowned at the memory. It was a long time ago, but the feeling of hurting someone who didn't deserve it still came with a twist in the gut. "After that, I just thought I wasn't meant for a relationship."

Toth's mouth twisted with a wry smile. He didn't say so, but he thought Sol didn't really know what living a solitary life was all about. "Then you met Jordan."

Sol nodded. "Then I met Jordan. I resisted her." His eyes squinted shut and he grimaced at the memory of how he'd pushed her away. "I resisted her with everything I had."

"Clearly you lost that battle," Toth said.

Sol blew a breath out. "Spectacularly."

Toth chuckled at this and hunkered down deeper into his scarf.

Sol smiled and looked at the Nycht. "So, what happened to Nieve?"

Toth let a few heartbeats pass before he spoke. "Nieve was born with a weak constitution. She could never fully adjust to the Arpak rhythm that drives life in Rodania."

Sol shifted uncomfortably against the tree. "But how did she die?"

"That *is* how she died, Sol."

Sol gaped at the Nycht, his jaw soft with disbelief. There was nothing in the Nycht's face which spoke of a lie or a bad joke or even an exaggeration.

"I can see you do not understand, and it comes as no surprise. Though you are among the best of them, you are Arpak, after all."

Sol's mouth opened and closed, searching for a response, but there was too much shock and drink in him for something rational to surface. "But... she died?" He shook his head. "There must have been something else."

"There wasn't anything else, Sol. Nychts are nocturnal. You know this the way you know that the sky is blue and the sun is hot, but you don't *know* it the way we know it. Strong Nychts can and do adapt, but it costs them. It costs all of them. For some, the weaker ones, it can cost them everything." The words were plain, like Toth was explaining how to bake bread, but there was pain in his eyes. "Over time, a debt is built up; the sun does its damage. For a weak heart especially, nighttime sleep is not restorative enough."

Sol could still barely believe what he was hearing. Could it really be true, that living against their natural rhythm could kill a Nycht over time? "Why didn't she live as a nocturnal creature, then?" Sol struggled to understand. "I mean, if it was killing her——"

"We didn't know it was killing her. We knew she was weak, but we didn't ascribe it to her lack of daytime sleep. She took a trip to Maticaw with Arth and Mareya one day. She'd never been, and had always wanted to go. Our mother was very protective of Nieve, never letting her leave Rodania. Arth had to make a delivery to someone in Maticaw who bought one of her items, and Nieve begged Arth to take her. Told her it was her dream to see the mainland. Arth agreed. They made the delivery during daytime hours, the way every other delivery is made. Nieve made it to Maticaw, but she collapsed on one of the docks. She was never one to complain. She had spent a lifetime hiding her suffering from us, keeping secret anything that would make us worry more or hold her back."

Toth was silent for a time.

"She never recovered," Toth continued. "They took her to a doctor, but he couldn't explain what was wrong with her. Arth sent for a Light Elf, but it was too late. The Elf arrived after Nieve had passed on. It was only then, using their magic, that they were able to discover the cause of her death. It was simply a life lived against what her biology needed to thrive, the forced continuation of insisting on the body when it's begging for otherwise."

"I'm sorry." Sol finally cobbled together a response, and it fell like dust from his mouth, hollow and meaningless in the face of such a tragedy.

"If you're really sorry, then find a way to help me change things. Nieve is why Caje and I left Rodania. For all the good it did us."

"Are there others?"

"Nychts who died because they're forced to live the Arpak way? Of course there are. Not many, but there have always been some Nychts born with a compromised immune system or a weak heart. Their deaths are ascribed to the diagnosis given at birth, but in how many cases might living in accordance with their biological imperative strengthen them enough to live a full life? Nychts thrive in moonlight, and they are forced to live in the sun. Many of them do not even know themselves how damaging this can be over time."

Sol swallowed down his horror. "Why don't the Council know about them? These Nycht deaths?"

"They do," muttered Toth, all his bitterness finally emerging.

"What are a few lowly Nycht deaths in the face of keeping Arpaks in control of Rodania?"

Sol found his gaze cast down between his booted feet, unable to look at Toth anymore. Shame burned through his insides in the same way the offensive alcohol had set his stomach and throat afire. "I never knew."

"Now you do," said Toth. "And you can't un-know it."

CHAPTER 16

They approached the caves of Golpa in the black of night, since harpies were not nocturnal. In this way, they wouldn't alert any harpies that might be out hunting nearby, and they could utilize one of the Nychts' more deadly assets--sonar.

The temperatures were now well below freezing. Every piece of cold-weather gear that had been brought along on the mission had been donned. Bags of food and supplies not needed for the attack itself were stashed among the rocks.

Scouts had reported in great detail the location, size, and surrounding terrain at the mouth of Golpa. They stammered through a description of a huge, yawning, toothy hole leading into the black belly of the mountain, and relayed the pungent odor of the harpy dung that littered the rocks and snow for a quarter mile leading up to it, in addition to the stench of death and decay, thick even on the frozen air.

When it was time for the party to see it for themselves, Blue and Red descended to join the Strix, landing on razor-sharp claws among the warriors, and blowing steam and smoke. A dim yellow glow emanated from the scales of Blue's belly where he'd stoked his inner fire. Red's scales glowed an angry scarlet, and were so hot that Strix who felt brave enough clustered around her for warmth.

The dragons crouched among the rocks, waiting with deadly patience for the Strix to move toward the cave entrance.

Toth made his way to Red's snout, approaching slowly and with his head down. She watched him through a calculating slash of a pupil, unblinking. The tips of her pearly white teeth could be seen even in the dark, giving her a chilly, predatory grin, and her jaws were so massive they could crush several harpies in one bite.

Toth stopped near her huge cheek, in the space between her and Blue, and rubbed his gloved hands together.

Blue swung his head toward the Nycht.

"This was your idea, bud. Are you ready?"

Blue snorted out a sharp, hot breath, which misted the side of Toth's face in mucous.

Toth wiped at his cheek and flicked the goop off his glove. "I'll take that as a yes."

Red's jaws opened, and Toth stepped back, observing the red glow that ran down her huge throat with watering eyes. Her jaws clicked shut and she shook her head, her leathery jowls swaying. She rose from where she lay and spread her wings, as Strix stumbled back from where they'd been basking in her heat. She took to the sky with slow, heavy beats of her wings, and Blue followed silently.

The Strix took to the air, staying behind the reptiles. They hovered at the huge black hole of Golpa and watched as Red floated into the darkness like a leviathan in the ocean. Her great form was swallowed up by the shadows, and Blue's disappeared shortly after. Only the beating of their wings could be heard, echoing up from the rocky cavern walls, growing softer by the second.

Toth held up a hand, signalling his Nychts to wait. Behind the cluster of hovering Nychts were the Arpaks, armed and waiting to do their job. The breath of the Strix punctured the air before every mouth. Two fat harvest moons had hoisted themselves into the frozen sky above them all, and the dome overtop Oriceran was a caul of stars. It was a beautiful sight.

When a blast of light and heat illuminated the mouth of Golpa, Toth signalled, and the Nychts moved forward.

The Arpaks watched the forms of their fellow warriors, silhouetted against the hellish glow, disappear one by one into the throat of the mountain. Shortly after, the screams and cries of outraged harpies echoed out to their ears.

Inside Golpa, the once frozen and dark-as-deep-space rock womb was now so lit with heat and light and blood, it seemed that the Nychts had found the location of hell itself. Staying far behind the dragons as they did their fiery work, the Nychts darted about the crags, stalagmites and stalactites, cutting down the panicked harpies that had been sleeping only moments before. Nests were discovered, eggs destroyed, young and old cut down without mercy. The smell of death and blood, smoke and scorched flesh filled the caves.

Golpa was not just one huge twisting hole winding itself deep under the mountain, but a stringy network of caves, mostly dead ends. Where harpies could go, Nychts could go with ease, but Red could only fit through the main artery; she wrought her deadly fire upon every hagbird she found there. The powerful sound of her fiery blasts emboldened the warriors, explosions of heat and light in hues of green, orange, and white lit up the mountain's interior, urging them on.

Sending sound waves from their throats too high to be detected by Arpak ears, the Nychts echolocated in places where the light of the dragonfire did not reach. With sonar, the Nychts could read where the harpies were, how big they were, how fast and in what direction they were moving—–meanwhile, the harpies were blind and terrified. Between the dragons and the

A.L. KNORR & MARTHA CARR

sonar, the scales of battle had tipped so steeply in the Nychts' favor that it was absurd.

The harpies screamed, panicked and disorganized. For them, armageddon had come. Even their superconsciousness was too startled to register what was happening. Surprise shattered any hope they might have had to organize a counterattack; it was every harpy for itself.

In places where the light did not reach, their sonar gave the Nychts perfect visuals of the chaos. The cold effectiveness of their strategy surprised even Toth, as he cut through a flaming harpy that was straining for the exit. He hovered for a moment to take in the scene around him: the Nychts were death on silent wings, and the caves were filled with the forms of darting, flapping, slashing warriors, and the tumbling, broken bodies of harpies. Far below his feet were the light orbs of abandoned nests, clustered with eggs. All of them would be destroyed before the morning sun lent its light to the frozen north.

The work Red and Blue were doing was too deep into the throat of the mountain to be seen. It was too hot and dangerous for any Nycht to venture close to them now, tempting though it was to watch the reptiles and their eye-watering, hair-singeing jets of flame. Judging by the state of the harpies that had survived the dragons' attack long enough to make it this close to the exit, Blue and Red were being thorough to the point of surgical.

And thus the night wore on.

* * *

SMOKE BILLOWED from the yawning mouth of the cave where the Arpak warriors waited. The light of early dawn welcomed the soot-blackened Nychts as they retreated from the hot, smoky belly of the earth. There, they joined the Arpaks and waited, with drawn steel, for stragglers.

Harpies that came screaming from the exit in panic were cut

166

down swiftly, their deaths upon them before they could register what was happening. At first, the harpies were many, exiting the rocky jaws with smoking feathers, some of them fully aflame. Then their numbers dwindled, and the screams that echoed from the throat of Golpa and into the crisp winter air abated.

Toth stepped back from the cluster of soldiers to wet his parched mouth with a drink of water.

A thick burst of black, resinous, and stinking smoke burst from the cave. A moment later, that same smoke was sucked back inside, only to be blown out again.

"Fall back!" Toth bellowed, the waterskin hovering in the air halfway to his lips. "Here they come!"

The Strix took to flight like a murder of startled crows, fleeing the entrance to Golpa like a spray of shrapnel. A triumphant, bestial roar shook the walls of the cave, and rocks loosed from their places in the overhang, falling to the rubble below with a clatter.

Blue burst from the mouth of Golpa first, his wings beating out a rapid, tight rhythm. He loosed an excited shriek that made the Strix soldiers cringe and cover their ears, but also grin with cold satisfaction. A blast of grimy smoke preceded Red, and all heads tilted back to watch the scarlet-scaled zeppelin emerge. She floated from the cave and darkened the sky as she passed overhead. Her wingbeats were slow and powerful as she caught up to Blue. The dragons climbed skyward, screaming their victory and trailing smoke.

The Strix lifted their weapons and cried out a collective reply, saluting the reptiles——it was the dragons' victory, not their own.

Toth bared his teeth in a satisfied grimace; the unpleasant mission was almost done. He knew there were harpies out in the wild world that had been missed. The next mission for his fierce Strix soldiers would be to break into smaller parties, hunt down the missing harpies, and exterminate them.

Toth's eyes shuttered closed for a moment, and he thought of

Caje. "For you, brother," he murmured before taking several long draughts of the cooling water.

A shadow fell over him as Sol landed nearby, his face as black as the earth of the southern Conca. He was coated with soot, and his teeth were a white blaze in his face.

Toth handed him the waterskin, and Sol took it and drank. He handed it back, his shoulders and chest still rising and falling from the exertion and exhilaration of their success. Toth reached into a pocket and took out a hunk of leftover cheese. He held it out to Sol, who took it, broke off a piece, and handed the rest back. Toth pocketed it for later.

"That went well," Sol said, the cheese a bulge in his cheek.

"Not so well for the harpies."

"No, not so well for them."

They watched as a few remaining harpies were cut down at the exit. A cluster of Strix still stood or hovered in the air in a semi-circle around the entrance. When a harpy emerged, whoever darted forward first finished the beast off. It became a bloody game.

There was a feeling of relief that the plan had gone so well, but death was unpleasant work. The mood was somber, for these Strix were not ruthless mindless killers. They were civilized men and women from all kinds of educated backgrounds. They knew what they had done was genocide.

Toth watched his soldiers finish off whatever came out, until the emergence of a screaming smoking hagbird dwindled to less than one every ten minutes.

"Were we right to do it this way?" Sol asked quietly from Toth's right side. Sol had not expected to feel the sadness that was rising up in him as the full extent of the damage they had done sank in. His own feelings baffled him. They had been victorious; he should be screaming triumph to the sky. But the victory felt hollow and pricey.

Toth knew what Sol was asking. Had they the right to exterminate an entire species, gruesome and vile though that species was?

"They were an unnatural breed," answered Toth. "They should never have happened in the first place." Toth rinsed his mouth out again and spat off to the side, hooking his waterskin onto his belt. "Rodania is safe again. From harpies, anyway."

The soldiers had begun to prepare for a journey home, cleaning their weapons, drinking and washing the smoke and blood from themselves as well as they could. Someone was lighting a fire to melt the snow so they had something warm to wash with.

A small figure on a clifftop over Toth's shoulder made Sol squint his eyes. "We've got an audience," he jerked his chin toward the silhouette.

Toth looked over his shoulder to where Sol had directed, but the sun glinted off the snow and obscured his vision. He lifted a hand to shade his eyes, and the figure become more defined. Toth frowned. *It's a child.* He or she was just standing there, still as a wax figurine, watching the smoke pouring from the mouth of Golpa and the Strix soldiers clustered around it.

"What's a child doing way out here?" Sol echoed Toth's own question. "There must be others nearby."

"Could be gypsies, though I thought they were allergic to cold weather. I'll find out."

Toth's wings opened, and Sol put out a hand and started to tell the Nycht that he would go, in case it was some kind of trap, but the words died on his lips. Toth was not that kind of captain. If he thought there was danger, he was more likely to lead the way or go by himself. Many of the Strix combatants thought this was foolhardy, but it was hardwired in Toth to behave this way. He'd been a solo mercenary for too long. So Sol only watched as he ascended from the barren valley floor toward the clifftop.

As Toth closed the gap between him and the child, the child

sprang into action, turning and running across the rocks and snow like a deer.

It's a girl, Toth realized, as he saw a long tangle of wild red hair the color of strawberries at the height of summer. He expected there to be a camp on the horizon, a nomadic village set up along the cliffside——though why any nomadic people would set up camp this close to Golpa was beyond him. But the child did not run to any camp. There was no tent in sight.

Toth flew overhead as the child ran, her fur-bound feet lightly springing between the sharp jutting rocks and ice without faltering. She headed for a copse of scrawny-trunked trees, where an arch of rock with a wide split in its face swallowed her up. Just outside the jagged crevasse were the ashes of a dead fire and a cobbled-together spit for cooking.

Toth landed just outside the copse of trees and made his way slowly through them toward the crack in the rock where the girl had disappeared.

"I won't hurt you," Toth called, and then repeated it in three more languages, hoping one of them would be hers. Toth knew most of the dialects of The Conca well enough to communicate, having defended it and made deals with its inhabitants for over a decade.

There was no reply.

"Are you alone?" Again, he asked this in multiple languages. He crouched at the remains of the fire and held a hand over the ash. It was warm. There were coals banked beneath the earth's surface. Toth's eyebrows shot up with surprise. *Clever girl.* How long had she been out here, living like this? His eyes took in the girl's camp, the surrounding terrain. His ears perked for sounds that might suggest some kind of ambush, but there was nothing but the wind and the sound of dry snow spraying against cold rock.

"Do you need help?" Toth waited for a response, but when

none came, he stood. Bemused, he posted his hands on his hips and chewed his cheek.

He wouldn't go in after her and drag her out; for all he knew, she was part of a tribe of hunters who would return with their kill and make a feast for her to eat. But Toth's gut told him this was not the case. Looking around, he saw only the tracks of a child in the snow, no others. There was an overturned metal pot full of dents——probably what she used to boil snow for water.

"I'll leave you, then," said Toth, rattling it off in multiple tongues. He turned to leave, still hoping the child would show herself. He walked slowly.

Something small bounced off Toth's shoulder and landed in the snow. Toth looked down. She'd thrown a pebble. He smiled and stopped walking. His gut had been right. She didn't want him to leave. He turned to face the crevasse just as a loud sneeze emerged from the crack. A white face appeared in the wall, half-hidden and with a purple smudge under the visible eye.

"Are you hungry?" Toth opened his satchel and retrieved a hunk of cheese, unwrapping the cloth encasing it and holding it out. He took a few slow steps forward and crouched again, trying to make himself as friendly looking as possible. Armed to the teeth and with sharp dewclaws arched over his head, Toth did not cut a friendly figure. But the girl didn't run away again.

The girl took a step forward where Toth could see her better. She was wrapped up in rough clothing made from animal skins. A hat that might have once been white, but was now a dingy gray, encased her head, and square flaps came down over her ears. Her boots were tied on with leather thongs, and her pants were shaggy with tawny fur——probably from one of the mountain goat species of the Northern Conca. Her jacket though, that was different. It had likely once been a bright blue-white, the color of an iceberg. Wooden toggles held it closed, and thick white fur sprouted from the cuffs and along the front, and lined the oversized hood, which hung against her shoulders. Mittens dangled from strings that hung from each sleeve. The mittens were leather and also lined with fur. Someone once cared very much about this girl, enough to outfit her in the warmest of handmade clothing.

Her eyes were the color of honey, her skin pale and lightly freckled. Her lips looked painfully chapped, and her child's cheeks were too hollow for Toth's liking. She was starving. There was no one else here. No one to look after her. She couldn't have been much older than seven or eight. It must have taken great effort to run from him with such vigor over the snow.

Toth stretched out further, urging her to take the cheese from his hand. "Would you like some cheese?"

She nodded, but she didn't come any closer.

"I'll toss it to you." He wrapped the cloth around the hunk and threw it to her. Her pale hand snaked out and snatched it from the air. She rooted in the cloth and broke off a piece of cheese, shoving it into her cheek and chewing with her mouth open, desperately.

"I have more food," said Toth, whose knees were beginning to protest at having been crouched for so long, but he didn't want to scare her by towering over her. "It's not good to eat too much too fast, but I think we can make you some broth with the supplies we have." He jabbed a thumb over his shoulder, toward the way they'd come. "In the valley, where you saw my soldiers."

She looked at him with those pale amber eyes, wanting but uncertain.

"How is it you can be so close to the harpies? They don't hunt you?" Even the crevice, as deep as it was, would offer very little protection from a harpy who was of a mind to make a snack of her.

She shook her head, gobbling down more cheese and licking her fingers.

The girl has to have magic.

"What is your name?"

She picked up a stick from the fire and wrote in the snow. She understood English, clearly, but her writing skills in English weren't strong. Toth could make out the name, after studying the letters carefully.

"Tashi," Toth read. "Is that right?"

She nodded.

"My name is Toth. I'm not going to hurt you. I think you know that."

The girl nodded again.

"Is there somewhere I can take you? Where are your people?"

Using the stick, Tashi wrote another message in the snow. She moved the stick uncertainly and slowly.

No one.

Toth considered her. There was no way he was going to leave her here.

"Listen, Tashi." He moved from his crouch to his knees, bringing his icy blue eyes on the same level as her golden ones. "I'm from Rodania. Do you know where that is?"

She shook her head.

"It's my home. All of those winged people you saw in the valley, they're from Rodania too, and I have to take them home. Would you like to come with us?"

The girl didn't hesitate to nod.

"Are you afraid to fly?"

Tashi shook her head.

Toth opened his arms wide with invitation. Tashi stepped fearlessly into the circle of the mercenary's arms. Wrapping her thin arms around his neck, she let him lift her and carry her away.

CHAPTER 17

"Wait," said Eohne, pressing her palms firmly against Linlett's skin. "There it is," she breathed.

"Harpy? We've found one?" Linlett's voice was simmering with excitement. "Finally. I can't believe it's taken us this long."

Eohne nodded, tuning in to the vibration just a little longer to be certain. "Yes. It's harpy. I'm sure of it." She removed her blindfold and looked at the filament pinched between Linlett's brightly lit fingertips.

"It originates here," Eohne said, watching as the pulses of light that travelled along the thread originated from the orb near their feet, "at this station."

She and Linlett shared a look of foreboding. They were to inform Balroc of any developments immediately. Now that they had the origin station of one of the harpies, the border guards who worked it would be taken in for interrogation. Every border guard had already been questioned, but now that they had some evidence, they knew who to press on. Eohne didn't want to think about the methods Balroc might employ to extract the information he was looking for.

"I'll let Balroc know," said Linlett soberly.

CHAPTER 18

On the journey home to Rodania, the Strix warriors broke into groups of twos and threes and spread out, since the need to stay together and travel in formation had passed. Though they were to watch for harpies who might have evaded them, the mood was one of relief. They hadn't suffered a single loss, and their plan had gone off without a hitch. Everyone wanted to get home to their loved ones and celebrate the end of a long rivalry.

Toth had used a batch of Eohne's messenger bugs to send word ahead, informing Rodania of their victory. The Strix anticipated a hero's welcome.

In the evenings, when camp was set up and fires made, Tashi stayed close to Toth's side, observing the Strix around her through wide eyes that missed nothing. During the day, she flew with him, cradled in a makeshift carrier that Chayla had fashioned out of her bedroll.

The weather grew warmer, and the cold weather gear was stowed away. When the floating masses of Rodania appeared on the horizon, a shout went up from the Strix nearest the front, which was echoed by those at the back.

Toth and Sol brought up the rear, with Tashi bound to Toth's chest.

The Strix approached the training islands first, and a few dozen of them descended to clean and organize their weapons and mingle with each other before saying goodbye and heading home. Sol and Toth descended to the largest training ground, and Sol unhooked Tashi, setting her down on her feet.

"We won't stay here long," he told the girl as he unstrapped her and let her down to stand on her own legs. "I'll have to take you down to a border station and register you. You can't see it, but there are three big islands just East of us. That's our home. You can come and stay with me."

Tashi was all eyes, wide and staring, taking in everything around her. She searched the horizon in the direction that the Strix around her were looking, but could see nothing but horizon.

"It's part of the magic that protects us," Toth explained. "Once you register at the border, you'll be able to see them, too, and always and forever after that."

Tashi pulled her scarf away from her face——which she'd kept on to keep the wind from buffeting her as they flew——and followed Toth. He found Teetch, and the brothers spoke about getting together the next day for a debrief.

"Hey!" A shout went up from the crowd of Strix. "Looks like the palace has sent a welcome party!"

Four Arpaks dressed in matching uniforms featuring Rodania's colors, blue and white, were winging toward the training grounds in tight formation.

"They look pretty grim for a welcome party," said one of the Nycht warriors. "Didn't anyone tell them we won?"

"Yeah! We won!" Someone belted out at the approaching foursome.

Toth and Sol shared an uneasy look. If the palace had wanted to send a welcome party, they wouldn't have sent armed Arpak soldiers from the king's own Royal Guard.

"Arpaks?" Sol mouthed to Toth, a question in his eyes.

Toth knew what Sol was thinking. The Royal Guard was sixty Strix strong, but fifty-five of them were Nychts, since Nychts made for better night guards. The fact that all four of the guards now approaching the training island were Arpaks seemed a strange but strategic choice.

The Strix warriors parted to leave room for the Royal Guard to land. The Arpaks were big and stoic. Wide jaws, broad hands and shoulders, huge wings. These Arpaks were of the kind who were born to be physical, born to fly. It was this kind of Arpak, not unlike Sol, who chose the life of a soldier because it was what they were best at. There was not a smile or a soft eye among them. One of the Arpaks with a crest over his heart that signified an elevated position, broke ranks and approached Toth. The three others followed behind, marching together in unison.

Apprehensive looks were shared among the Strix warriors, and there were murmured questions among the crowd.

Tashi inched closer to Toth and hid behind him, peeking out at the Arpaks from under his wing.

"Toth Sazak?" the first guard addressed Toth with a booming voice. "You're under arrest for treason against the crown. Hand over your weapons. You'll be coming with us."

An angry cry of protest went up from the crowd, intermingled with disbelieving laughter. Toth's expression was one of stone, but some of the color in his cheeks, heightened by the wind and the spirited journey drained away.

"It's a joke?" someone asked.

"This is no joke. Weapons please." The guard gestured to the multiplicity of Toth's scabbards and holsters. His own hand was on the pommel of his dirk.

Sol moved in. "You're making a terrible mistake," he said. "This man is a hero to Rodania, not a traitor. When The Council hears of this, you'll be punished and humiliated. You don't want that, now, do you?" His flinty blue eyes flashed steel, but his tone was light and cajoling.

The guard's cold and precise gaze fell on Sol. "You're the courier who got expelled for abandoning your post, aren't you?" His lip curled in a sneer.

"To get the guns that helped save your ass," snarled Chayla, as she emerged from the crowd.

"Solomon Donda? Perfect. You're under arrest, too. Thanks for making it easy."

Chayla ripped back the black cowl which had been shrouding her face and stalked between Toth, Sol, and the guard, shoving herself in the middle of them, and met the accuser nose to nose. The guard almost took a step back from her but stopped himself. Chayla bared her teeth in his face. "Go home, shithawks. You're not taking these Strix anywhere."

"Step back," the Arpak guard snapped, his hand tightening over the pommel.

"Or what?" Chayla's eyeteeth glittered in the afternoon light, her eyes lit up with a dare.

"Chayla," said Toth, his voice calm. "It's alright." Fighting the Royal Guard wouldn't lead anywhere good. "It's just a misunderstanding. I'm sure we'll get it sorted out."

Chayla ignored him.

"Listen to your captain, hagbird." The Guard put a hand on Chayla's shoulder and shoved.

Chayla's fist was a blur. The guard's head snapped up and back, blood flying from his nose as he staggered back with a cry. He recovered himself, the blood flowing freely down his face and into his teeth. He spat off to the side and pulled out his sword.

Chayla had two short spears in her hands, and one of them did a graceful twirl as a slow smile spread across her face. Her body lowered, as tightly wound as a clockspring.

Suddenly all the guards had weapons drawn and moved into a

widely spaced, back-to-back formation. The Strix warriors closed in, blades and teeth bare. The sound of multiple pairs of wings snapping open punctuated the air. The guards shifted into a circle in small, tight steps, their wings opening, preparing to take off and fight in the air if need be.

"At ease! That is an order!" Toth bellowed.

The Strix warriors glanced at one another, unsure of what to do.

"I won't say it again."

One by one the Strix put their weapons away and stepped back. The four guards watched, eyes shifting——mostly to Chayla.

"Chayla." Toth put a hand on her arm and pushed the short spear down. "This isn't the way." Toth began to unbuckle and unstrap his weapons. "I need you to take Tashi. After you register her, take her to Mareya. She'll look after her until I get this dealt with. Whatever *this* is."

Chayla's eyes widened and shifted to the girl, who stood in Toth's shadow, trembling. Chayla nodded. She held out a hand to Tashi, but Tashi moved further under Toth's wing and hid there. Up until they'd arrived on the training island, Tashi and Chayla had had no interaction, and Chayla's face was still lit with a fierce anger, her movements abrupt.

Toth dropped his scabbard and knelt to face his new ward.

"I know she looks scary," Toth said, a ghost of a smile playing at the corners of his lips. "But Chayla will take care of you. She'll take you to my sister, Mareya. She has a big house and a big yard, and lots of delicious food. You'll have a room to yourself until I come for you. You can take a bath and sleep as long as you want. Okay?"

Tashi shook her head.

"You can't come where I am going." Toth stood and put a hand on the girl's flaming red curls. "I'm sorry, but I'm sure I'll see you soon."

Chayla reached down and took Tashi's hand. The girl looked up at the fierce Nycht woman, but she didn't pull her hand away. Her honey eyes were huge and shining, lined with unshed tears.

Toth stood and faced the guards, alongside Sol, who had also shed his weapons. As the soldiers stepped forward and cuffed Toth and Sol, Sol stared into the face of the Arpak who was chaining him, his expression full of disgust.

"That's why they sent Arpaks," Sol said, "isn't it? Because there is no way even the Nychts of the Royal Guard would dare arrest the captain. They won't admit it out loud, but Toth is a hero to them. No one would take the post but you four sorry palace-crows. Am I right?"

The Arpak Guard snapped the handcuffs closed and stepped back. "Shut your mouth, traitor," he said. But his words lacked venom, and he didn't look Sol in the eye.

Chayla, Tashi, and the rest of the Strix warriors watched as the Royal Guard flanked Sol and Toth, and the six Strix took to the sky in the direction of Upper Rodania.

CHAPTER 19

The beating of wings outside the apartment brought Jordan hurrying from the bedroom, where she'd been tidying up. Jordan had slept only fitfully the night before, and was becoming well acquainted with the feeling of malaise and agitation. If the palace had received news about the Strix party, it hadn't yet been shared with the rest of Rodania. Foremost in her mind was the safety of Sol and her fellow Strix warriors. Secondary to that was what on Oriceran the Council was up to. Eight days had passed since King Konig's death. Balroc had said it would take a number of days for all the Council members to return home and have their hearing, but... over a week?

When she heard a Strix outside the apartment, her heart leapt into her throat. Hopeful for good news or Sol in the flesh, she dropped the bedsheets she'd been wrestling onto the bed and hurried to the terrace.

"Jordan Kacy?"

An Arpak courier greeted her instead, the same one who had delivered Sol his discharge papers when Sol had skipped work to go to Earth with Jordan.

Jordan's face fell, and she worked to fix her expression into one of stone. "Yes?"

"You're wanted at the palace," he said, his voice monotone. He focused on something over her head. "I'm to escort you." His arms were crossed, his expression flat.

This Arpak was giving nothing away. *If he even knows anything.* Jordan reminded herself that couriers were not often privy to the contents of the messages they delivered. This courier wasn't delivering a message per se, he was coming to bring her back to the palace, but it was likely he didn't know why.

"Fine. Give me a minute." Jordan turned away from him and headed into the kitchen.

"No weapons," the Arpak said, hovering gracefully just beyond the tile balcony. He uncrossed his arms and shook a finger at her like she was a petulant child. "No weapons," he repeated.

"I got it the first time," Jordan muttered, looking longingly over her shoulder at the closet where her knives, spears, and holsters were hung.

She pulled on her boots and tightened the stays on her vest, before spreading her wings and leaving the balcony. She wondered distractedly whether she'd ever return to the apartment she shared with Sol. A feeling of foreboding grew in her stomach as she winged ahead of the Arpak courier. At least they hadn't sent a bunch of guards to retrieve her. That would have sent her into a proper fit of panic.

"Not that way," called the courier to Jordan when she headed up toward the same terrace where she and Ashley had delivered the fungus to Juer. "There." He pointed to a terrace on the second floor. A long line of arched windows lined the black marble of the balcony. Jordan landed and folded up her wings, and the Arpak courier landed beside her. He stood at the balcony's edge, arms folded, watching her. The windows were dressed with gauzy blue curtains, and lights behind them lit the fabric to make it glow.

At a nod from her escort, Jordan pushed her way through the curtain.

Inside was a vast, long room, high-ceilinged, like every other room in a Strix abode. There was a gaping, cold fireplace, a long wooden table with high-backed chairs, and huge mirrors leaning against the wall. Jordan caught a glimpse of herself in one of these mirrors, her shape made long and lean by the angle of the glass. What she saw was a pale, frightened Arpak with lines of confusion on her brow. Her lips were tight, their corners pulled down. Jordan tried to relax her face and mouth; whatever was going to happen next, she didn't want those she faced to know just how frightened she was.

She looked back through the crack in the curtain in time to see the courier spread his wings and take off.

"Jordan Kacy," said a voice at her elbow.

Jordan turned to see a tall Nycht dressed in the blue and white of the Royal Guard.

"Yes. Who are you?"

"It's not important. Follow me, please." He spoke kindly enough, and his eyes didn't look through her the way her escort's had. Jordan took comfort in this and fell into step behind him. The small amount of reassurance she took from his attention evaporated when another Nycht fell in behind her.

Where are these guards coming from? She could have sworn when she arrived this room had been empty.

"Oh, hello," she said over her shoulder to the Nycht now flanking her. She kept her voice light. "You boys really know how to move quietly." She almost gave a nervous laugh, but the words echoed hollowly with no response from either guard. She bit her laughter back, swallowed hard, and shut her mouth.

The guards took her through the mirrored room, to an arch at the end. On the other side was a circular foyer with three doors and a huge table, on which sat a vase full of spectacular, ornamental grasses. It reminded her of her own foyer back in

Virginia, where both Cal and Maria used to place similar vases full of plants on the big circular table that welcomed Jordan and Allan home every weekend. A shard of homesickness pierced her momentarily.

The Nycht guard opened the door on the other side of the foyer, and stood aside for Jordan to enter. Warm yellow firelight flickered from inside.

"They're waiting for you," the Nycht said, his eyes taking her in. If Jordan wasn't mistaken, they were not cold or distant, but filled with curiosity.

A door behind her opened, and she turned toward the sound.

Ashley and Allan entered.

"Dad!" Jordan threw her arms around her father. "What are you doing here?" Her heart seemed to resume something of its normal rhythm, and she marvelled at the steadying influence her father's presence had on her physiology.

"A courier came to get Ashley, and there is no way I'm going to let you two go through this alone," Allan looked at one of the guards. "Provided they let me in, of course."

Jordan glanced at the Nycht guards waiting by the door. They seemed unconcerned about Allan's presence.

Jordan looked at Ashley. "You ready for this?"

Ashley nodded, his mouth a flat line. "Let's get it over with."

Jordan, Ashley and Allan stepped through the doorway to face whatever was on the other side.

* * *

ONCE THROUGH REGISTRATION, Chayla winged to Mareya's house as fast as she could manage without frightening the little girl. Tashi clutched Chayla's hips and torso with her arms and legs, pressing her face to the Nycht's armor.

The warrior landing in her backyard with a grim look on her face and a child wrapped around her was enough to bring

Mareya rushing out. She had been wiping her hands on a towel, and she threw it over her shoulder and reached for the girl without hesitation.

"What's happened? Who is this?" She kept her voice soft and light. "What's your name, sweetheart?"

Tashi released Chayla and stood on her own feet. She allowed Mareya to put her face between her hands and look at her.

"So far, she hasn't spoken. But Toth rescued her from Golpa and asked me to bring her to you. Her name is Tashi."

Mareya looked up sharply at mention of Toth. "Where is my dear brother?"

Chayla took a breath to calm her pumping heart before saying, "He's been arrested."

Mareya straightened, her back rigid as iron. "Excuse me?"

"That's why he had me bring you Tashi." Chayla glowered, and Tashi cowered behind Mareya at the fierce look on the warrior's face. "They've accused him of treason. The bloody lot of them are..."

"Fools," Mareya hissed. She turned and went into the house, taking Tashi by the hand. "Just let me gather a few things and I'll be off. Would you mind staying here with Tashi? I'm alone today, otherwise I'd ask Shad to look after her."

"I'm not a babysitter," Chayla snapped, following Mareya but stopping before entering the house. "I'm going to find out what's going on."

Mareya ushered Tashi inside. "I'll be right there, honey. There are some freshly baked krutch cakes on the table. Help yourself." Tashi disappeared inside, and Mareya closed the door before turning to face Chayla. Her face was like thunder.

" I have connections. I know things about what is going on in the palace that you could not possibly know. Stay with the girl until I get back."

"Forget it!" Chayla put her hands on her hips and opened her wings with a snap. "My captain is in trouble, and you want me to stay here, playing nanny and eating sweets? Are you out of your mind?"

"Chayla…" Mareya began, ratcheting her tone into a much more reasoning inflection. "I am in a much better position to help him than you——"

Chayla took off into the air before Mareya could persuade the stubborn Nycht to see her side. Mareya cursed as she watched the warrior disappear. Taking a steadying breath, she stepped into the house where Tashi was just polishing off her third krutch cake.

"It's an exciting day for you apparently. Tashi, was it?"

The girl licked her fingers and nodded.

Mareya sat opposite the girl and fixed an excited expression onto her face. "How would you like to see the palace?"

CHAPTER 20

A murmur of voices greeted them, along with the faint smell of bread, wine, and meat. The room had a V-shaped table open toward the door. Men and women were seated around it as well as standing behind it, holding drinks and talking quietly among themselves.

The Nycht guard led Jordan, Ashley and Allan to the floor in front of the open V. "Council of Ten," he said loudly, coming to a halt and setting his shoulders back. "Your requested subjects, Jordan and Ashley Kacy, as well as their adopted father and citizen of Earth, Allan Kacy."

At this, Ashley glanced at Allan, who gave him a close-mouthed smile. Neither of them bothered to correct the Nycht.

The talking ceased except for someone thanking the Nycht and dismissing him. Arpaks who were standing now moved quietly to their seats. Two Nycht servants cleared away bowls, plates and cutlery from the table and left the room.

Jordan recognized Balroc and Darber, but the rest of the Council were strangers to her. All Arpak, half of them female, half of them male, they were well dressed and well groomed.

Most looked over the age of sixty, except for Balroc and two of the women. *The old guard*, she thought errantly to herself.

One of the older women stood up. "Come closer, please. We won't bite. My name is Marli and I've been elected speaker today." Her elegant pale hands were folded in front of her waist. She lifted her chin as she spoke. "To state the case so we are all of one understanding, you're here because you've made a claim for the throne. As proof of your recognition, you present Doctor Juer Donda, the late king's physician, as witness. Is this correct?"

Ashley and Jordan both nodded and murmured their agreement.

"Fine. Is there anything else that you would like to present as proof? Anything at all?"

"We have nothing else," Jordan said. She looked at Ashley. "Unless you've come up with something over the last couple of days?"

Ashley shook his head. "We are willing to present ourselves for blood-relation testing," he said, addressing Marli. "If the color of Jordan's eyes is not enough for you."

"The question lies not in your being a blood relation to King Konig. None of us dispute that——or care, frankly. King Konig had many illegitimate children, as have all the kings of Rodania, and some of the queens before him. The question is: did King Konig recognize you irrefutably and formally before he died? And the answer to that is no, he didn't." The room fell silent for the space of a few heartbeats. "The only evidence we have is the claim that you two," she pointed a finger at the twins, "and Doctor Juer, witnessed the king write in light-ink that you are his children, and that he had a desire to recognize you formally. This is simply not enough. We need material proof."

The doors behind the twins and Allan banged open, and Prince Diruk stalked into the room. Jordan, Ashley and Allan turned to face the intrusion, and the Arpaks at the table got to their feet, startled.

Ten of the Royal Guard followed the prince, including a Nycht who was simply enormous.

Jordan's skin prickled with horror at the sight of him.

Dark bristles for hair, and a face more scarred than smooth, including a scar that crossed his upper lip and lifted it into a perpetual snarl. He would have dwarfed even Caje. The man had cold, hard eyes and a presence that went through the room like a shockwave. His razor-sharp dewclaws curled high above his head like scythes, and his wingtips crossed over one another behind his ankles, curving up and away from the floor, out to either side. Anyone standing within an eight-foot radius of him risked being knocked over by his thick, leathery appendages.

Jordan had never seen him before and wondered why such a powerful and obviously battle-hardened Nycht had not fought with the Strix warriors against the harpies.

The prince's wings spread up and out as he entered, their golden shimmer framing him as he walked in and giving him a godlike appearance. They stretched wide and held for a moment as Diruk scanned the room.

"There," Prince Diruk pointed at Jordan, and his wings folded away. "Arrest that Arpak!"

Allan stepped in front of Jordan. "You'll do no such thing!"

A guard shoved Allan into Ashley, who caught him before he fell.

Two of the guards, both Arpak, seized Jordan by the shoulders. She found her wrists bound with manacles connected by a link of chain. A stone-cold shock rocketed through her as she stared down at the iron. She tried to form the single worded question 'why?', but all that came out was a rasp.

"What are you arresting her for?" asked Marli from the table.

"Highly unusual, a prince making arrests," said another feminine voice, quieter than the first.

"She's a traitor," Prince Diruk seethed, his lip curling. He stood in front of Jordan, shoving his nose into her face. "You disgust me," he sneered.

Jordan drew back from him, repelled by his expression, his very being. Her knees trembled, and her stomach was filled with cold lead shot, but she wasn't going to give him the satisfaction of seeing her fear. "I have no idea what you're talking about." This time the words came out properly, but her voice was hoarse.

"Rodania will be free of you and your friends soon."

Jordan's heart plummeted into her shoes. She was about to ask which friends he was talking about, when Balroc asked for her.

"Who else have you arrested?" His voice was filled with alarm as he came around to the front of the table.

"Toth Sazak and Solomon Donda, traitors both. The three of them have been conspiring to destroy Rodania."

"That's ridiculous," said Balroc with an actual laugh. "Sol was an Arpak courier and is a Strix warrior, honored after the harpy war for acts of bravery and selflessness. And Toth," Balroc huffed another disbelieving laugh, "I recruited Toth to protect Rodania, and he has done just that. He wouldn't even be here if I hadn't invited him. He'd be back in The Conca, fighting for someone else!"

"Then you're a bigger fool than most," Prince Diruk replied. "I have proof."

"What proof?" Allan barked. Ashley had his hands on Allan's upper arms as though afraid the man would fly at the prince and make the situation far worse than it already was.

"What proof?" Balroc had asked at the same time. He held up a hand. "No, wait. Bring them here. Now. I propose that this charge can be refuted and resolved quickly and quietly."

"Yes!" Prince Diruk's eyes lit up at the idea. "The Council is all here." He threw his chest forward and opened his palms, his head at a cocky angle. "The faster we convict them, the sooner we can have all the threats removed from Rodanian skies." He turned to the guards who had followed him. "Bring the prisoners!" He beckoned to the monstrous warrior Nycht, who approached and tilted his ear down to the prince. Diruk whispered some instruction, and the Nycht nodded and left the room.

There was a murmur of talk as the Council members stirred and got to their feet. Their faces were a mixed bag of interest, fear, curiosity, and excitement.

"Jordan," Allan whispered, pulling away from Ashley and straining toward his daughter, against one of the guards that flanked her. "This is not good. We have no idea what he's up to. It's a trap! We have no time to form a defense."

"Get him away from the prisoner," the prince barked, and Allan was restrained and pulled away from Jordan, while still trying to speak to her.

Sweat beaded his pale brow, and his glasses slid forward. He shoved them back in an agitated motion. "Council members," he said, his voice loud and firm. "Surely this requires proper consideration and time. We do not yet know the charges, and there is already to be a trial?"

Prince Diruk's eyes gleamed. "Do you believe her to be innocent?"

"I know it!"

"Then she'll have nothing to worry about."

"But——" Allan's expression grew more desperate, and he searched for a friendly face among the Council members.

But all eyes were now on the door, where a cluster of Strix had appeared.

The room fell into a hush.

Toth and Sol, with their hands chained in front of them, were shoved forward. Their ankles had been manacled to their wrists, and they walked with slow, shuffling steps. Both their expressions were wooden.

Jordan wanted to scream at the sight of Sol and Toth bound like criminals. The injustice of it filled her with a cold fury, and she could hear the sound of her own molars grinding against one another. Her own arrest had not elicited even close to the reaction her body gave as she saw her friend and her lover humiliated like this.

Sol and Toth saw Jordan at the same time, and their reactions were as opposite as fire and ice.

"Jordan!" Sol barked. His teeth bared as he glowered at the prince. "She is innocent. Let her go," he growled. His cheeks flushed with pink, and his hands clenched into fists.

"Is that an admission of guilt?" Prince Diruk asked smoothly.

"You know it's not."

Toth's eyes were frozen and cold, his face expressionless and impossible to read. He didn't seem surprised to see Jordan there; then again, Toth never gave anything away. His icy gray eyes found Balroc and gripped the Councilman's face. There was no accusation there, but Balroc imagined what Toth might be thinking: that he should have said no to Balroc's offer, that he should have stayed in The Conca, that Rodania's corruption ran so deep it was beyond redemption.

Balroc's mouth turned down at the corners, and his eyes narrowed at the prince, as malevolent as a flesh-eating reptile on its prey. Toth watched the anger play out across the Councilman's face before he squashed it with effort and the cool, detached politician was back. Balroc looked behind the table where the Council's guards stood at the rear doorways. He jerked his head at one of them, calling him over. The guard went to Balroc, and Balroc whispered something in his ear. The guard nodded and left the room through a back door.

No one seemed to notice this except for Toth. All other eyes were on the main doorway, where another small group of Strix and one wingless, human form wearing a dress entered the room.

Jordan's eyes opened wide with surprise as she recognized the woman. She looked similar to the last time she'd seen her, except her shabby clothes had been traded in for much finer ones, and her simple bangles had been traded for beautiful golden wrist-cuffs encrusted with semi-precious stones. Her hair was glossy and richer in color, and the kerchief that held it up was shot through with gold thread. Her purple skirts floated and swirled beautifully around her like fine chiffon.

Jordan's mind skittered for the name of the gypsy who had sold them Blue back in Maticaw. It came to her suddenly.

"Berla," she muttered. Her surprise at the gypsy's appearance could not have been deeper had Blue himself strolled in wearing nail polish.

"You recognize this woman?" Prince Diruk said, pouncing on Jordan's utterance.

Sol's eyes fell on the gypsy, then they too widened with surprise and then shot back to the Prince. He mouthed a few choice curse words, and Toth shot him a warning look. Sol yanked against the chains and they clinked loudly, emphasizing his frustration.

"We met her in Maticaw," Jordan said, fighting to keep her tone even and losing. Her voice quavered. "She sold us Blue, the dragon that saved you all." She couldn't help but add the last bit and narrow her eyes, reminding them that they were alive thanks to Blue and his companion.

"That's what you'd like us to think," Prince Diruk said coolly. He extended a hand to Berla, and his face melted into an expression of concern and care so artificial and syrupy, it made Jordan's gut roil with disgust. "It's alright. Don't be frightened," the prince crooned. "They won't hurt you."

Berla took the prince's hand and stepped forward.

Jordan thought that Berla looked older; her olive skin looked paler, and the purple smudges under her eyes had not been there before. She was stressed out.

"Do you recognize these Strix, Berla?" the prince gestured to the three in chains.

"Only those two," Berla replied, pointing at Jordan and Sol. "It is as the woman said, we met in Maticaw."

"Tell us about that meeting," Prince Diruk directed.

"The lady, Jordan, she was drawn to a dragon hatchling I had for sale."

"You told us it was full grown!" Sol spat and lunged for her against his chains. A guard yanked him back. It appeared to Jordan that Sol, normally so controlled and professional, had been pushed beyond his limit. The color was high in his cheeks, and his body was as taut as a piano wire. Her heart wanted to leap from her chest toward him, to do something to make him feel better. All she could do was watch him fume. She'd rarely felt so helpless, so sick with frustration.

"Let the woman speak!" Prince Diruk barked. "You'll get your turn."

Sol growled in his throat like an angry bear.

"I told them the dragon hatchling was of the *Tchielis vulgaris* breed and that if they were bound for Rodania, that it would not be allowed to pass through the border."

Jordan gasped and her jaw dropped at this bald-faced lie. She stared at the gypsy, and then at the prince who was watching the gypsy woman with a thoughtful expression painted on his face.

Prince Diruk made a sound of understanding in his throat. "I see. What did they do then?"

Just then a shape blocked the doorway, and Jordan looked to see the enormous Nycht return, ushering a much smaller, elderly Arpak in front of him. The Nycht bent down and said something to the Arpak, who nodded and went to stand quietly against the wall with his hands behind his back. His hair was white as snow and he observed the goings on through cool, detached eyes.

Jordan's stomach sank further. She didn't know who this Arpak was, but if he was delivered by the terrifying Nycht, then he couldn't possibly spell good news for them. It seemed that

Prince Diruk had been thoroughly planning this and had all his chess pieces in place.

"They spoke to each other," Berla was saying, "talking about how the dragon could easily pass for a Predoian Miniature. They agreed that he was perfect for what they needed."

Sol and Jordan stared at one another in horror.

"And what did they need the dragon for?" Prince Diruk prompted. "Did they tell you?"

Berla shook her head. "No, they didn't share their plans with me. They just purchased the dragon, as he seemed to like the woman, and went on their way."

"And what of the paperwork you gave us?" Sol asked the gypsy. His voice was under better control now, but red dots of anger still marred his cheeks. "Or have you been bought off to lie about that too?"

Her eyes shifted from the floor to the prince to the Council members engrossed by the scene unfolding before them. She avoided all eye contact with Jordan, Sol and Toth. It was painfully obvious the woman was not a practiced liar. Jordan almost felt sorry for the woman and wondered what Prince Diruk had threatened her with if she did not comply.

"I did provide registration, of course," Berla admitted. "But they asked me to change it."

Sol's eyes nearly bugged out of his head, then they rolled as he let out a frustrated groan. "You've got to be kidding me."

Jordan closed her eyes against the nightmare that seemed to be swallowing them whole. The gypsy was weaving their destruction with every lie that dripped from her lips.

"How did they ask you to change it?"

"They asked me to change the breed from a *T.vulgaris* to a Predoian Miniature."

"Why would you comply to such a thing? This is illegal," Balroc interjected for the first time. He looked drawn and irritated by the circumstance unfolding in the room.

Jordan was certain he knew just as well as she and Sol did that the woman was lying through her teeth. But a glance at the other Council members said they were buying her story, swallowing it whole, no matter how much Jordan and Sol looked aghast at her words.

"The man," Berla nodded toward Sol without looking at him, "he threatened me."

Sol rolled his eyes skyward again. "What a farce."

"Keep quiet, traitor," snapped the prince. "How did he threaten you?"

"He said he knew where I lived, knew who my children were. If I did not comply, that something ugly would happen to them." Berla's voice broke on the word 'children' and a few of the Councilwomen's faces melted with empathy. There were a couple of nasty looks shot in Sol's direction.

The prince scanned the Council members faces, strutting before the long table. "I can provide more evidence, but I think you've seen plenty. These Strix have worked together to bring an illegal species through the Rodanian border. Jordan Kacy and Solomon Donda," the prince jabbed a finger at each of them in turn, "arranged for the dragon's procurement and smuggled him through using illegal paperwork. As you know, the magic system that protects us relies on our guards to take blood samples and introduce them to the network. Once the blood has been submitted, the being it came from is perpetually permitted entry. Our border guards were presented with seemingly legal registration papers by Arpaks; there is no question as to why they were trusted. Look at them. Do they not look trustworthy?"

"Why would Arpaks betray their own country?" asked one of the Councilmen, a balding Arpak who was wider than he was tall, with thin droopy wings.

"For this man and his kind," Prince Diruk said, now pointing at Toth. "They've been partners in an elaborate scheme this entire time. A scheme to undermine our border system and allow harpies to breach our security and invade Rodania, at great cost of life, real estate and commerce."

"I must be missing something," said Marli, brows drawn and long, slender arms crossed. "Are you accusing them of importing an illegal species? Or sabotaging our system so that harpies could enter at will?"

"Both together." A glittering smile spread across Prince Diruk's face, the proverbial cat who got the cream expression. "What they know that you don't is their secret weapon. I have here one of our eminent scientists to explain." Prince Diruk crooked all the fingers of his left hand at the white-haired Arpak who was hovering against the wall. He stepped forward and passed through the cluster of guards and the bound Strix to stand in front of the table.

"Most of you know me already," he rasped in a reedy voice. "But for those who don't, I have worked at the Rodanian Institute of Biology for the last forty-seven years. My name is Doctor Krost. I would like to emphasize that I am a scientist," he said, putting a hand against his heart. He rotated as he said this, eyeing Toth, Jordan and Sol as well as the rest of the room. "I am not invested in one side or the other of this mess. I am simply here to share facts which will help to enlighten you." He faced the Council's table again and took a breath, seeming to savor the attention now being lavished upon him. "It is common knowledge that the harpies of Golpa are——"

"Were," said Toth.

"Excuse me?" the doctor turned to find the speaker.

"The harpies of Golpa *were*," repeated Toth. "The dragons and my Strix warriors have exterminated them."

Doctor Krost looked momentarily stunned by this. "Can this be true?"

"It's true, although there may be stragglers," Toth nodded. He spoke with such an unruffled calm that Jordan's deep respect for the Nycht mercenary swelled. "I have assigned warriors to hunt and exterminate them, as well."

"Job's done, then," barked Prince Diruk. "You no longer need them, since you've now positioned yourself as Rodania's savior." The prince gave Toth such a look of utter contempt that Jordan wanted to scream and hurl herself at the monarch, to rake his face with her nails.

Toth just gazed at the prince, his icy eyes cool.

"You seem awfully cocky for someone staring excision and a trip to Trevilsom in the face," Prince Diruk said.

"Truth will find its way out," Toth replied calmly.

Prince Diruk looked discomfited for the first time since entering the room, like a bad smell had assaulted his nose. He sniffed and beckoned that the doctor continue.

"If this is true, then it is a remarkable feat," the doctor added. At a deadly look from the prince, he cleared his throat and went on. "Harpies are a result of an abominable cross between the Greater Vultures of the Northern Conca, a grotesque breed in their own right, and the dragon species known as *T.vulgaris*."

There was a murmur among the Council members at this, and it was clear for whom this was new information and who had been aware of it already.

"*T.vulgaris* is characterized by a form of telepathic pack-mentality we call a superconsciousness."

Jordan might have given a delighted gasp at this information had the situation not been so dire. It made perfect sense to her that Blue and Red shared thoughts, and that their appearance in the skies over Rodania during the worst of the harpy battles had been so timely.

"The harpies inherited this from the *T.vulgaris,* and it is what makes them able to hunt so efficiently in packs when they choose to. They are able to, on some level, talk to one another. We suspect that the older the harpy is, the stronger her mental energy, and the more she is able to dominate and direct the others."

"It still doesn't explain how the harpies breached our borders in the first place," said Marli.

"Yes it does," said a voice from the door.

The room turned to see a tall, slender Light Elf with strange markings on his face enter the room.

Behind him, was Eohne.

CHAPTER 21

"Who are you?" Prince Diruk demanded, his eyes flashing to his Nycht and back to the Light Elf. His look was slightly reproachful, as though the mountainous Nycht male should not have allowed anyone in the room that the prince himself hadn't approved of. The Nycht looked mildly dazed at the appearance of the two Elves.

Jordan's heart leapt for joy to see her friend's face, and wondered if perhaps the Light Elf had dazzled his way past the Nycht with magic.

"My name is Linlett," the Light Elf said cheerfully. "Hello, Balroc!" He waved to the blue-winged Arpak, who nodded back with a close-mouthed smile.

Jordan thought Balroc looked as though he was hopeful that the tides were about to turn, but wasn't sure of himself——not by a long stretch. She imagined that the bringing in of the Elves was a stab in the dark; after all, they would know more about the border magic at this point than anyone else.

"Did you know there is quite a gathering of warriors outside?" Linlett said to the room, his tone downright jovial. "They seem very interested in what is going on in here. Some of them seem rather put out, to put it delicately. Your guards at the outer doors have their hands full, and I'm not entirely sure there isn't going to be some sort of riot."

Prince Diruk looked alarmed and glanced at his brutish cohort. He opened his mouth to speak, but someone else got there first.

"Allow no one else inside unless they have permission from myself or a Member of Council, please," Balroc called to the guards at the door. "Tell them their captain and their colleagues are unharmed, and we are in session." He nodded to Linlett. "Go ahead, please."

Linlett smiled. "Very well. Hello, Councilpeople, what a pleasure to meet you all. I recognize some of your faces and, of course, how could I not recognize the Heir Apparent," Linlett said smoothly, with a flourishy bow to the prince.

Prince Diruk glowered.

"Though I haven't met many of you, you'll know already that I was sent by the Light Elves to assess and repair the damage to your magical borders, if any was found. This is my partner," he gestured to her, "Eohne, of the Charra-Rae Elves."

Eohne nodded to the Council members and to the prince.

"My colleague has made some very interesting discoveries recently, which have bearing, I understand, upon the fate of these Strix who stand accused." Linlett nodded to Eohne, encouraging her to take the floor.

Eohne stepped into the circular space in front of the table of Council members, flanked by Strix both in chains and out, by the scientist, and by Berla the gypsy.

Jordan's mouth went dry for her friend as all eyes fell on her. Prince Diruk's eyes were narrowed and hard as he watched carefully, his arms folded over his chest and his wings tight behind him. Jordan was reminded of a cobra standing up, his hood open in consideration of a strike.

She thought Eohne had never looked stronger. Her iconic scythe-shaped blades were hooked to her back, the grips protruding from behind her shoulders, ready to fall into her palms at a dizzying speed. The fact that she still had her weapons was proof enough to Jordan that she and Linlett had passed by the Royal Guard using magic. Her dark hair was pulled back and up in a line of tails down the center of her head, giving the fierce effect of a mohawk. In short, she looked ready to do battle, and yet, her hands hung relaxed at her sides and her face was serene.

"What you say is true," she began, nodding at the scientist. "The harpies and the *T.vulgaris* do share the superconsciousness and pack mentality. The border magic recognizes the life force of an individual when blood is introduced. But what even the Light Elf engineers could not have foreseen when they developed the magic was that a group telepathy of this nature would be recognized by the system as a single life force, rather than multiple."

"So, you confirm it then," Prince Diruk said with a smile. "The illegal introduction of the dragon Blue allowed for the harpies to enter as well." He nodded at the Council members. "This is what I have been trying to show you all along," he spread his palms, "she only validates their guilt."

"No," Eohne contradicted. "The introduction of the dragon did not spontaneously permit harpies to pass through the border, only other *T.vulgaris*; the red dragon who arrived in time to save us all is proof of this."

"Then how did the harpies get in?" Balroc asked.

"There has been sabotage," Eohne spoke slowly and clearly, as calm as a winter's night.

The room was filled with murmurs, and Prince Diruk visibly stiffened. His eyes darted around the room, falling on the huge Nycht at the rear momentarily, before finding Eohne again.

"But it had nothing to do with the dragons," Eohne spoke loudly enough to be heard over the din. The crowd quietened to hear her speak. "Each incidence of blood in the system results in the production of a magic filament. Each filament is linked to the being whose blood it came from, and thickens over time. By measuring the thickness of the filament, we are able to determine with pinpoint accuracy, the day it was created."

Prince Diruk's mouth opened, and he seemed about to speak, only nothing came out.

"There was a single introduction of harpy blood made, *before* Blue the dragon ever entered the system. The magic cannot be wrong in this for there is no way to manufacture a filament. Someone introduced harpy blood one time," she raised a single finger to emphasize, "and by doing so, gave all of its kind permission to enter forever after."

"This is enough to dismiss the accusations that these Strix," Balroc gestured to Jordan, Toth and Sol, "are responsible for the harpy threat." He turned to his colleagues. "Do you all agree?"

"Wait!" Prince Diruk said sharply. "The Nycht has motive to sabotage Rodania, and make himself into a hero in order to sway our upcoming vote. He may still be the one who sabotaged the system."

"Seems a bit absurd to me, after all the trouble he went to to *save* Rodania," Balroc replied. "Do you know he lost his brother in battle? Along with many of his friends?"

"Loss of life does not affect his kind. It is a small price to pay to win a kingdom," Prince Diruk snarled.

"Surely the border guards have all been interviewed," added Marli. "Have they not been able to pinpoint a saboteur? Perhaps one of them was in on it? Or threatened if they did not comply."

Balroc opened his mouth to answer to this, when a small girl's pale face appeared between Toth's wing and side. Her appearance was so unexpected and comical that some of the Council members laughed.

Toth looked down at the girl, his eyes expressing something positive for the first time since he'd been brought into the room. Jordan thought she'd never seen a more beautiful look grace the mercenary's face. His expression was radiant with delight and love.

"Tashi!" he said, his voice full of surprise. "What are you doing here?"

The girl did not answer, only reached for Toth's face.

"Hey! Child! Get away from that prisoner!" It was the voice of Prince Diruk. "Guards! How did she get in here?" There were footsteps on the floor as a guard approached.

Reflexively, Toth bent down toward the girl. Tashi placed her fingertips on his temples. As her fingers touched his skin, Tashi and Toth froze. A blue orb of rippling light wrapped itself around them.

The guard reached for Tashi, and there was a sizzling sound as his knuckles bumped against the blue ball of light. He snatched them back with a yelp. "Damn thing burned me!"

There were cries of surprise and dismay. Everyone got to their feet and craned their necks to get a better look at the light surrounding the child and the chained Nycht. Their forms were visible inside the orb, but unmoving, still as porcelain sculptures.

"Move back," said a sharp voice, and the guards stepped away.

Marli came around the table and walked toward the blue orb. The glow reflected in her face as she approached with curiosity. She looked to where Linlett and Eohne stood.

"What is this magic?" she asked. "One of you Elves must know."

"I do," replied Linlett, his voice soft. "The girl is of The Ash."

Immediately there was a reaction. People mumbled to their neighbors, and there were some murmurs of understanding. Clearly, 'of The Ash' was a term which was not completely foreign to some in the room. Prince Diruk's face was unmoving, his eyes flinty.

"Rodanian intelligence is under the impression that the People of The Ash are extinct," Marli said in a hushed tone.

"Apparently not." Linlett waved a hand at the blue ball of light enclosing Toth and the girl. "That orb is impenetrable. No weapons in this world, or in any other that I know of, could destroy it. There is nothing to be done but wait until she is finished."

CHAPTER 22

*T*oth was lost in a world of particulate grays. He blinked rapidly, trying to clear his vision, but color did not return, and his view did not sharpen to his satisfaction. The world around him was made of small, shifting particles in gray scale, everything moving like softly drifting sand. The edges of everything were slightly blurred, as though an artist had used ashes in shades ranging from near-white to soot-black to paint a scene on a canvas, outdoors, in a gentle breeze. It was difficult to lock in detail, but the overall image was plain.

Toth looked around. There was a mountain range on the horizon, but before it was the edge of a cliff, which disappeared from view. Snow-dusted rocks spread out around them. *It looks like the terrain around Golpa.* The scream of a harpy made Toth wince and look up. Three harpies winged by overhead. He instinctively reached for a weapon before reminding himself they couldn't be seen. There was no clink of metal as he moved, and he looked down to see that he was no longer in manacles.

A wind blew, lifting dry snow and dust particles into the air, but the Nycht felt nothing on his skin. The temperature had not changed from the room in Rodania. He looked at his hands, holding them out palms up. His skin had color, as did his clothing. He himself was not drawn in ashes, just his surroundings.

"Tashi," he whispered.

His voice echoed as though he was inside a cave, and he looked around with a start, remembering the last thing that had happened was her face appearing beside him, and her fingers reaching for him.

He found the girl standing just behind him. She too was in full color. She stepped close and looked up at him, her face calm. The wind did not lift her hair or shift her clothing.

"You're of The Ash," Toth said wonderingly.

Tashi nodded.

"Is this your memory? Or someone else's?" Toth asked.

People of The Ash had the ability not only to share their own memories, but to acquire, store and replay the memories of others. Toth had never met anyone of The Ash——at least, not knowingly. They were reclusive and rare, and many even believed them to be extinct.

Tashi walked forward and stopped at the edge of the cliff. She looked back at Toth, pointing down.

Toth came to stand beside her, where they had a view of the cave. The last time Toth had seen Golpa, black smoke had been billowing from its mouth, and soot staining the rock of its upper edges.

There were no soot deposits around the cave's entrance now.

Toth registered two figures in the valley in front of Golpa. One figure, small and further back, was clearly Tashi herself.

This gave Toth a bit of a start. He'd never been treated to a memory from someone of The Ash before, let alone met one. He would have assumed the memory would be through Tashi's eyes, rather than as an outsider, but apparently their magic had a way of presenting the memory as though viewed through the eyes of a ghost.

The gray-scale version of Tashi was dressed in the same garb she'd been wearing when Toth had found her, only it was brighter, whiter and not tattered. Tashi was far back from the entrance to Golpa, crouched behind a rock outcrop and so still as to be nearly invisible. Puffs of vapor hung in the air in front of her mouth, otherwise Toth might not have seen her at all.

The black and white Tashi of the past peered over the edge of the outcropping and peered down into the valley, drawing Toth's eyes to the second figure. A man dressed not unlike Tashi, in bleached skins and wool with rough footwear held on by leather thongs, moved toward the entrance to Golpa. His back was to Toth, but Toth felt instinctively that the man was related somehow to Tashi, perhaps even her father. There was something in the way he carried himself that was familiar: a lilt to his walk, the chest thrown confidently forward, that reminded Toth of Tashi.

The girl had come by her stature honestly.

The man looked back over his shoulder once to where Tashi was hidden, and Toth could make out his face. He took a quick intake of breath. The man's eyes were without pupils and glowed with an otherworldly blue haze. It wasn't unlike the luminescence King Konig's eyes had taken on when Toth had seen him on the balcony... only this man's eyes glimmered with a sharp brilliance that had been lacking in the monarch. There was no illness in them.

His skin was leathery and deeply tanned. A scar seamed his cheekbone, and heavy scarring on both cheeks spoke of more than a passing acquaintance with fire. He wore a hat similar to the one Tashi wore, but it appeared gray rather than white. Toth supposed it could have been bright cardinal red in real life, there was no way of knowing.

A harpy scream echoed from the cave, and the man crouched low in response. Toth's heart began to pound. The man carried no weapons that Toth could see, only a gnarled staff. He held his breath as a huge female harpy emerged from the cave, in flight and screaming. Her head tilted and her jowls swung as she turned an eye downward at the small form of the man. She screamed again, and her talons flexed. She dove.

The man lifted his hand to the harpy, fingers curled in a strange symbol.

The harpy matriarch pulled up at the last moment, her heavy wings gusting snow across the valley floor. She landed with her talons buried in the rubble of Golpa, and lowered her toothy beak to the man.

Toth watched, awestruck, as the large female tucked her chin down and set the tip of her beak between her talons, almost like she was bowing.

The man relaxed his hand, and that same hand disappeared into a pocket among the folds of his clothing to retrieve something too small for Toth to make out clearly. He approached the harpy and put a hand on the greasy feathers at her neck. His fingers were lost beneath her plumage. Toth's eyes narrowed, trying to discern what he was seeing.

The man pulled away from the harpy, tucking his hand into his pocket again and turning away from the cowed hagbird. He began to walk away from Golpa, his gait relaxed. The harpy lifted her head and her wings shifted and rustled, but she did not attack. She screamed again.

The man lifted his hand and made the same symbol he'd made before, the first three fingers flexed so strongly that they seemed to curl back and make a fan, the baby finger bent in two, the thumb jutting out to the side.

The harpy took off into the sky with a scream and flew back into the cave.

"Does that symbol work for anyone?" Toth asked with a chuckle.

Tashi smiled but it did not reach her eyes. She brought her delicate hand up toward her shoulder and flexed her fingers, palm out.

The world of ash exploded into a cloud of swirling gray. Vertigo swept through Toth as he and Tashi were swallowed in a blizzard. There was no sensation here, not even the feel of solid ground beneath his feet.

Shapes materialized as the ash settled. A blurry white light sharpened into a campfire, where Grayscale Tashi and the same man who had subdued the harpy sat in its glow. The man's eyes were no longer lit with a blue light, but were now plain and deceptively dull by comparison. Some small creature who had fallen prey to the man had been skinned and was roasting over the flames. The hissing sound of fat dripping into the fire added to the sizzle of wood burning, which was a little too wet to be ideal.

The pair was sheltered by a rock overhang, and Toth recognized the narrow black crevice dividing the rock in two——it was the same place where Toth had found Tashi.

The two he was seeing had hiked out of the valley to their camp. Toth wondered if what he was seeing happened later the same day.

Tashi and the man conversed in a language Toth was not familiar with. He spoke most of the languages of The Conca, at least of the south end, but their dialect had a harsh, guttural quality that was unfamiliar.

Toth glanced at Tashi.

"So you can speak," Toth said quietly. "You just choose not to. Not even in your own tongue?"

It seemed as though Tashi didn't hear him; she was watching the pair in front of the fire. A tear tracked down her cheek, its trail gleamed in the firelight.

Alarmed, he was about to ask Tashi what was wrong, when the man tapped memory-Tashi on the arm and gestured to the crack in the rock. Tashi dashed into the crevice, turning sideways to slip through. She disappeared soundlessly from view.

Wingbeats could be heard in the distance, and then the sound of a body landing in the rocks on booted feet. The crunch and squeak of snow under the gait of a heavy man preceded the man himself.

Not a man.

A Nycht.

"Bryc!" Toth couldn't help but gasp in surprise as the prince's right-hand materialized in the glow of the campfire.

The huge prehistoric-looking Nycht stopped just inside the circle of firelight. His broad wings were held up and out, making him look even more intimidating. His eyes glittered, homing in on the much smaller man seated in front of the fire.

"What are you doing out here, you crafty, primordial bastard," Toth seethed.

"You have what I need?" Bryc's voice was a deep growl.

Tashi's companion ducked his head once, and Bryc moved forward and stood over the man, looking down. He finally put his wings away with the heavy rustle of thick membrane. His dewclaws curled inward like scythes in a motion that was now familiar to Toth. Bryc held out a gloved hand.

"Hurry up. I've no interest in freezing to death in this godforsaken place."

The man gazed up at Bryc, his face impassive. He chewed something slowly, turned his head to the side and spat. His gaze returned expectantly to the Nycht. The message was clear, *I am not afraid of you.*

Bryc muttered something under his breath. One hand disappeared into some pocket inside his fur-lined cape and produced a bag. There was the clink of coins, which Bryc then dropped on the ground.

The man snatched up the bag and upturned the contents into his open palm.

There was a beastly, close-mouthed growling sound, which for a moment made Toth turn to look for the source, as it seemed to be coming from everywhere. Then he realized it was coming from Bryc.

The man reached into the folds of his furs and pulled out something small, which he held up for Bryc to take.

Bryc swept the item up and held it in his fingertips, low so the firelight backlit it.

It was a small vial, and in the light it glowed red.

"How did a puny waste of skin like you manage to extract living harpy blood?"

The man responded by leaning forward and turning the roasting meat on its spit. "You have three days," he rasped in roughly accented English. "Three days only, before the blood dies." He settled himself back on the log and pulled his furs tighter around him. Again, he spat off to the side. He didn't look up at Bryc as he spoke. "Waste time insulting me, or take it and go."

"And what if the blood is dead by the time I arrive?" Bryc knelt in front of the man, teeth bare. "We'll have paid you for nothing."

"Not Dieffe's problem," the man husked.

As unexpectedly as a fork of lightning across a clear blue summer sky, Bryc's fist snaked out and closed around the man's throat. The man's hands flew to Bryc's fingers as a choked garble issued from his throat. His face turned red, then purple. Try as he might, he could not loosen the grip around his windpipe.

Toth stepped forward on instinct before remembering there was nothing he could do to help.

"I say it is," Bryc said into the man's face, spittle spraying onto his chin. "I say you're coming with me as collateral. The prince gets what he pays for, or you die."

"The prince," Toth echoed.

He looked down at where color-Tashi stood beside him, watching. She looked up at him and made a face that said, *'now you get it?'* Her eyes were shining with unshed tears. Toth lifted a hand and rested it on her shoulder, and she moved closer to him, pressing against his thigh. She crossed her arms over her chest and let out a shuddering exhale.

It must be hell for her to see this again, thought Toth.

Tashi's father was choking. His eyes flickered with that blue light, on and off, like sparks trying and failing to catch on tinder.

Toth saw the pale moon of grayscale-Tashi's face peer from the crevice, frightened and uncertain what to do, unseen by Bryc. His heart ached for her, and he pressed color-Tashi closer against his side, wishing that he could have been there, could have done something. The fact that Tashi had been alone when he met her meant that her father hadn't gotten out of this alive.

Toth dreaded going further in the memory, but had no choice.

Dieffe's feet came off the ground as he fought Bryc, his eyes still flashing but not catching and holding. He dropped one hand and spread the fingers out, palm back, giving the hidden Tashi a sign to stay back, a motion which Bryc didn't see.

Ash-Tashi retreated into the crack again, swallowed by the shadows.

That same hand made a fist that came around to Bryc's eye in a rapid arc. Bryc's face turned to the side with the force of the blow, but his grip didn't loosen. His enormous leathery wings snapped out and caught at the air, lifting the two off the ground.

Dieffe still struggled and kicked as Bryc lifted him higher and higher. Bryc turned and picked up speed. They were becoming a strange, misshapen shadow as they left Toth and color-Tashi behind.

Bryc took Dieffe high above the mountains and flew away to the East, toward Rodania. As the Nycht and the man passed in front of one of Orcieran's moons, there was a flash of bright blue light, and a deep-throated bellow of pain.

Suddenly, Dieffe was falling. Soundlessly and limply, his body plummeted past the horizon's edge and disappeared into the black.

Ash-Tashi cried out and dashed from the crevice. She leapt over the flames and ran into the darkness.

Toth looked down at the girl by his side, understanding. She'd lost her father, been left alone to fend for herself, and that was how Toth had found her.

"I'm sorry," said Toth. "Bryc will be made to pay, as will the prince. But you'd better take us back now, so we can let the truth out."

The ash lifted and swirled, and the world lost all definition.

CHAPTER 23

*T*oth gasped as Tashi's fingers broke away from his temple. The courtroom snapped into focus, in full color and in painfully vivid detail.

Voices droned urgently overtop of one another, a question in every tone. Hands pulled Tashi away from Toth, and he tried to reach for her but was reminded he was in chains.

Prince Diruk barked. "Bind that girl! Immediately!"

"Don't hurt her!" cried another voice.

Toth felt dazed. His eyes found the speaker, and recognized Marli as she reached for the girl.

"I'll take her." Marli took the girl from the guard and knelt down to murmur words of comfort to her.

Tashi turned away from Marli and strained against her, wanting to go back to Toth.

"Permission to speak," Toth ground out, finding Balroc in the crowd.

Balroc lifted a hand. "Speak! For God's sake, man, speak! We're all dying to know what just happened!" He turned and bellowed at the crowd in the room. "Shut up, you fools!"

The crowd calmed, and the room became quiet again. The

faces of the Council members were alive with curiosity. A few were frightened and drawn, while others were alert and hopeful.

"She's of The Ash," Toth said, his voice strained, and his eyes on The Council.

"They know." Linlett was leaning against a pillar, one foot crossed over the other. "I told them."

"Good. Then I don't need to explain that she just shared a memory with me." Toth looked to Tashi. "Are you willing to show someone from The Council what you've just shown me?"

"We don't have time for this!" barked the prince.

"All due respect, Your Majesty," replied Balroc. "We are not in a rush. They were gone for barely a full minute."

Toth blinked at this. It had felt as though they'd been gone for half an hour.

Balroc turned to The Council. "I don't know about you, but I think that if she has evidence to show, we are duty-bound to view it. My understanding of The Ash memories is that they cannot be simulated or tampered with. Is this true?" he addressed Linlett.

"It's true. Those of The Ash can only present what they themselves have seen, or what another Ashling has shared with them. Their images are true recordings of actual events."

"Good enough. Come here, please," Balroc held out a hand to Tashi, beckoning her closer. "Don't be afraid. No one will hurt you."

Tashi approached. She lifted her fingertips toward Balroc's face.

"Wait," the Arpak said. "What is your name?"

"Tashi," Toth answered for her. "Since I have met her, she hasn't spoken. But she understands just fine."

"Where did you get this girl?" Prince Diruk demanded.

"Why should I answer any of your questions," Toth replied, his tone icy. "You don't believe a word I say."

Jordan thought the air seemed to vacuum from the room at

this. Shocked looks were exchanged at the disrespectful and mutinous words Toth had said to his monarch. Jordan shared a look with Sol and pinched her lips together to bite back a grin.

Whatever Toth had seen, it must have had a massive impact.

Toth knew there was nothing the prince could do to stop this entire room from seeing the same critical moment in history the girl had just shown him.

Toth's eyes slid to Balroc. "She'll show you all you need to know."

The prince looked as though he had a mouth full of rusty tacks.

"Shall we vote on who goes first?" Balroc asked The Council.

"That should be me," Prince Diruk said, striding toward Tashi. The Ashling shook her head and put her hands behind her back. "What's the matter with you, girl?" The prince made for her, as though to force her to put her hands against his head.

"Why don't we let the girl choose," suggested one of the Council members, a tall, slender Arpak woman with curly gray hair piled on top of her head.

There was agreement on this.

Tashi pointed to the woman who had suggested it, and the woman looked pleasantly surprised. She stepped forward and knelt before Tashi. "I'm Ninfa," she said, eye-to-eye with the girl. "Nice to meet you Tashi. I've never met anyone of The Ash before."

Tashi looked at her with those soulful amber eyes and gave the Arpak a close-mouthed smile. She reached her fingers up.

Ninfa took a breath, closed her eyes and tilted her head down.

Toth watched breathlessly as the girl and the Arpak were swallowed by the pulsating blue orb. Their features became blurred and lost behind the light. Now he understood why no one had interrupted them. A deep respect for Tashi's ability grew in him. He was beginning to understand just how special the girl was.

Moments later, the blue orb disappeared and Ninfa rose, her face pale, her brow damp with sweat. "Thank you, my child." Toth noticed that she did not look at the prince. He couldn't blame her.

"Well?" Prince Diruk barked. "What did you see?"

"I think it is wise not to speak until we've all seen what Tashi has to show us," Ninfa said. Her voice was reedy and trembled noticeably.

Tashi was already standing near Balroc, looking up expectantly. Balroc knelt and was swallowed by the blue orb. When the orb disappeared, he looked unsettled but not surprised by what he had seen.

Jordan saw Toth visibly stiffen as Tashi lifted her fingertips to Darber's temples. Darber had always been a disciple of the prince's. When the blue orb had done its job, Darber lifted angry eyes to Prince Diruk, his face flushed with rage.

"You," he seethed. "It was you all along! How could you terrorize your own country like this? You..." he spluttered, his face now purple and apoplectic, "You... betrayer!" He bellowed this at the top of his lungs. "Traitor! Apostate!" Spit flew from his lips and trailed down his chin as he lunged toward the prince. A pair of guards swept in like water to protect Diruk against the enraged old man. "You dare accuse an innocent, you poison us all against them, and it was you! All along, it was you!"

The guards holding Darber cast about the room for guidance, their faces agitated. One of them looked downright distressed as the old man wailed and screamed until he began to choke. Jordan wondered if he might give himself a heart attack.

"Take him away so he can calm himself," Balroc cried to the guards over the wailing Arpak, whose face was now wet with angry tears.

Darber's voice was cracking under the strain of his cries and was thick with heartbreak.

Chaos swept through the room like a hurricane as Darber

revealed the secret. Those few Council members who had yet to see the memories looked shocked and frightened; those who had, either joined in the angry tirade, or tried to calm everyone down so they could continue.

The prince gathered some understanding of what Tashi was showing the Council members and screamed, letting out a stream of curse words. He headed for the girl, his hands curled into claws. Toth lunged out of instinct, trying to get between Tashi and Diruk, but his guards and the chains jerked him to a stop.

"Detain him!" Balroc barked.

Two Nychts from the Royal Guard grabbed the prince as though they had been waiting for years for just such an order.

"Bryc as well! Seize him!"

The mountainous Nycht was already halfway to the door when guards dashed after him. Bryc turned and punched one of them in the face. There was a brief scuffle as more Royal Guards stepped forward to execute the order, all of them Nychts. There were cries of terror and bodies dashing for cover as the sounds of steel being drawn and the thuds of fists against flesh filled the room. Guards were flung as Bryc did what he was good at. He made for the door, with more guards in pursuit. He slashed at them with his dewclaws before exiting the room.

There was the sound of a pair of massive wings opening out and taking to the air as Bryc took to the skies outside.

Linlett was at the door in a flash. He was out and through it before those hiding under the table and behind furniture even realized the Light Elf had followed Bryc out.

Sounds of a scuffle and yelling voices drifted in through the doorway before all went quiet again. A moment later, Linlett reappeared.

"He's been neutralized," the Light Elf said with a grin. "Even a brute that big can't face odds like that and come out ahead." Linlett gave Toth an admiring look. "You've got some very impassioned soldiers there, if I might say so. Especially the woman with the teeth." The Light Elf bared his own teeth and pointed to his incisors. "Very intimidating."

Jordan thought she heard Eohne snort deep in her throat at this comical display.

Balroc looked pale. "They didn't kill him?"

"No, no." Linlett patted the air in a *'don't worry'* gesture. "He's on his knees, though."

Tashi was allowed to continue, and in less than ten minutes, the remaining Council members were shown the memory. Now that the prince's betrayal was known, the Council members came out of the memory without surprise, only a grim resignation.

Jordan, Sol, Ashley, and the others in the room were each given their turn.

It took some persuasion from Toth, but Tashi gave the prince the memory while the guards held him still. While Prince Diruk was ensconced inside the blue orb, the Council talked among themselves. When the blue orb disappeared and Tashi stepped back, a pin could have been heard hitting the floor. Everyone watched as Diruk returned to the present after seeing what they'd already seen--irrefutable evidence of the utter betrayal of his people and his country.

Prince Diruk looked completely gray, like a man who was watching the construction of his own coffin.

"Prince Diruk of Rodania, son of King Konig, you are under arrest for treason," said Balroc. His tone was weary but satisfied. "Take the manacles off them," he gestured to where Jordan, Sol and Toth stood. "They do not deserve another moment in those restraints."

Their chains were removed.

Jordan flew toward Sol and Toth and wrapped her arms around both of them. Her heart pounded with relief and her legs felt like they were made of jelly. Another set of arms wrapped around them, and in her periphery, Jordan caught a flash of brunette hair.

"Thank you," she whispered to her Elven friend.

"Don't mention it," Eohne whispered back.

At the sound of little footsteps, the party broke apart just in time to see the little girl leap into Toth's arms and wrap both her arms and legs around him, clinging like a monkey. She planted her face in his neck, her red hair spilling down over her shoulders.

Sol and Jordan shared a shiny-eyed look at the sweetness of the moment.

"You did good, Tashi," Toth whispered in her ear as he held her tight. His expression was dazed and full of joy. "You did so good."

* * *

Prince Diruk was removed from the room and taken to the cells beneath the palace to await his sentence. The room was loud with astonished conversation. Some Council members sat in their seats, pale with shock and unable to speak. Others remarked to one another in hushed and excited tones. It was not difficult to tell which of the Council members had backed Diruk, and which were ready for a regime change.

Balroc crossed the floor to where Toth, Jordan and Sol stood. Toth set Tashi down on her own feet.

"My deepest apologies will never be enough, I'm afraid," Balroc began. "Even I had not imagined the depth of evil in Diruk's nature."

"Thanks to this little one," Toth replied, a hand resting on Tashi's shoulder, "things are finally about to change for the better."

"But where did you come from?" Balroc asked as he smiled

down at Tashi, a bemused expression on his face. "Your presence here seems near miraculous."

Toth looked around the room. "My sister is not far away, I'd wager."

"And you'd win." A strong, confident female voice penetrated the room. "I brought the girl." Mareya materialized from the back of the crowd. "I know this palace better than anyone. There is a secret entrance behind that tapestry. When she wriggled away from me and disappeared in the crowd, I almost had a panic attack. Now I understand why you ran away," Mareya touched Tashi's cheek. But her gaze shifted to Jordan, where the Arpak was staring in pure astonishment. "Hello, you."

"Maria!" Jordan put a hand on her old nanny's arm and squeezed, just to make sure she was actual flesh and blood and not a figment of her imagination. She looked no different than the last time Jordan had seen her in the driveway of the plantation home outside of Richmond.

Except that Maria had big, dark Nycht wings folded up behind her, with dewclaws framing her face.

"You're a Nycht?" Jordan's wonderment went to the very soles of her feet.

Mareya nodded. "I am. Hello, Jordy."

"How?" Jordan pulled back, keeping her hands on Mareya's shoulders for fear she might vaporize. Then she looked around, eyeballing the room for Allan. "Dad?"

Allan shoved his way through the crowd. "Maria!" he croaked, putting his hands on her shoulders too, making sure for himself she was real. "Is it really you?"

"Hello, Allan. I'm sorry I couldn't come see you before now. You'll understand everything soon, I promise." She gave him a hug, still chuckling at the dazed expression on his face.

Toth looked at Sol, a question on his face. "Maria?"

"Jordan's old nanny, from Earth," Sol whispered back, amazed. "She's your sister?"

Toth shrugged. "I guess. I had no idea. No one in my family tells me anything."

Mareya laughed. "I couldn't tell anyone! While on Earth, I took a more common name, one I knew I could still answer to, but would draw no attention to me when I emigrated."

"Emigrated..." Jordan echoed. Her mind felt as though it had choked to a stall and was incapable of starting up again, possibly for good.

But Mareya had something else on her mind. Members of the Council were milling about, and Mareya raised her voice."While Council members are still here, there is an urgent matter I've come to address with you."

"It's been a harrowing day," replied Marli. "Are you certain this can't wait?"

"It concerns the proof you require in order for Jordan and Ashley Kacy's recent claim to the throne to be upheld."

"We didn't actually make a claim," Jordan mumbled, but pressed her lips closed with a sheepish smile at a look from Sol. Jordan had forgotten Ashley in all the excitement, and looked around for him. She spotted him behind Linlett and shot him a smile. He smiled back and gave her a nod.

A murmur went through the room. Mareya's words had gotten the Council's attention. They returned to their places at the table.

"You all know who I am," Mareya addressed them. "I was in the employ of King Konig for the last twenty-eight years. I began work at the palace as a chambermaid, and became a nanny and a nurse as needed. Some of you have been on The Council for as long as I served the king. You know that King Konig trusted me. You'll also remember a span of thirteen years where I was largely absent from palace life, only visiting for a few weeks out of the year. I doubt any of you had enough curiosity or awareness to inquire after the absence of one of the king's more trusted servants.

"Twenty-five years ago," she went on, "Rodania was visited by a travelling merchant named Torpizar. You'll remember him because he visited us once a season for twelve years. He once brought a beautiful human slave with him, before King Konig had banned merchants and traders who kept slaves. This human woman had fallen through a portal, was snatched up by gypsies, and sold to the highest bidder––Torpizar. But when King Konig saw her, he fell in love. King Konig bought her freedom and gave her a room in the palace. Her name was Jaclyn Kacy."

Mention of the name 'Kacy' sent a ripple through the room. Some Council members shared looks of growing concern, while others seemed to be eager for Mareya to continue.

Jordan listened, still feeling breathless and amazed to have set eyes on her nanny once again.

"When Jaclyn became pregnant, she became demanding. Understanding that even illegitimate children could be recognized by the crown and made legitimate if the king wished it, she put pressure on King Konig to recognize her baby while still in the womb. King Konig grew worried for Jaclyn and the unborn babe's life, since the queen was also pregnant with Prince Diruk at this time."

Mareya paused. Not even the rustle of feathers was audible in the room, so still had the audience become.

Jordan could hardly believe what she was hearing, but all the pieces fit. The room seemed to disappear. The Council members faded into the background. Only what Mareya was saying mattered in that moment. She felt movement beside her, and Sol's warm hand slipped into her own and squeezed it. She flashed him an amazed smile.

"Jaclyn became insistent that King Konig acknowledge her baby, and was becoming increasingly difficult to silence. King Konig loved Jaclyn, you have to understand, and he also loved the unborn baby. But the queen..." Mareya took a long breath. "She'd have none of it. Afraid for Jaclyn, and understanding that the queen had resources at her disposal, and would not hesitate to kill to protect her own child's inheritance, King Konig sent the pregnant Jaclyn back to Earth against her will."

Jordan looked for her father and spotted him just behind her. He had one hand thoughtfully crooked over his mouth, and he smiled at Jordan. It was a sad smile, and Jordan thought she knew why.

When she'd returned to Allan, Jaclyn was in a sorry state. He'd always thought it had been because of her ordeal, but the real reason she'd been so upset was finally clear.

"When Jaclyn's pregnancy had come close to term," Mareya continued, "King Konig sent me to Earth to check on her. I was able to report that Jaclyn had actually given birth to twins, a boy and a girl, and that the girl was born first."

At this, Sol squeezed Jordan's hand again. Mareya had just answered another big question, which had been on both their minds. Jordan was the eldest.

"Unfortunately, I also had to report that Jaclyn was depressed and unstable. Out of concern, King Konig sent me more frequently. When Jaclyn disappeared and took her son, leaving two-year old Jordan and a bereft human husband behind, he bade me go back for the long-term. When Allan, Jordan's Earthly father, put a posting for a nanny to help him raise Jordan, it was the perfect opportunity to ensure that King Konig's daughter was well looked after. I applied for the job, offering the name of Maria, and Allan hired me, believing me to be human.

"I stayed with the Kacys and became the only mother Jordan ever had," Mareya's eyes crinkled at Jordan as she walked about the room. "Not until Jordan was thirteen and old enough for me to leave her, did I come home to Oriceran to live permanently. Neither Jordan nor her father Allan ever knew my true Nycht nature, until today.

"When I returned to Oriceran, I reported to King Konig, as I had been doing every year since I left Rodania. He gave me back my station at the palace and no one questioned it. The queen had died, and Prince Diruk was Heir Apparent."

"Did the king have any intentions of ever bringing Jordan back from Earth?" someone from the Council called out to Mareya.

"Not initially, no. I reported that Jordan had a good life with Allan, that she was well looked after and lived as well as any Earthling could hope to. To bring her to Oriceran, give her wings for the first time, and integrate her into life here would have been disruptive and shocking. King Konig didn't want that for his daughter.

"But after the harpy battle, everyone in Rodania knew about the dragons and the woman who seemed to control them. I learned that Jordan had found her way to her true home, against all odds."

There were not just whispers but full-voice discussions that sprang forward at this.

Someone yelled, "Why didn't you come forward with this information as soon as you knew the king had died?"

Mareya turned toward the voice. "I wanted to wait until the Strix warriors returned, most importantly my brother, Toth. I wasn't sure if there would be trouble with Prince Diruk," she answered boldly and without shame, "and wanted some security. When I learned that my brother had been arrested, I came to the palace as quickly as I could, bringing this young lady," she gestured to where Tashi stood next to Toth, "with me."

Mareya then retrieved a small black leather bag from the belt at her waist.

"King Konig gave me these." She upended the bag into her palm, and out tumbled two rings and a clear sphere.

Mareya held the sphere up between a thumb and a forefinger so all could see. "This is an Elven nephogram. What it is about to play back to you is a true residual which cannot be manufactured, as I'm sure Linlett here will corroborate."

Mareya set the nephogram on the floor and stepped back. She invoked it with her voice, and a stream of light shot from the orb, projecting an image of King Konig sitting up in his bed. The recording had clearly been taken not that long ago, as the King was slender and pale, but he still had his powers of speech.

"I officially recognize Jordan Kacy as a legitimate heir, and Ashley Kacy as next in line to the throne." The words boomed and echoed around the room, startling everyone with their power and resonance.

The image blinked, and King Konig repeated the sentence again. Mareya let it play several times over before closing the vision off with a command.

The room fell silent.

Jordan closed her eyes for a moment, letting what had just happened sink in. When she opened them, she looked over at Ashley. He was looking at her, his expression serious but relaxed. He gave her a slow respectful nod of acknowledgment, and she could almost hear him saying, 'My Queen'.

It was done then.

Mareya turned her shoulders toward Jordan and extended her hands out. "Ladies and gentlemen of the court and Council, I present to you, your Heir Apparent and future queen."

Jordan watched, speechless and in utter astonishment, as Mareya bent her head in deference, and the rest of the room followed.

power. "From now on, I want us to remind each other that we do not have a right to forget where we came from and what we have, because most of our citizens are not as privileged. And if we do not make every effort to understand their perspective, then what right do we have to make decisions that affect them? We are not allowed to put our own ambitions ahead of what is right for Rodanians.

"I understand the seductive nature of politics better than you might think. I grew up in a political family; I watched it spoil my father's happiness, and I have learned that the quest for power made a tyrant of my mother."

The Arpaks were openly staring at Jordan now, mouths hanging agape. The green team were sitting ramrod straight, some of them nodding. The red team were shriveling like tender stems of grass under a baking summer sun.

"But I digress," Jordan softened her tone. "If there are no illicit behaviors to be found, then you have nothing to fear. All in favor of implementing Eohne's magic before every vote, hands up."

The green team reached skyward. The red team looked completely flummoxed, outraged, and dazed.

Darber slowly raised a quivering hand, bringing the vote to five for and five against.

Jordan raised her hand.

Balroc clapped his hands together with a single loud snap. "And the Heir Apparent's vote takes it to a 'yes', seven to five. Oh, this is most excellent."

There was a smattering of applause around the table, but the Arpaks who voted against looked as drawn as though they'd just been condemned to hard labor for the rest of their days.

"Wonderful. Eohne, shall we run the magic now so we can get on with the main vote of the day?" Jordan rubbed her hands together.

"Wait!" Daegan stood. He swayed unsteadily on his feet and his uneven breathing was audible. "I think," he rasped before clearing his throat. He tugged at his collar, mustering as much dignity as he could manage. "I think it would be pertinent at this particular juncture, for me to tender my resignation."

"Oh," Jordan feigned a disheartened look. "Are you certain, Daegan? After all, you've been running this country since before I was alive."

Marli pinched her lips together against a laugh.

"I'm certain, Your Majesty," he said. "I'll take my leave." He stepped out from behind the table, pushed his chair back into place, patted it twice, and left the room.

Silence descended.

"Does anyone else feel the same way?" Jordan invited.

Darber and Pasco rose at the same time, looking drawn and deeply unhappy. Piaget followed a moment later, as did Banerai and Naste. Each of them mumbled something about resignation and left the room with their eyes down.

"Goodbye, red team," Jordan murmured.

"Your Majesty?" Marli was peering at Jordan, bemused.

"Nothing," Jordan folded her hands. "Well, we're looking a skinny bunch, aren't we? Look at all those empty seats."

The remaining Arpaks looked around at one another, mildly astonished at what had just taken place. It felt as though a hurricane had swept through the room, and then vanished.

"Shall we proceed with the vote of the day, then?" Jordan continued brightly. "How many of you are in support of allowing Nychts on Council?"

"Wait, Your Majesty," Balroc put up a hand. "What about Eohne's magic?"

Eohne gave Balroc a smile. "That was it."

CHAPTER 25

*J*ordan stood in the Council's chambers, looking at the empty table surrounded by empty seats. It was the morning following the upset and the vote, and she'd hardly been able to sleep for all the changes that had happened so suddenly.

Her eyes skimmed the leatherbound volumes that filled the low bookcases skirting the entire room, and the tall arched windows with gilded frames. The winged logo of Rodania had been rendered in stained glass at the apex of each window. She moved closer to look up at the symbol, her eyes studying its two disembodied, feathered wings, reaching in opposite directions as though from one invisible spine. Beyond the windows, many of the spires of the castle were topped with the same symbol, only manufactured out of wrought iron.

"That," Jordan said quietly to herself, "will be one of the first things to change."

"What will be one of the first things to change?" came a man's voice from the doorway.

Jordan turned to see her twin wander through the open door. She was pleased to see he looked well rested and relaxed, fully recovered from the brutality that Bryc had rained on him in Maticaw.

"The Rodanian crest." Jordan pointed to a stained glass rendering of it. "One of those wings needs to look entirely different."

Ashley gave an agreeable grunt but he didn't comment on the logo. "Sure sign of old age when you start talking to yourself." He cocked an eyebrow and gave her a half-smile. His face completely transformed into that of a young man who loved to laugh and had been missing it in his life.

Jordan was reminded suddenly that even though she'd spent some time with Ashley in the last several days, she really had no idea who her twin was. They'd been under so much stress and uncertainty about their futures that they hadn't been able to relax enough to talk as siblings. They'd been pitted against one another by their mother the moment they met. So what kind of person was he when he wasn't held under Jaclyn's thumb? It was possible that even he didn't know.

"I thought I was alone."

Ashley rested his hands on the back of one of the chairs and gave Jordan a level look. "I suspect you will never be alone again, so long as you live." He took a breath and dipped his chin, adding, "my Queen."

Jordan rolled her eyes. "Don't remind me."

Ashley strolled into the room, his movements casual. He came to stand on the other side of the table and face his sister. "You've kicked all the corrupt Arpaks off the Council, you have only to nominate the Nychts you want and the government you've been striving for will fall into place. The security breach has been solved, and all this in a matter of hours. Rodania will look very different a year from now. Especially for the Nychts. Well done."

"And what about you, Prince of Rodania?"

Uncertainty shrouded his features. He was opening his mouth to respond when a Nycht appeared in the doorway.

"Excuse me, Your Majesty." She bowed her head. "I'm sorry to interrupt you."

"Come in. You're not interrupting." Jordan shivered at being bowed to twice in a matter of moments. *This is going to take a lot of getting used to.*

The Nycht entered the room, and Jordan realized she had never seen her before and wondered just how many servants now answered to her bidding that she had never met. She made a mental note to call the palace staff together so she could meet them.

This Nycht had soft tawny wings and matching hair piled up high on her head in a spiral bun. Her skin was pale and she looked just as tired as every other working Nycht Jordan had seen.

"What's your name?"

The Nycht hesitated before answering. "Aysha, Your Majesty."

"Nice to meet you, Aysha. Starting right now, Nychts who would rather work a night shift can talk to Balroc about getting switched immediately."

"Night shift?" Aysha blinked. "Will there be service roles at night? I'm afraid it's all I have ever done."

"Half of our Council will soon be Nychts, and they'll be needing help; so yes, there will be some. There'll also be a re-education program for those who feel like they've been mis-utilized."

"Thank you, Your Majesty." Aysha looked astonished.

"Don't thank me," Jordan reddened. "I'm only undoing what should never have been done in the first place. What did you come to say?"

"The guards have a woman outside who is desperate to speak with you."

Jordan bristled and she and Ashley shared a look.

Aysha didn't miss it. "Should I have them send her away?"

"Did she give her name?"

Aysha blushed. "Not a name, no. But..." She shifted, and her eyes dropped to the floor.

"What? What did she say?"

"It's just a ridiculous ploy, Your Majesty. I have no desire to repeat it."

"It's alright, Aysha. I have a feeling I know already."

Aysha cleared her throat. "She said she's the queen's mother."

"Oh, boy," Ashley said under his breath. "Here we go. That didn't take long. Woman doesn't miss an opportunity when she sees one."

"Actually," Aysha's blush deepened. "Slight correction."

"Let me guess," Ashley crossed his arms. "She said she's the *Queen Mother?*"

Aysha nodded, and Ashley shot Jordan a smug look.

Jordan couldn't stop a snort from sounding in the back of her throat. The gall of Jaclyn would never fail to surprise. "How did she get here so fast, I wonder?"

"She may have already been on her way," explained Ashley. "She knows that Rodania is where I fled to, and she'll want to repair things with me. Her spies would have told her what has transpired here, and that you're about to be coronated, and she would have then adjusted her plans en route."

"Is she really so efficient?"

"She's a practiced opportunist. The best I know," Ashley said sourly.

Ashley and Jordan stared at one another and an understanding passed between them that shook Jordan to her core. Maybe it was the connection that twins shared, or maybe it was a fluke, but she *knew* what Ashley was thinking. Somehow, she knew.

She also knew that Ashley knew what *she* was thinking: face Jaclyn now, on their own turf.

"Send her in," the twins said at the same time.

Aysha nodded and moved toward the door.

"Wait!" Ashley put a hand up. He moved toward Jordan and whispered in her ear. Jordan nodded. "Have her wait in the courtyard," he instructed Aysha, "the one just in front of the tower. Have her wait for two hours. Then have her brought to the throne room."

"The throne room." Aysha looked to Jordan for confirmation. "Your Majesty?"

"Yes." Jordan nodded.

Aysha left the room.

* * *

THE DOORS to the throne room swung wide. Jaclyn's slender outline was dwarfed by the doorframe and by the Nycht guards who flanked her. Jaclyn waited to be announced and, when no announcement came, she peered around in confusion. One of the guards made a gesture saying, *'you can go in'.*

Jaclyn began the long walk toward the throne, where Jordan was seated and Ashley was standing at her right hand. Neither of the twins moved or made a sound. They simply watched Jaclyn approach.

Her chest was thrust forward, her head held high. She passed column after column and window after window, her footsteps amplified on the marble floor and echoing around the space. The throne room was empty, save for a few guards lining the way to the throne, and they too were as still as statues.

Jordan fought to keep her face neutral as she watched her mother approach. Jaclyn wore a gown of emerald and sage. It was cinched in at the waist, displaying her hourglass figure. Her brown hair was pulled back and up, and her face was made up to highlight her huge eyes and pouty mouth. She barely looked older than Jordan herself, and Jordan marvelled at how well her mother had kept over the years.

How is it that a person with such a deceptive heart can be so beautiful?

Jaclyn stopped in front of the steps leading up to the throne and dipped into an elegant curtsey. Her movements were practiced, liquid, and full of irony.

Jordan and Ashley had taken the two hours they'd made Jaclyn wait to put on beautiful clothes and explain to the guards how they wanted them to behave.

Jordan wore a purple satin vest with black trim, over a white blouse with billowy sleeves. Her legs were encased in black leather leggings and black knee-high boots. Jordan had thought long and hard about wearing armor, but in the end had decided to wear a black scabbard, which held a shortsword along her thigh; anything else, and sitting on the throne would have been unbearably uncomfortable. She didn't choose to arm herself because she thought Jaclyn was a threat——after all, she had a palace full of guards to call on now. But Jordan no longer felt quite like herself without some kind of weaponry. She was a warrior, and that made her a warrior queen.

Ashley, however, was armed to the teeth in his usual style, though he had exchanged his rough boiled leather for a purple vest that matched Jordan's.

The throne Jordan sat in was nothing less than spectacular.

A white marble base cradled a polished blackwood seat and a back that arched high above Jordan's head. The Rodanian crest had been carved into the throne's back and a torch placed a distance behind the crest in a holder specially made. The flames danced and crackled, visible through the crest to anyone standing in front of the throne. A shadow of the crest was thrown onto the floor in front of Jordan, quivering there, bringing the Rodanian symbol to life.

The throne would have to be remade, and the crest altered to include a Nycht wing.

Jordan and Ashley watched Jaclyn bow in silence. When she

straightened, they still did not speak. They did not speak for such a long time that Jaclyn shifted from one foot to the other.

It was the first clue that she was uncertain of herself here——which, all things considered, was astonishing. It was also astonishing that Jaclyn had journeyed to Rodania only in the company of a few hired men, and that she had not brought them to the palace with her.

This was a strategic move in true Jaclyn style. She would not give any clue that she was in a precarious position, maintaining the image that she was innocent and entitled.

Jaclyn finally spoke. "When is the coronation?"

"Next week," said Ashley, his voice flat. "And you'll address Jordan as 'Your Majesty'."

Jaclyn's hands clasped in front of her gown, and a muscle jumped in her jaw. "I shall remain onhand until then, if you might have someone show me to my rooms."

It took everything Jordan had not to fall off the throne with shocked laughter.

"Your... rooms." Ashley repeated. His voice remained so void of emotion, so bored and uninterested, that Jordan almost applauded.

"Of course." Jaclyn's chin lifted defensively. "The Queen Mother must have her own suite of rooms."

"You tried to have me killed," Ashley leaned forward, a subconscious movement Jordan recognized as a preparation to attack. His voice was hostile, and Jordan's body tensed, but Ashley did not attack. "You tried to have me kill Jordan. You've been conspiring with Diruk against the king, and hampering trade of important medicine, all to keep the king on the edge of death until you were ready to deliver the fatal blow. You are not royalty. You are a traitor."

"I did *not* try and have you killed," Jaclyn drew up tall, and her surprise at this was so genuine that Jordan almost believed her. But the fact that it was the only thing she denied in the long line of accusations was laughable. "I would never. I love you! You are the reason I have done everything I have since leaving Earth!"

"You have one chance," said Jordan. Both Ashley and Jaclyn fell silent and looked at her. "Explain your actions to the daughter you abandoned. If your story makes sense, you'll be allowed to leave Rodania alive, merely banished. If not," Jordan shrugged. "You'll have the traitor's trial you deserve."

Jaclyn did not hesitate. "Leaving you behind was the hardest thing I have ever done, and my biggest regret."

"What a load of——" Ashley began. Jordan raised her hand to stop him, and he closed his mouth.

Jaclyn's words were exactly what Jordan had been hoping to hear when she had first found her mother hiding in the trade office, off the coast of Maticaw. The child that Jordan had been yearned to believe them, needed to believe them. But the woman she had become knew better. Still, she was determined to give Jaclyn her say, once and done forever.

"I could only take one of my children, and in the state I was in, I was not confident I could even care for you properly," Jaclyn said, looking at Ashley. Her eyes had grown soft, the eyes of a mother. "I don't know what your father," she looked back at Jordan now, "Allan, told you, but I had very bad post-partum depression. I could not stay on Earth; it would have been a death sentence. I am human, but I have never felt like I belonged. After falling through the portal the first time and meeting Torpizar, who then brought me to King Konig, I knew I was meant for more. For only here could I fulfill my destiny. Only here could my offspring fulfill theirs."

"His destiny," said Jordan.

"Better one than none," Jaclyn responded, quick as a snake. "Make no mistake, neither of you would be here now if it weren't for me. Look how beautifully everything turned out for you. You are rulers, you have inherited your rightful places. If I had not come back from Earth, if I had not clawed my way up from nothing, if I had not allied myself with the prince, you," she seemed almost to sneer the word as she jerked her chin at Jordan, "would still be in Richmond. Maybe you had the smarts to become a lawyer or a doctor, or maybe you would have followed in Allan's footsteps and gone into politics, but here," Jaclyn laughed and it was a sound that made Jordan shiver. "You are a queen!"

Jaclyn's eyes were alight with mania, and Jordan watched her with a growing sense of pity and sadness. Jaclyn believed what she was saying, the delusions ran so deep.

Suddenly, Jordan had no desire for revenge; she felt weary to her bones. Weary of conflict and confusion, weary of feeling angry, weary of politics and false accusations and selfishness.

Jaclyn was still speaking. "I was the one who was strong enough, brave enough to do the hard thing. Do you think any family achieves greatness without someone in the background willing to do the dirty work?" Her voice was growing harder. "The two of you are where you are now because my actions have bestowed it upon you."

At this, Ashley reached a hand over and laid it on Jordan's arm, squeezing gently, as though frightened Jordan might fly from her seat and tear Jaclyn's head from her neck. But there was no risk of that. Jordan lay her other hand on top of Ashley's, telling him it was okay. She was no longer angry——only terribly sad.

Jaclyn's eyes fell on the connection between the twins, and her face went white with rage. Her seething gaze lifted to Ashley's face. "After everything I have done for you, everything I have given you. You *dare* to call me a traitor? You dare to turn your back on me, now that my plan to see you get your inheritance is complete? You ungrateful little maggot." She spat this, and her face transformed into a Medusa-like mask of wrath.

Ashley's hand spasmed on Jordan's arm, his fingers clenching.

Jordan looked over at him. His face was white as a sheet, and there was green around his mouth, as though he needed to be sick.

"You are dismissed," Jordan said, alarm bells going off in her belly.

"You *will* give me the respect and position I am due," Jaclyn continued as though Jordan hadn't spoken. "My children are the royalty of Rodania, *my* children!" her voice rose finally, to a pitch that echoed through the throne room. "I carried you! I birthed you! I am the Queen Mother!"

Jordan shot a look at one of the Nycht guards, and he moved forward to Jaclyn's right side. Another guard closed in on her left.

Jaclyn's hands curled into claws and she made to go toward the steps leading up to the throne when the Nychts took her by the upper arms.

"Release me!" she screamed, her face now nearly purple.

Jordan could feel Ashley quaking beside her.

"Take her to one of the rooms in the East tower and put guards on her, please," Jordan said numbly. Her face felt wooden, and her heart ached.

The Nychts dragged Jaclyn backward, still screaming to be released. Halfway to the door, Jaclyn seemed to get a hold of herself and, instead of being dragged, began to walk. She stumbled twice, and both times Ashley visibly winced.

Then the doors to the throne room were closed, and the twins were left in silence.

Jordan watched as Ashley slouched forward in agony, his face in his hands. His whole body trembled.

"What would you like to do with her?" Jordan asked. "We'll have to make a decision quickly. We can get her help and do so quietly."

"Help?" Ashley turned to look at Jordan, aghast.

"She is very sick."

"Then put her out of her misery!" Ashley barked. "Send her to Trevilsom, where traitors belong."

"You don't mean that."

He let out a long sigh and raked a hand through his hair. He looked over at Jordan, and his expression was grief laced with respect. "It is a very lucky thing for her that you were born first. She has taught me to be brutal and unforgiving. I would not be merciful. You decide what to do with her; I'll not protest."

Ashley rose and headed for the door behind the thrones, his shoulders drooping, as though he carried the weight of the world on them.

CHAPTER 26

*J*ordan lay awake, listening to Sol's deep breathing. She tried timing her own breath to his, hoping it would help her slip down the slide of slumber and give her mind and heart a desperately needed reprieve from emotional turmoil. Somewhere in the belly of the palace, her mother was contained in a room, awaiting some form of judgement.

What to do with Jaclyn?

She turned her head and looked at Sol. His face was relaxed with sleep, and his exhales were flirting with the idea of turning into full-blown snores. Her eyes drifted beyond him, to one of the three balconies attached to their room in the palace. She let out a long sigh and blinked like an owl. She missed their little apartment, but as Heir Apparent——and soon to be queen——the palace was now her official home.

Heavy is the head that wears the crown, she thought.

She was acquiring a far too intimate understanding of just how heavy that crown was. She had a feeling she was only getting a small taste of what was to come.

She rubbed at her face and rolled out of bed, slowly, so she didn't wake Sol. Her bare feet found the cool hardwood floor, and she got up and grabbed the robe that had been tossed over the back of the chair near their bed.

It had appeared there as if by magic. It was disconcerting, having servants do things for her. A pot of tea of some mystical sleep-inducing blend had appeared in front of the fireplace, hot and steaming. They'd drunk the entire pot, but it hadn't done its job——at least not for Jordan.

She visited the water closet and then went out onto the balcony. Oriceran's two moons hung low in a blanket of stars. Upper Rodania was a dark landscape dotted with warm yellow lights. Streets and terraces were illuminated by nighttime lamps. All was still, peaceful.

Jordan leaned her elbows on the railing and rested her chin in her hands, trying to focus on the wind tugging at her hair and ruffling her feathers. She failed, and her mind was pulled back to Jaclyn and Diruk as if by magnets.

Diruk was to be sent to Trevilsom according to Rodanian laws; there was nothing that could be done about that. He was a traitor; he'd caused the deaths of hundreds of warriors and citizens, and the destruction of dozens of villages. He claimed his intention had been to only allow one harpy through the barrier, to distract all of Rodania from the upcoming vote in order for him to create the right political climate that he could win.

It didn't matter, his fate was death.

Jaclyn was a different story. She was not a citizen of Rodania, which meant that there was no protocol for her offenses. It was the Council and the reigning monarch who were to decide her fate. The Council had made their preference known——ban her from Rodania and remove her from her post at the trade office. Balroc even preferred Trevilsom for her, but the others thought it was too harsh a sentence.

What do you think, Your Majesty? Balroc had asked her.

As if she was capable of passing judgement so easily. As if Jaclyn wasn't her biological mother.

Tears blurred Jordan's vision and threatened to spill, her view of the stars becoming a muddy panorama. Jordan didn't want the responsibility of deciding Jaclyn's fate, but she couldn't leave it up to Ashley, either. Her brother was angry enough with Jaclyn to make a rash decision.

'Do you believe in rehabilitation?' Sol had asked her before they had fallen asleep.

Jordan had replied that yes, she did. She was inclined toward mercy. They could never have the kind of relationship Jordan had always wanted with her mother, but it didn't mean she deserved death.

Sol's hands slipped around Jordan's waist, and his lips pressed against her shoulder, pulling her away from her troubles.

"Is my snoring keeping you awake?" His voice rasped with sleep.

"No."

They stood there for a time, looking at the stars.

"I'm going to let her go," Jordan said quietly.

Sol nodded against her back. "It's not like you to do anything else."

"She can't keep her post, though. She's too treacherous."

Sol made a sound of agreement. "What about sending her back to Earth?"

"I did think of that. It might be for the best, but what would she do there? She'd have to start over."

"That's not your problem, love. If anyone has proven that they can go from nothing to something in no time, it's Jaclyn. She's like a..."

"A what?"

"Nevermind. It doesn't matter what I think. She's your... mother. Biologically, anyway."

Suddenly Jordan knew what Sol was going to say. "Like a cockroach?"

Sol chuckled. "Mmhmm." He kissed her cheek. "Can I get something for you? Something to help you sleep? More of that tea?"

"I guess. Can't hurt, anyway. Aysha will be nearby."

"I'll make it for you. I still feel weird asking servants to do things for us." Sol moved away from her, and she heard their door open and close.

She smiled. He wouldn't make it very far before Aysha would pounce on him. Sol would likely never make another pot of tea in his life.

Jordan shivered when a cool breeze moved over her, tousling her feathers. She retreated into the room and closed the terrace doors.

"Look at you now. Queen of Rodania."

Jordan whirled, her heart in her throat. "Sohne!"

In the middle of the room, having appeared as though she was a ghost, was the Elf princess. The torches around the room flared to life with Elf-light, casting shadows against every wall and illuminating the women in that unusual blue-white glare. Jordan hadn't seen that strange Elf-light since she had last been in Charra-Rae.

Sohne wore a long ethereal gown of pure white. Her red hair appeared the color of blood in the light, and her skin seemed to glow. The gown was sleeveless, with a neckline that plunged almost to the Elf's belly button. The skin of Sohne's stomach was decorated with Elvish symbols, just like the ones that wound their way up Jordan's arm.

Jordan straightened. It was on her lips to ask how the Elf had gotten in, but it was a foolish question. Sohne had powerful, penetrating magic. Jordan doubted there was anywhere that could keep her out, if she had a mind to get in.

"You've come to collect." Jordan's heart was hammering

around inside her ribcage like a frightened bird. She folded her hands in front of her to keep from wringing them. She began to walk slowly around the perimeter of the room.

"Congratulations on your elevation in life." Sohne inclined her head in a movement of exquisite grace hiding layers of meaning. It was the nod of acknowledgement of Jordan's new station, but it was devoid of submission.

"You knew this was going to happen." Jordan's eyes narrowed. "A promise from some random Arpak is almost meaningless, but a promise from a queen…" she trailed off.

"I am not your enemy, Jordan." Sohne crossed her arms and began to walk in the opposite direction that Jordan was moving in.

The two women circled one another slowly. To Jordan, it felt like skirting a snake in the middle of a hiking trail. Her eyes shifted to the door and back to Sohne.

"Sol won't be back until we're done here."

Damn. I really need to work on my poker face.

"What do you want?" Jordan couldn't help but bare her teeth. Her skin prickled with distrust.

"Nothing you won't be happy to give me. Haven't I proven several times already that we have common interests? I have no desire to make an enemy of Rodania."

"Spit it out."

Sohne looked down with a small smile. She continued walking slowly around the room, her knees pushing at the fabric of her dress, making it float as though it were made of cobweb. "Some time ago, before you and I ever met, I was visited by an emissary who made the very long journey to Charra-Rae in order to deliver a foolish threat." Sohne's voice took on a lyrical quality. "They told me that if I were to sell any more of my fungus to anyone aside from Jack, the Trademaster at the port of Maticaw, that Charra-Rae would burn to the ground."

Jordan's blood turned to ice. "Jaclyn," she whispered. How foolish her mother had been.

Sohne inclined her head. "I'm not sure why your mother thought that an alias and staying behind closed doors would protect her." She spread her hands. "For here we are. Her own daughter is going to give her over to me. It's poetry. Don't you think?"

Jordan's hands turned to ice, and a feeling came over her like all of the water in her body was draining toward her feet. Her legs felt like lead. "You want my mother?"

"That's right. I would ask for Prince Diruk as well, since the threats were made by both of them as a way to prevent King Konig from becoming well again. But I know that Rodanian law demands he be sent to Trevilsom." She smiled. "I think this punishment is adequate."

"What are you going to do with her?" But Jordan already knew the answer. Jaclyn was going to be gnashwitted–– sentenced to live the same day over and over in perpetuity, without functioning memory, reasoning, logic or emotion.

"Why do you care?" Sohne's elegant eyebrow arched. "I'm making a difficult decision easy for you, taking care of one of your problems." She flicked an invisible piece of lint off her dress. "You're welcome."

"I don't understand. Of all the things you could ask for, why this?"

"There is a special place in my heart for those who threaten Charra-Rae. There is an art to my vengeance; it's my calling card, let's say. Jaclyn will lose everything, and it will be a direct result of being handed over to her enemy by the very daughter she rejected. Nothing hurts more than regret, and she'll feel plenty of that, believe me. In fact, she is feeling it even now, before she yet knows the true punchline."

"How long have you been planning this?"

"Since the day you unwittingly stumbled into my forest."

Jordan sank into a chair that sat against the wall between two of the balconies. Her knees were shaking. She found it hard to label the feelings bubbling up inside her, there were so many of them: humiliation at being tricked into making a decision that went against her will, revulsion at the intentions Sohne had for Jaclyn.

The gnashwits had inspired horror and pity in her when she'd been in Charra-Rae. It was a fate she'd thought no one could possibly deserve.

Jordan's eyes lifted to the redheaded Elf. She couldn't look at Sohne without thinking of Eohne. A white-hot anger laced through her. "I've never met anyone more manipulative and controlling than you. I think you might even be worse than Jaclyn."

Sohne's eyes widened before she wrested her surprise under control. "I really thought you'd be happy about this, Jordan."

"It's worse than a death sentence."

A glimmer of concern passed over Sohne's face and was gone, her stoic expression fixed back into place. "Are we going to have a problem?"

"Yes." Jordan got to her feet. "This isn't going to happen your way."

Sohne's perfect pale brow wrinkled. "You're willing to die for that woman?"

Jordan's lips pressed together. "No. I'm willing to let you take her. But you have to give me something in return."

Sohne laughed with genuine surprise. "You have no cards to play, no leverage at all. What are you talking about?"

"Eohne."

The smile disappeared. Understanding dawned slowly, like moonlight crossing a moor. "You fool."

Jordan bit back a cry of pain when the markings on her hand began to burn. Some invisible hand was trailing a white-hot poker along the glyphs written on her palm. The burning sensation began to travel slowly up her arm, following the trail of marks and migrating to her wrist. A light drew Jordan's eyes down, and she saw with horror that the glyphs were smoldering like there was fire beneath the surface of her skin. The heat and pain of it made sweat spring out on her forehead.

"The Unbreakable Promise cannot be broken, Jordan." Sohne's face was impassive. "You have only moments before it reaches your heart."

A low moan leaked from Jordan's throat. She began to pant against the pain. "Let Eohne go, and you can take Jaclyn." Jordan knew Sohne didn't want her to die. She was the Heir Apparent and soon-to-be Strix Queen. Killing her would make war between Charra-Rae and Rodania. If she had to hand Jaclyn over to Sohne, she was determined to get something out of it. Jordan cried out in spite of herself. The burning sensation deepened, scorching Jordan to the bone of her forearm. The red light igniting her flesh began to brighten, and a sizzling sound reached her ears. Tendrils of smoke drifted toward the ceiling. Jordan clenched her teeth against a scream.

"Stop this now," Sohne snapped. "I cannot halt the Promise from doing its work. The magic is beyond even me."

"Don't stop it," Jordan said through clenched teeth. The white-hot agony had reached her elbow and was blazing its way up towards her armpit. It felt like her arm was filled with red-hot lava. Sweat dripped down the side of her face. A deep moan vibrated in the back of Jordan's throat of its own accord. She panted the words, "Just release Eohne. It's all you have to do." Jordan's body began to quake, and she thought that her knees might give way.

Sohne's expression had gone from uncertain to profoundly disturbed.

Jordan lifted a shaking right hand and pointed with her trembling finger at where the fire was crawling toward her heart. The glyphs were blazing with red light, smoke trailing as the magic moved.

Sohne's crossed arms dropped and her face lost all its color.

"Give Eohne her freedom." Jordan's heart hammered, and her entire arm was buried in a bed of hot coals. "Give her the right to visit Charra-Rae, come and go as she pleases."

Jordan let out her first real wail of pain and crumbled to the floor ,where she rolled onto her back, her wings spreading out and spasming with the agony of the Promise. Sweat soaked her hair and her brow and trickled over her scalp. She opened her eyes and tried to focus on Sohne. The Elf looked blurry.

"Free Eohne, or it's war with Rodania." She bared her teeth in a grimace of pain, her back arching as she screamed out again. "Decide! Now!"

Sohne bellowed and went to her knees on the floor beside Jordan. "You treacherous Arpak! Eohne will be free! Say the words! SAY THEM!" The Elf was screaming in terror, watching the red light as it burned its way toward Jordan's heart.

"You can..." Jordan panted and squirmed across the floor, as the fire penetrated her left armpit and lit up her arteries and veins like nitroglycerine. "...take Jaclyn!"

She said the final words on a moaning exhale, as the fire was mere centimeters from her sprinting heart.

The effect was immediate.

The moment the words passed Jordan's lips, the pain stopped. Jordan's body slumped flat against the cool hardwood floor. Her chest heaved, and her heart was riding hard behind her ribs. She lifted her trembling left arm and looked at it.

Where there had once been Elven glyphs, there were now scars. They had the texture of melted skin, hairless and shiny, marks that only fire could leave behind. White and puckered, they looked years old, rather than seconds. The landscape of her arm had been forever changed.

Jordan looked at Sohne, who was still on her knees beside her.

Her face was a mask of shock and violence. She too was panting. Jordan had never seen the Elf look so discomposed and confounded. Sohne had not been able to foresee this outcome; she was not in control, and she hated it.

Arpak eyes met Elven ones, flint striking against stone.

Sohne let out a long, predatory hiss of frustration and got to her feet. Jordan got up more slowly, flexing and shaking her left arm to make sure it was fully functional. She got her feet under her and folded her wings back neatly into place, her eyes on the infuriated Elf.

Jordan gave Sohne a smug smile. "Good call."

CHAPTER 27

The sounds of laughter and conversation filled the dining room. A floor below Jordan and Sol's bedroom in the palace were the private living quarters of the reigning monarch. Jordan had arranged for a dinner and invited all her beloved people to see her new home and eat there with her and Sol.

Sol, Eohne, Allan, Arth, Toth, Tashi, Mareya, Linlett, Shad, Eade and Ashley sat around the table, reliving the past week's events. Their meal had come and gone, and the dessert of pink plums with a buttery custard was nearly finished.

Jordan watched Toth and Tashi as the girl sat on Toth's knee and tried pink plums for the first time. Jordan had never seen Toth so attentive to anyone the way he was with the little orphan he'd found at Golpa. Even Arth had made a comment that her glacier of a brother was beginning to drip a little as Tashi melted him. Toth would only smile a little sheepishly at the comments and return his attention to the girl.

"Look at them," Sol leaned over and whispered to Jordan. "He looks so..."

"Happy?" Jordan supplied. "Yeah, or at least like he knows he'll be happy again soon."

Sol nodded and kissed Jordan's cheek. "And you? Are you happy?"

Jordan turned and put a hand on Sol's face. "Who knew that fateful day when you crash-landed in my tree that it would lead to all of this? I'm overwhelmed."

"Any regrets?"

"I just wish King Konig could have stayed alive long enough for me——" Jordan nodded toward Ashley where her twin was deep in conversation with Arth, "*us*, to get to know him."

"Of course. At least everything he did as king was recorded; it's in the public record. You can access it anytime you want."

Jordan nodded. "And I will." She took a sip of wine. "My first order of business will be filling the empty seats of the Council." Her eyes drifted back to Toth. "Speaking of which, I'll be right back." She kissed Sol on the lips and got up, dragging her chair over to where Toth sat.

"Do you like it?" Jordan asked Tashi, who had pink plum juice running down her chin.

Tashi nodded and licked her lips. She picked up her bowl and tilted it into her mouth, slurping up the remaining plum sauce and custard.

"I have something to ask you," Jordan said to Toth. "You don't have to answer now, but I hope you'll take some time to think about it."

Toth eyed Jordan with a crooked smile. "I think I know what you're about to ask."

"You do?"

"You want to offer me a place on the Council."

Jordan nodded, brightening. "You'd make a wonderful Councilman! You're the first person I thought of, and the best choice for Rodania."

"No, I'm not, Jordan."

Jordan's smile melted away. "You're not?"

"I appreciate the offer, really I do. I'm flattered. But I'm not a politician. My goal was always to get Nychts a place at the table, not to be at the table myself. I'm a mercenary, always have been. And——" Toth paused.

"What?"

"And I already find myself in a far more important role." Toth gazed at Tashi as she licked her spoon clean. "That of a father."

Jordan suddenly found it hard to speak around the lump in her throat.

"Thank you for asking me, it means the world," Toth went on. "But I have plans to leave Rodania shortly."

"Leave?" Jordan felt as though he'd knocked the wind out of her. *After fighting so hard and losing so much for his country, he's planning to leave?* Jordan swallowed down her disappointment. Rodania without Toth just didn't seem right to her. "I wasn't expecting that. Where would you go?"

Tashi set her spoon in her empty bowl and squirmed down from Toth's lap. She wandered in the direction of a large crystal sculpture of Rodania, the two upper tiers floating as if by magic, and the middle one slowly rotating, mimicking real life.

"I found Tashi in Golpa. I don't know where she's from or which people she belongs to. We know she's an Ashling, and that her father was killed. But she must have more people than him. She hasn't shown me anything about her family or where she's from yet, but I'm hoping she will. I feel duty bound to find them. For her sake. Don't you think I owe her at least that much?"

Jordan was full of conflicted emotions, but she could set aside her own heartache at the idea of Toth leaving to see that, for him, there was no other option.

Jordan nodded. "We all owe her. That little Ashling saved our lives."

Toth nodded, smiling as he watched Tashi run a hand through

the air underneath the crystal rendering of Upper Rodania. "She certainly saved mine."

* * *

ON HER WAY around the table back to Sol, Jordan passed by Allan and Linlett, who had their heads bent together and looked to be chatting about something serious.

"What are you two gentlemen plotting?" Jordan asked, putting a hand on each of their shoulders.

Allan looked up, brightening. "Linlett has been helping me think through what to do with our holdings back on Earth." He patted her hand. "We've been awfully distracted with what's been going on here, of course. But I will have to go back and deal with all that, and the sooner the better."

Jordan nodded. "I know. You're right. We shouldn't leave it any longer."

"I was thinking..." Allan's forehead furrowed. "What would you think of passing the deed to our plantation over to Cal and his wife? They've looked after that place since you were a baby; I figure no one deserves it more than they do. They could live in it or sell it——either way, they'd be set for life."

A look of pleasure crossed Jordan's face. "I love that idea!"

"Good." Allan cleared his throat. "I was also thinking that we need to make a statement, letting our acquaintances and the authorities know that we're okay."

Jordan noticed his deliberate use of the word 'acquaintances'. This struck her momentarily. She might have used the word 'friends' in this case, but looking back at the relationships she'd had on Earth, and comparing them to the relationships she had here in Oriceran——with the people in the dining room, and others she'd come to know and love while training or fighting alongside them——her previous relationships paled.

Being affluent, in the public eye, and with her father in politics, Jordan had met people easily. There were no shortage of people who wanted to be her friend. The challenge lay in finding those she could trust. Showing vulnerability in the circles they had been in wasn't an option. Jordan was painfully aware that anything she said, even by accident, could be used to put her father into a negative light.

On Oriceran, she'd been vulnerable from the start. She'd learned what it really felt like to need someone, to need them and trust them.

There was no one she'd missed so much from home that made her feel the need to go back. What her father was suggesting seemed like the right thing to do.

"What would you want to say? How would you want to do it?" Linlett asked, his face ruminant.

"I think a handwritten letter, including fingerprints from both Jordan and me to help prove its authenticity, might be enough. We will explain that we are safe, that there is no one to blame, but that we've decided to go traveling for the long-term. Then we'll put all of our wealth into a twenty-year trust. We can decide what to do with it as it's needed. Give it to charity, or bring it over in the form of gold and put it to work for Rodanians."

"You think they would believe the letter to be real?" Jordan chewed her lip doubtfully. "What if they think we've been kidnapped and the kidnapper forced us to write the letter? They might link it to Cal, since he'd be the one benefiting from the gift of the house."

"I would send a letter to my lawyer and move the house into a trust. Cal would continue on as the groundskeeper according to my wishes. That bit we can make public," Allan added as a side thought. "Once the whole matter has blown over, the lawyer would release the deed to Cal and Mary in private. No one would need to know they're the new legal owners."

"Might work," said Jordan finally. "Let's try and look at all the things that could go wrong for Cal, though, before we do anything. I would want to be really sure that nothing we did could get him into hot water, especially after all he's done for us."

Allan nodded. "You're right, of course. We'll do that." He patted her hand.

"I wouldn't worry," said Linlett. "I'm happy to contribute magic, both for traveling back and forth as often as required to get the job done, and also to help ease the situation on Earth. Because the gates between Oriceran and Earth are waxing open right now, magic endures for longer there than it has for more than twenty-five thousand years. If there was ever a good time to do this, it's now."

"Thank you, Linlett," Jordan and Allan spoke in tandem.

"My pleasure," the Light Elf said, his tone lyrical.

"Do you have plans to return to your home soon, Linlett? Now that the border situation has been resolved?"

Linlett's eyes flicked to Eohne, and he looked hesitant. "I'm still... trying to figure that out. I should say 'we', if I'm truthful. Eohne and I have been discussing a more... permanent partnership. We've so enjoyed working together."

"Well, I also have something for you to consider," Jordan said, speaking on inspiration. "I'm looking for a non-Strix representative for the new Council; someone who can give insight on behalf of our wingless residents. I think life here could be vastly improved for them. I'm also looking for a Light Elf to sit on Council, I feel like it would be excellent to have a liaison with our most powerful allies here in Rodania. If you'd take a place at the table, it would be killing two birds with one stone." *And all the better if it means Eohne spends more time in Rodania,* Jordan added to herself.

Linlett laughed, and the sound sent a pleasant vibration through Jordan. "I have a feeling I know what you're doing." He grinned at Jordan and winked at Eohne as she looked over at them from where she sat chatting with Sol. Her cheeks flushed pink and she cocked her head with curiosity. "I promise I'll think about it," said Linlett, "Your Majesty."

* * *

JORDAN SPIED Mareya ducking out onto the balcony, a wine glass in her hand. With all the bodies in the room, stomachs full and drinks being nursed, the room had grown stuffy. Jordan grabbed her own glass and followed her nanny-of-times-past outside.

"I was hoping I'd have a chance to catch you alone," Jordan went to stand by Mareya at the railing.

Mareya set her glass on the marble banister and opened her arms to Jordan, who stepped into them for a hug. The women squeezed one another, and the familiar smell of her nanny made Jordan's eyes tingle at the corners and her nose threaten to run.

"You'll always be 'Maria' to me," sniffed Jordan, stepping back and smiling at her nanny. She wiped at her eyes.

Mareya's teeth caught the moonlight, gleaming as she smiled. "I don't have a problem with that. It helped me, that name."

"It did?" Jordan turned and set her back against the railing.

Mareya leaned her elbows on the marble and gazed down at the glittering lights of Rodania, far below them. "It was difficult, you know. Leaving for such a long time. No wings, no identity there on Earth. Not knowing anyone. Not really understanding the culture or way of life when I first arrived. Not seeing my husband except a few weeks out of the year."

Jordan nodded. "I can only imagine. And you managed to have a son somewhere along the way."

"Yes," Mareya laughed. "Shad came along six years before I was able to go home and be with him full-time. I have an amazing husband."

"How did you..." Jordan paused, doing the math and shuffling through her memories, then made a sound of understanding as the story clicked into place. "When you left us to go back to Belize for seven months."

Mareya looked up at Jordan and nodded. "That's right. I was pregnant with Shad. I left just as I started to show, and did not return until Shad was two months old."

"You told us your sister was sick."

"Yes. And Allan brought in a temporary nanny for you. Angela was her name, was it?"

"Angel." Jordan shuddered. "Awful woman. We were thrilled when you came back." Jordan's eyes softened as she looked at Mareya. "How did you manage to leave a two month old baby at home?"

"King Konig asked it of me," the Nycht replied, picking up her glass and straightening. She shrugged. She took a sip and looked up at the moon. "I loved my king and I'm loyal to a fault. At least, that's what Eade would tell you. Shad spent much of his first six years with an absentee mother. But Eade is a fantastic father, and Arth stepped in as much as she could."

"I noticed Shad and Arth seem to have a special bond."

Mareya's face reflected some sadness. She nodded. "They do. And I'm glad for it." She put a warm palm on Jordan's arm. "But I owe you information. Anything you want to know?"

"When did Konig send you to Earth permanently?" Mareya had implied that she had gone back and forth from Earth to Rodania a few times after Jordan was born, but that eventually, she'd stayed.

"It was when Jaclyn disappeared again. I watched you from afar since you were an infant—–you and Ashley both, and Jaclyn too. Although, to be honest, I never cared a whit what happened to that woman." Mareya frowned when she thought of Jaclyn. "She made her bed. When Jaclyn vanished and took Ashley, I reported it. King Konig was frantic when I told him, and sent Strix to search for them." She shook her head. "Jaclyn was very clever. Staying underground."

"Surely she could have been found using Light Elf magic? After all, she wasn't even that far away."

"We tried that, but we underestimated her... as I suspect everyone who has ever met her has been doing since the day she was born." Mareya frowned. "She commissioned magic to cloak herself and Ashley from prying eyes." The Nycht shook her head. "I suspect it was black magic she bought. Coming into contact with that kind of sorcery never goes well. Insidious stuff. It will bring out every negative trait you have and suppress your good qualities. The longer you use it, the worse it gets."

Jordan mulled this over. "Are you saying that maybe Jaclyn wouldn't have been such a horrible person if she hadn't used black magic to hide herself for all those years?"

"I'm saying, it sure didn't help. We'll never know, I guess. Anyway, King Konig was distraught when we couldn't find Ashley and he was worried for you, having lost your mother and your twin. So, he bade me find a way to insert myself into your life."

"Easy enough, when Allan posted an ad for a nanny."

"Yes." Mareya smiled. "It was perfect."

"Any regrets?"

Mareya made a *tsk* sound and laid her palm on Jordan's cheek. "I lost time with a son, but I gained time with a daughter."

Jordan's throat closed up. She couldn't speak for fear of losing control. It was a beautiful thing to be wanted, to be cared for. Neither her mother or her father were blood relatives, and it didn't matter one bit.

She swallowed and fought to keep tears from spilling over, even though no one had seen the young Jordan cry more often than Maria had. She turned her back to the door, in case someone came out and saw her looking overwrought.

"I'm sorry, Jordan." Mareya put a hand on Jordan's back. "I'm sorry about your mother. Sorry for what happened to you. Sorry I had to keep so many secrets from you."

"Why couldn't you just tell me?" Jordan swiped at her face where a hot tear jumped ship and tracked down her cheek.

"I wasn't allowed, honey. King Konig swore me to secrecy. He was never planning to have you come back to Rodania, to uproot you from your Earthly life. He thought it would be too hard on you." Mareya paused, hesitating.

"What is it?"

"Well, it was why I gave you the locket in the first place. I disagreed with his decision not to bring you home to Oriceran. I thought you were strong, and you would have made the transition well. I couldn't actually *say* anything to you about the locket, because I had sworn not to, but I was hoping it would bring you home."

Jordan's eyes widened at Mareya. "I could have been killed, though! I almost was. Sol saved me so many times, and Toth saved me even more."

Mareya gave a sort of grimace. "Well, I sure didn't expect you to make the journey on the very same day I gave you the locket. I thought it would take weeks, maybe even months, before you came through, or that you wouldn't come at all. I had intended to formulate an anonymous magic message for you, something crafted by a Light Elf, to help you find your way but that wouldn't break my promise to King Konig. I couldn't do that until I got back to Oriceran myself, and by that time, you had already left Earth. It all happened so fast. By the time I got organized enough to have a Light Elf track you, you were with my very own brother and I knew he'd keep you safe."

"You couldn't have sent me a message?"

Mareya sighed. "I wanted to. But I'd used up my savings just to try and find you. Light Elf magic is so expensive. Plus, the harpy attacks started then, and it was madness around here. King Konig was getting steadily worse, and you were busy with Toth, training and fighting. I knew the right time would come, and it did."

Jordan went silent for a time, thinking about King Konig and the warm way he had welcomed her and Ashley.

"I'm pretty sure the king wanted Ashley and me to come and find you. He started to write the words *'ask for'*, but got too tired and had to put his arm down." Jordan gazed at Mareya. "I would bet anything that he was going to write your name."

Mareya nodded, her mouth a sad line. "Yes. Since he could no longer speak, in order to acknowledge you formally, he'd have to have a Council member present, as well as me with the nephogram. Thankfully, it all worked itself out in the end."

"What was he like?" Jordan asked quietly. "My father."

"Ah." Mareya emptied her glass and set it down. "King Konig was a complicated Arpak. He was a man of big appetites and an even bigger vision. I loved him, but he was far from perfect. At least he was for equality for the Nychts. The queen and Prince Diruk——" she shuddered. "If it was up to them, they would have kept us down forever." Her eyes softened and she gazed at Jordan. She swept a blonde lock back from Jordan's face and tucked it behind her ear. "Thanks to you, we'll never be kept down again. Rodania 'lucked out', as Earthlings like to say, to inherit you as their queen, Jordan."

"Thank you. I have no idea what I'm doing, but..."

"You'll figure it out." Mareya jerked her chin toward the door where laughter and voices were spilling out. "You have a good advisory board, and will soon have a balanced Council, finally. You're not alone."

Jordan straightened, blinking as an idea struck. "Would you consider a place on the Council, Mareya? I can't believe I didn't think of it already!"

Mareya grinned. "I thought you'd never ask."

"Really?" Jordan's heart jumped for joy. "Why didn't you say something?"

"I didn't have to, you came around to the idea on your own." She gave Jordan a serious look. "I'd be honored. You can't imagine, all the years spent at the palace as an underling, how many stupid decisions and deceptions I saw." She shook her head. "Ten years ago, I would have said no to that kind of responsibility. But now." Her lip twitched in a smile. "I have so many ideas, and I'm ready to share them."

"Wonderful! I'm so pleased!"

"And what of Ashley?" Mareya asked, eyeing Jordan carefully.

"I don't think Council is the right place for him, at least not right now. But did you notice that he and Arth hit it off? Couldn't stop talking over dinner, and still haven't shut up."

"I did notice that, in fact. What were they talking about?"

"Technologies from Earth. Seems Arth and Ashley have this interest in common."

"Why don't you see if she'd take him on as an apprentice?" Mareya suggested. "Arth has been looking for help at her workshop and needs a keen mind. Perhaps he'd like to learn how to engineer properly."

Jordan nodded, liking the idea. "I'll speak with them both about it."

Footsteps on the balcony tiles made the women turn. Eohne hovered at the doorway.

"Might I have a word?" she asked shyly. "I know you have a lot of catching up to do, but…"

"Not at all," Mareya replied, straightening. "We have plenty of time to catch up." She kissed Jordan's cheek and disappeared inside.

Eohne wandered to the balcony, her expression tentative. She came to face Jordan. It was the first moment the two friends had been alone since the princess of Charra-Rae had been to visit Jordan.

Eohne's eyes drifted to Jordan's left arm, which was covered by the long billowy sleeve of her blouse. The Elf reached for Jordan's hand and held it, turning her palm over in the torchlight. She ran a thumb over the puckered scars running up Jordan's wrist. She unbuttoned Jordan's cuff and slowly rolled the sleeve up her arm, revealing the marks left behind by the Unbreakable Promise. Eohne's eyes grew glassy as she traced the leftover glyphs with her fingertips.

"No one has ever done anything like that for me before," the Elf said, her voice cracking. She lifted her eyes to Jordan's. "Thank you. I don't know how I can ever repay you."

"I would do it a thousand times over, Eohne. And you don't need to repay me. You've done so much for me and my Dad. It's I who owes you."

Eohne shook her head and sighed, pulling Jordan's sleeve down and buttoning the cuff.

"Did Sohne come to see you before she left?" Jordan asked.

"Yes. She almost gave me a heart attack. She appeared in my room sometime before dawn, right after she'd been with you. Her face was like thunder." Eohne took a breath. "I have never seen her so furious. I thought for sure she'd come to punish me, to take me home for good right that minute. I could hardly believe it when she gifted me with the freedom to visit Charra-Rae as I wished instead. She didn't explain why, or what happened, so I was very confused at first. Then, over dinner just now..." Eohne blinked rapidly and brushed at her eyes. "I spotted the scars on your palm when you picked up your wine glass, and figured it out. I'm grateful, but that was either very brave or very stupid of you, Jordan. You could have died."

Jordan shook her head, thinking back on the pain, which she could now hardly even remember. "I knew Sohne wouldn't let me die; that has never been what she was after. Even less so, now that I'm Queen of Rodania."

Eohne nodded, smiling at her friend. "And what a queen you'll make."

EPILOGUE

Jordan stared at her reflection in the mirror. Her hair was swept up and back into a low braid and lay over her shoulder. Simple pearl earrings sat in her ears and tendrils curled from her temples and hairline. The low elegant hairdo had been crafted by Mareya, and left room for the crown Jordan would be coronated with in less than an hour's time.

She wore a floor-length gown in white with delicate trim in blue, Rodania's colors. The gown was long-sleeved with a wide neckline that exposed Jordan's collarbones. The dress was plain on purpose; it left room for the sash and gilded crest that would be placed over Jordan's left shoulder and right hip. The crest had already been altered: one of the two Arpak wings had been removed and replaced with a Nycht wing. Jordan had refused to be coronated under the old symbol, so there had been a flurry of activity throughout the palace to update every crest.

The distant sounds of a crowd gathering drifted in through Jordan's open terrace door from the park below. She was alone with her thoughts, but not for long. Mareya would come to fetch her in less than fifteen minutes, along with Ashley and Sol and four members of the Royal Guard to escort the group down to the park.

Jordan bowed her head and closed her eyes, shutting out the room and her reflection. She put her hand on her heart and felt it beating. Little butterflies danced up and down her spine, and her palms felt a little damp, but she was relieved that there were no more nerves than this. It was a big thing she was doing today. It signalled the true end of her life as an Earthling. Not that she was ever considering going back, but the promise she was making today meant that she was no longer living her life for herself, but for the citizens of Rodania.

She opened her eyes and nodded to her reflection.

"We can do this," she said to the soon-to-be-Queen looking back. "Thank God we won't have to wear a dress if we don't want to, though. I miss my leggings." She blinked. "Oh my God, I'm talking to myself." She looked to the wall, where a portrait of King Konig was hung over the fireplace. His teal eyes looked down at her, and she imagined him winking. "Did you talk to yourself? Of course you did. All the great leaders did, right? I think I read that somewhere. Great, now I'm babbling."

There was a tap at the door, and it opened a crack.

"You look so beautiful," said Sol, entering and shutting the door behind him. His eyes drifted over her appreciatively. "You look like a queen." A doubt crossed his face. "You're not going to wear dresses all the time, though, are you?"

"Absolutely not."

"Good, because I already miss the leggings and daggers." Sol crossed the floor to her and kissed her on both cheeks.

Jordan threw her arms around his neck and squeezed him tight. His warmth and solidity filled her with confidence.

"Are you ready for this?" Sol asked into her hair.

"I'll never be readier, let's put it that way."

"Good enough." Sol's hands slipped down her arms to her hands. "Shall we?"

"I was expecting Mareya. And where is Ashley?"

"Ah. Yes, there's has been a change of plans. They've gone down ahead of us." Sol pulled her through the open terrace door and onto the balcony where the sounds of the crowd below had grown louder. "It's a bit last minute, but we thought of a more appropriate entrance for you." Sol gestured to the sky. "Your escort awaits."

The sound of great wings beating at the air approached, and Jordan looked down, her own wings vibrating with joy. "Blue!"

Her reptilian friend gave a piercing whistle followed by a long throaty roar as he hovered beside the balcony.

Jordan hiked up her gown, spread her wings wide, and took to the air. With Sol at her back and Blue leading her, they flew down to the park together where a nation of Strix, their friends, and a colossal red dragon waited to celebrate the coronation of their rightful Queen.

The End

AUTHOR NOTES - A.L. KNORR

WRITTEN MARCH 17, 2018

So, here we are at the end! What a ride! The Kacy Chronicles book 4 marks the completion of my first full series of books. Began in July 2017 and completed in March 2018.

When I was a kid, my greatest wish was to be able to fly. I loved laying in the grass on the farm I grew up on in Southwestern Ontario and watching the birds glide and swoop across the backdrop of infinite blue. How incredible to be that free. How amazing to have a view of the world from up there. I thought nothing could be better, and dreamed about it during my waking hours as well as at night.

When I was sixteen I had an idea for a race of winged people, a nation united by their ability to fly, but divided by the differences in their anatomy, a nation of those with feathers, and those with the membranes of a bat. When Martha Carr asked me to join her and Michael Anderle's Oriceran universe, I dusted off this idea and fleshed it out. This is how the Arpaks and the Nychts got their start. I'm thrilled to have finally brought an idea to light which I wasn't sure would ever surface. Check. Dream fulfilled.

I can't say enough thanks to Nicola Aquino, Shandi Petersen, the JIT Team at LMBPN Publishing, Steve, Jen, Martha and Michael at LMBPN, and last but definitely not least the group of fans and readers in my VIP Reader's Lounge on Facebook. I feel like pretty much the luckiest writer ever to have had you all at my back.

I try to respond to what readers want, so even though The Kacy Chronicles are complete, I have a couple of spin-off stories in mind for Toth and Eohne. If these are stories you would like to read, please either email me directly or message me on Facebook.

I hope you've enjoyed the adventures of my winged creatures as much as I've enjoyed dreaming them up. I am a little biased, to be sure, but I think there is a little Strix in all of us, a winged creature waiting to burst forward and take to the skies.

A.L. Knorr
    Written in London, England.

Okay, Abby Lynn Knorr (Abs to a lot of us) is the perfect author for these author notes. The girl knows how to live a full, rich balanced life and keep things in perspective. Has anyone seen the video of her Irish step dancing on Facebook lately? I look forward to seeing her pictures of Italy or even her small hometown in Canada and then there's the side trips to Scotland. No wonder she can write so well in Fantasy. She's feeding her imagination and giving herself time to breathe.

Which brings me to my last conversation with Magic Mike. The main takeaway for me was that I wasn't looking at how I could take the most from this experience and create the ideal life for myself. It's easy to let things get away from you. My first job was at 15 years old, and I was a single mother, and then the Great Recession and along came cancer over and over again and paying back big cancer bills.

I have been on survival mode for so long that switching over to thrive is taking some doing. Who knew? That's where I'm downright blessed to be surrounded by people who do it so easily like Abs and Mike.

Letting go of doing as much as possible just in case takes time and happens in layers. But it's happening... Instead of wondering how I could punch out another series and find a few more hours I'm thinking about how I can write and edit... and embroider, and go out with friends, and take boxing lessons (yes, boxing but no in the ring sparring... sorry Mike and Craig), and travel, travel, travel. And then there's that thing about meeting a hot 50-ish guy. Why not?

But it has to start with me being willing to ease my foot off the gas and work on being the best possible, happiest, THRIVING version of myself. Otherwise I could get caught up in pointless competition with others, or more likely – myself, and miss the whole point of being alive. To have some fun in community with others and be of service where I can while writing about Elves and Witches and Trolls. Suddenly, I am looking forward to what this year has to offer even more... More adventures to follow.

PUBLISHER NOTES - MICHAEL ANDERLE

WRITTEN MARCH 18, 2018

First, THANK YOU for not only reading our stories, but also our author notes in the back!

If you haven't yet checked out Abby's Elemental Origin's tales, I'd encourage you to take a look on Amazon and see if these books are something you would like to read.

In the last book (Combatant), I spoke about my first series coming in the Oriceran Universe, and I can share with you a bit as it is due out in the next few weeks.

I jump ahead about twenty (20) years into the future from these stories, and we follow a Bounty Hunter as he works to keep his area of Earth (Los Angeles) clean of hoodlums that are using the integration of Earth and Oriceran with magic and technology as a way to push their criminal ways.

The Police have chosen to offer bounties for different levels of criminals, and our protagonist James Brownstone has been doing this for a while.

So, we don't learn how he became unbelievable. The story we step into isn't truly about his abilities, but about his *relationships*.

What we find out is he is a guy that does his job, goes home, watches HGTV shows (predominately about BarBQ) and looks into the next bounty.

You know, someone who needs a female...or two... to shake up his existence.

Enter Allison and Shay.

One is a teen that has had her mother kidnapped, the other is a person leaving her past behind, and working to become a well know tomb raider for Oriceran artifacts.

James Brownstone's future just became complicated, and he will (eventually) understand why relationships are a good thing.

Eventually.

If you are looking for something to read and haven't read The Leira Chronicles by Martha Carr and myself, you can ALWAYS give that a try.

Or Protected by the Damned, The Kurtherian Gambit... We have others.

Just be warned, anything with Martha or myself should have a warning sticker with the label "Excessive Snark" right on the cover.

I look forward to seeing you after your next reading binge!

Ad Aeternitatem,

Michael Anderle

WANT MORE FROM ORICERAN

JOIN THE EMAIL LIST HERE:

http://oriceran.com/email/
Find the Oriceran Universe on Facebook:
https://www.facebook.com/OriceranUniverse/
Find the Oriceran Universe on Pinterest:
https://www.pinterest.com/lmbpn/pins/

The email list will be a way to share upcoming news and let you know about giveaways and other fun stuff. The Facebook group is a way for us to connect faster – in other words, a chat, plus a way to share new spy tools, ways to keep your information safe, and other cool information and stories. Plus, from time to time I'll share other great indie authors' upcoming worlds of magic and adventure. Signing up for the email list is an easy way to ensure you receive all of the big news and make sure you don't miss any major releases or updates.

Enjoy the new adventure!
A.L. Knorr and Martha Carr 2017

A.L. KNORR SOCIAL

To be the first to learn about new releases and special offers, sign up for A.L. Knorr's newsletter here: https://www.alknorrbooks.com/

Facebook: https://www.facebook.com/alknorrbooks/
Instagram:
https://www.instagram.com/alknorrbooks/?hl=en
Twitter: https://twitter.com/ALKnorrBooks
Pinterest: https://www.pinterest.com/ALKnorrBooks/

MARTHA CARR SOCIAL

Website and Email list: www.marthacarr.com

Facebook Page:
https://www.facebook.com/ChroniclesofLeira/

Facebook Fan Group:
https://www.facebook.com/groups/MarthaCarrFans/

OTHER BOOKS BY A.L. KNORR

Pyro (including the novella Heat)
<u>Returning Episode II</u>